Courage Rises

A Pride and Prejudice Continuation

MELANIE RACHEL

Courage Rises: A Pride and Prejudice Continuation

Copyright © 2016 by Melanie Rachel

All rights reserved. No part of this publication may be reproduced, distributed, or transmitted in any form or by any means, including photocopying, recording, or other electronic or mechanical methods, without the prior written permission of the publisher, except in the case of brief quotations embodied in critical reviews and certain other noncommercial uses permitted by copyright law.

ISBN: 9781521247051

First printing 2017

Chapter One

COLONEL RICHARD FITZWILLIAM rubbed at tired eyes and tried to focus. Now that they had successfully crossed the Zadorra, the adjutant was outlining Wellington's plan to chase down the increasingly desperate French forces. As far as he could tell, it was not complex—overtake and overwhelm the enemy with numbers. Taking the high ground and finding the bridge unguarded had given them an advantage, but it had been nearly a fortnight of nasty business, and the men were growing bitter.

As he turned his head towards the door, he spied a familiar boy from the 95th in a green and black uniform caked in mud, a well-used but spotless Baker rife in his hand, a single captain's epaulette on his shoulder, tall black hat tipped slightly forward on his head. He was leaning against the wall next to a rather larger companion, listening but, the Colonel thought, given the boy's crossed arms and hearty frown, not approving.

At first, Richard focused only on the Baker rifle and thought, disjointedly, that he would very much like to own one. Without moving anything other than his eyes, he lifted his gaze. The light in the room was poor, and the captain's tall black hat was jammed down over his forehead, making it difficult to see his face. He had spoken briefly with the boy several times over the past few weeks, occasionally giving him orders to carry back to his own colonel. Blue eyes, he thought, trying to remember the face. The boy had intensely blue eyes and a fierce scowl.

Then as now, the captain had appeared young, and it had bothered the Colonel, though he could not say precisely why. He knew many young fighting men no older than the captain, even a few officers. He narrowed his eyes, trying to clear the fog from his vision. A few strands of sunny yellow hair curled out from under the captain's hat. He had known a few other men who looked boyish even in their thirties, but they were generally not soldiers. The captain was of medium height, but though strong, he was also slight of build. The boy's coloring, particularly the shade of golden hair, put him suddenly in mind of his young cousin Georgiana. Perhaps that was why he would feel better were the captain older. He quickly shook that thought away. He could not think of home now. If he hoped to return in one piece he would need to focus on what they were facing today. There was a grim job to be done and no easy way to do it. Despite all the talk, it would come down to what it always did, throwing men at the guns and hoping there were enough to overpower the defending army. That meant bullets, cannon, bodies. He ducked his head again and rubbed the back of his neck, trying to relieve the tight, knotted muscles.

The 95th was given its charge, to disrupt the ranks by targeting French officers before the real fighting began and then to assist Wellington and his men. By the twist of the boy's mouth and the brusque nod of his head, the Colonel could see that he was prepared. He jumped distractedly to another thought, that the 95th did not sell commissions as often as the rest of the army. He wondered whether the boy had won his promotion through competition or merit. The riflemen were far more likely to rise in such ways, and the captain had probably earned his rank. He grunted softly in approval and Wellington himself finally stood to release them with a wave of his hand.

Richard stood up, watching the general stride out of the room with his entourage, and stretched his aching limbs. He blinked a few times, trying to shake himself into wakefulness, and found the young man he had been watching suddenly at his side, shoving a mug of steaming hot coffee into one hand and a thick slab of folded bread into the other.

"You look done in, Colonel," he said in a voice hoarse with smoke. "We plan to be off soon. You had best eat."

"Thank you, boy," Richard replied, looking blankly at his hands for a moment before taking a gulp of the coffee. The hot liquid warmed his throat and helped clear his head.

Suddenly, it seemed important to ask, "What is your name?"

The boy looked up into the Colonel's face. Richard was tall, a good four inches taller than the captain, but it did not seem to bother the younger man.

"Captain Oliver Hawke, sir. Out of Kent."

Richard transferred the mug to his left hand and stuck out his right. "I am Colonel Richard Fitzwilliam." Captain Hawke narrowed his eyes, frowning, and Richard almost laughed. Apparently Hawke had already known who he was. He nodded, feeling a little better. "Kent. You might know of my Aunt de Bourgh."

"Lady Catherine de Bourgh?" the young man chuckled softly. "Yes, I suppose I have heard of her. More like *heard* her, if you do not mind my saying, sir. I was more acquainted with Miss Anne. Good girl, that. Made sure we was all fed and rested before setting off for Hythe. Quite kind. Your cousin?"

"Indeed," the Colonel replied, too exhausted to feel more than a small spark of curiosity. He had not thought Anne well enough to take an interest in much outside Rosings. He raised the mug. "Thank you again, Captain."

The boy nodded curtly and moved to go. He picked up his rifle, turning as he reached the door. "Godspeed, Colonel," he said gruffly. He clapped his waiting companion on the shoulder, and they both slipped through the door and were gone.

"Godspeed, Captain," said Richard softly, swallowing the bread in two bites. He tasted a bit of beef and wondered where the captain had managed to get it. He downed the rest of the coffee, sat the mug down, and walked out into the rapidly cooling summer night, calling for his horse. As he swung up in to the saddle, he gazed at the harvest moon sitting low in the afternoon sky. *Someday*, he thought, *it would be nice to visit Spain and Portugal without the need to be armed.*

***

Colonel Fitzwilliam had briefed his men. Now he swung up onto his horse, where, from his perch above the massing troops, he could just make out the green coats of the men working across the river and farther down towards town, already busy disrupting the lines by taking shots from distance at the officers following Gazan. The artillery was beginning to fire. He said a brief prayer, more out of habit than belief, and with a shout, began to move his men into position across the bridge and behind the 95th.

The order came to charge, and within a few moments, there was nothing to consider but the roar of artillery, the heat of fire, and the salty, metallic smell of blood. To the left of him, the ground heaved, showering him with dirt. He could hardly hear anything over the sound of the explosion. He fought to control his mount as they staggered to the right, though he managed to keep his seat. Another blast kicked up to the right and slightly behind him, and his horse reared in fright. Richard hung on with all his strength, but just as the animal returned to all four legs, there was a final blast, this one directly ahead. He did not see the bodies flying or feel the earth raining down upon him, because he was falling, his horse screaming as it lost its footing. He instinctively rolled away to keep from being caught under the beast as it fell.

He could have wept for his steed, lying there in the mud of the battlefield. Odd, he thought, detached, shots and canon firing all around him, that there was something more heart rending about losing the horse's life than his own. He crawled back to see whether he would need to spend a bullet to put the creature out of its misery, but this was not a country field and a simple broken leg. Instead, the entire chest of the animal had been torn to shreds by shrapnel. He cursed, checked his sword, grabbed his gun, and pushed forward.

He was well behind his men, now, and he hurried to catch up. He looked ahead and saw the men of the 95th streaming into the chase ahead of his men rather than keeping to the higher ground in their support position. He felt a fleeting annoyance. His own men were being detained, left out in full range of the cannons, while the battle plan was disregarded. At least some of the men of the 95th had clearly not wished to be used in support. He shoved up ahead, reaching his regiment quickly, when he heard some yell something about a cannon and then felt a slight but very strong body slamming into him, knocking him sideways behind the protection of a copse he had not observed before. As he staggered to the side, behind the protection of a few trees, the air was suddenly sucked from his lungs and a massive wind tossed him back through the air, pushing him to the earth at last as though an unseen hand had shoved him down from a great height.

Richard lay still, eyes closed tight and arms thrown wide while he struggled to fill his lungs. One arm was tangled in the brush, the other rested on tree roots. He felt a throbbing pain in his right leg, but could not sit up to evaluate the damage. After a long moment, his lungs filled and he gasped as though he had been drowning. He opened his eyes in time to see a young captain in a green and black uniform dragging himself slowly away from the trees on his belly, the back of his green coat torn in long, jagged, bloody lines. *Where is he going?* Richard thought hazily, watching him reach for something but not yet able to place where he was or what he himself was doing there.

He blinked a few times and tried to rise, but the ringing in his ears just became louder, more insistent. He rolled onto his side and lifted himself slightly on one arm, his head only slowly beginning to clear. As hard as he had been tossed, it took too long to recognize that there was a man standing above him and longer still to realize that the man was wearing a French uniform. Somehow, over the cannon, the shooting, the screaming, even the ringing in his ears, he still heard the unmistakable cocking of a pistol. Perhaps he only imagined he had heard it. Richard struggled to lift his head, to look the man in the eye. If this was to be his death, he would stare it down.

The shot came immediately.

Richard heard the shot, but did not feel it. He was almost angry. *How the deuce did he miss from so short a distance?* Then the soldier was falling, slumping to the earth, the pistol dropping harmlessly from his hand. Richard tried again to rise, but his body would not allow it. He laid his head back down on his arm and spied a shock of blond hair. It was Captain Oliver Hawke. The boy had lost his hat, his yellow curls bright against a face darkened with gunpowder residue, mud, and blood, and he was sitting on the ground in the Plunkett position, his legs stretched out before him, a thin curl of smoke twisting up from the barrel of his rifle. The captain slowly, carefully rolled over on his stomach and tried to push himself up, rifle in one hand, but his balance was unsteady, and as Richard watched the boy finally collapse in a bloody heap, he closed his eyes. *Just a little rest,* he thought, as a sunny slope in the north of

England and the face of his young cousin began to dance in his vision. *I am weary.*

Chapter Two

ELIZABETH DARCY WAS AWAKE. Though the sunlight was only beginning to seep weakly through the drawn curtains, she had been awake since her husband has risen some hours earlier. She watched the boughs of the trees swaying in the wind, heard them rubbing, one bough against the other. She pulled the covers up to her chin and sighed. It was not a pleasant dream or even a nightmare that had kept her from her rest, but the need to review her responsibilities for the day.

It had been nearly four months since their wedding tour concluded. Four months since she had arrived at Pemberley as its mistress, and understood, completely, what it meant to be Mrs. Darcy. Her husband had been involved in the final weeks of the planting, and she had been busy taking her place as Mrs. Darcy, greeting the neighborhood, becoming familiar with the tenants, and learning how to manage the house. During the day she was able to tuck the doubts away, but at night she had time to think and to worry. Today she was needed to go over the menus with Mrs. Cronk so that the cook could complete the weekly order. Both beef and sugar should be arriving today, and she would need to supervise the weighing of each parcel, comparing the weight against the charge. She had already discovered that the butcher had been sending slightly less beef than the receipts promised, in an attempt, she supposed, to test whether the young mistress would keep strict accounts. In some of the orders for flour she had discovered small rocks at the bottom of the sacks. Lately the orders had been measuring up nearly perfectly without such assistance, much to her satisfaction, but she was keenly aware that should her diligence waver in the least that many would be quick to take advantage. *Foolish,* she thought, *to risk losing as large an account such as Pemberley for a few extra pennies.*

She shut her eyes and rubbed one dark curl between her finger and thumb. Despite her husband's assurances, she understood human nature. While they would never show their disapproval in front of the master of Pemberley, she knew that the tenants of the estate, many of the townspeople in Lambton, the local gentry, even the servants were watching for her to make a mistake, to reveal in some way that she had not been the correct choice as his wife. She had heard the whispers and read the incredulous glances. The neighbors had been less obvious, but no less astonished. She would not have cared for their good opinion, she thought stubbornly, but she cared a great deal for her husband's reputation. She smiled to herself at the thought. How abominably proper she had become. Where was the spirited Lizzy of Longbourn now? No, if she were truly being honest with herself, she thought wistfully, it was more than their admiration and respect she wanted. She wanted, most of all, to feel herself worthy of them.

Elizabeth gazed around her room. It was all still so new to her, the intricately carved bedstead, the sky blue silk curtains, the thick woolen rug done in blues and greens that covered the floor. There was a new copper tub in the room just off her chambers, where she took a bath almost every night. It was the one luxury she had adapted to quickly and with joy. When Fitzwilliam teased that he had married a sister of Beau Brummel, she had replied, archly, that a bath every night would not hurt *him,* either, particularly when he had been out riding. She relished the deep baritone laughter that was his response.

She hoped that after finishing with Mrs. Cronk in the kitchen that she might be able to breakfast with Fitzwilliam before he rode out to the northern fields. He had mentioned the night before that he would need to inspect a tenant's barn roof damaged by a recent storm. Then she would answer her correspondence and take some food out to the Wrights, whose two little boys had been ill. After that, she would speak with the head gardener about planning the fall vegetable garden now that the summer garden was in and growing. Mrs. Cronk had gone over the needs of the kitchen with her the day before. She could have left this to Mrs. Cronk's care, but before she relinquished these kinds of duties, she wanted to understand them.

Elizabeth heaved a great sigh and thought she might as well get dressed and begin her day. As she reached for the bell to call her maid, there was a soft knock on the door, and Fitzwilliam stepped quietly inside.

"Good morning, Mrs. Darcy," he said with a gentle smile. She still blushed a little when he came into her chamber before she was dressed, and the gleam in his eyes betrayed his approval. His dark hair was tousled, as though he had already been outside in the wind.

Mrs. Darcy, he thought to himself as he gazed upon the lovely picture his wife made in her nightclothes. Calling her by his name was still unreasonably thrilling.

She smiled, but noted that he was already wearing his riding clothes, and tried to hide her disappointment.

"Are you on your way out?" she said quietly, looking up into his eyes. "I had hoped to breakfast with you before you left." She retreated to the bed to sit. He sat beside her and took her hand.

"No, better to conclude this business quickly. I have no desire to miss dining with you this evening." He kissed her forehead and she leaned in, laying her head on his shoulder.

"I will miss you while you are gone, but I promise not to allow the butcher to cheat us in your absence," she laughed lightly, and raised her head to look him in the eye. A stray lock of hair fell over his forehead and she reached out to put it in place. He grinned, a lopsided smile that smoothed his features and made him appear boyish. It was a smile Elizabeth adored, particularly because it appeared rarely, and nearly always for her alone. She touched his coat gently, quickly eyeing his apparel to be sure he was dressed warmly. Even in the summer the mornings were still damp and could be cool.

"I am certain he is ruing the day I married such a shrewd wife. He has probably been cheating me for years."

"Mrs. Cronk would never allow it."

"She has admitted that she was often occupied when his parcels arrived late, undoubtedly by design. She has said to Mrs. Reynolds that she is delighted with the young mistress taking him to task." He watched for her smile, but instead a silent blush spread across her cheeks.

Yes, she thought as she offered Fitzwilliam a kiss, this was just the beginning of her education. It was essential that she become the partner that her husband needed and deserved. For so long he had done everything himself. She wanted him to feel more at liberty to enjoy the estate from time to time, rather than always being required to run it.

She looked over his shoulder, lost in her thoughts, and a small sigh escaped her. Every day when she awoke, she prayed a short prayer, hoping that Fitzwilliam's belief in her had not been misplaced. She felt his warm hands on her shoulders as he pulled away to study her. She looked up into his face, which had become serious.

"Never doubt my faith in you," he said with a small shake of his head. She tilted her head quizzically and he raised his eyebrows. His blue eyes met her serious brown ones. Darcy watched, pleased when his young wife's expression changed from anxiety and embarrassment to its more natural state of cheerful mischievousness.

"Your face tells me everything I need to know," he said gruffly. "It is one of the reasons I love you. Now," he said, planting a kiss on top of her head and standing, "if I do not leave directly, I shall never get to the north fields today. Remember, as always, Mrs. Reynolds is a patient instructor should you need her, and John will accompany you and Georgiana to the Wrights this afternoon. I will see you this evening, my love." He tugged purposefully at his waistcoat.

"Very well," she said, smiling. "Georgiana and I will attempt to wait for you, but we shall be quite hungry by dinner and if you are not prompt I make no promises." With a chuckle and another quick kiss, he was out the door, and Elizabeth was ringing for her maid.

***

The parcels had been closely examined and exactly measured. After the last boy exited the kitchen, Elizabeth touched Mrs. Cronk's arm and laughed, "Do you think they are understanding us now?" The cook smiled broadly and nodded her head almost gleefully. Elizabeth checked her list. There had been far more activity than she had expected. The butcher had been there but there had also been separate deliveries of flour, sugar, eggs and vegetables from the home farm.

"I think they won't dare try an' cheat you again, ma'am," she said emphatically. "It does me good to see it, and I'm only too glad you have thrown a rub in his way. I will nay put up with his slum again." Elizabeth smiled, genuinely pleased at her approbation and shared a teasing glance with the buxom woman. She always felt something like an elf standing next to a giant with Mrs. Cronk, who was at least a head taller and twice as wide. Her wild curls had once been red, but were now streaked with gray, and no matter how she attempted to subdue them, a few always managed to escape her cap. Elizabeth had rarely met as amiable a woman or as capable a cook, and was pleased to have her confidence.

Mrs. Cronk drew herself up proudly, feeling a good deal of pleasure in Mrs. Darcy's clear approval. By God, she had not been at all sure when the master had brought this pretty young woman home. Many of these young new wives, guided by the fashion edicts of London, wanted men to run their kitchens and

French cooks at that, but not Mrs. Darcy. Near the end of the meal at their first dinner party, the new mistress had been asked whether there would be a change in the kitchen. Mrs. Darcy, bless her, had stated quite pleasantly, and for all to hear, that her singularly accomplished English cook was a treasure she could never willingly relinquish.

Mrs. Cronk had been thrilled and grateful to have been so publicly praised. She knew the mistress would suffer some gossip in the neighborhood on account of that statement, and her loyalty had been unfailingly engaged. Jacob, one of the footmen who had helped serve the meal, had further reported that the bold but quite proper pronouncement had made Mr. Darcy glance at his plate and smile. As young and pretty as she was, the mistress had some steel in her.

"If he does, we shall know how to respond, Mrs. Cronk, shall we not?" Elizabeth squeezed the older lady's arm affectionately and then said slyly, "I am off to breakfast. Do you think it will be quite up to expectations, as you were engaged with me this morning?"

Mrs. Cronk was indignant. "Of course, Madam. Everything on the table has been properly supervised. I. . ." she stopped suddenly as she realized she was being teased. "Off with you, then," she said in good humor as the mistress pretended to be scandalized at her familiarity. There was something to be said for young women who did not always stand on fashion or rank, she thought, as Mrs. Darcy walked away with a light step. She would do very well. Very well indeed.

***

Fitzwilliam Darcy guided his horse along the road to the northern fields of the estate, distracted by his early morning conversation with Elizabeth. He was proud of how well she had adapted to her new role as mistress of Pemberley, but she still seemed dissatisfied with her progress. He would find a way to show her that it was only her own expectations that she yet to meet. *Stubborn woman*, he thought with affection. She seemed to be attempting to become a Darcy with everything that she had, but she had not been raised to be a Darcy, and he thanked God for that. There were two in residence at Pemberley already, and that was quite enough. Once his lovely young bride fully accepted that he needed her to be only who she was, everything would turn out right.

He spurred his horse to a trot, eager to finish his business and return to his wife. He heard the familiar footfalls of a trotting horse on the road and looked to his left, where his steward, Mr. Harrison, was riding to meet him.

"Morning, sir," said Harrison. He was a short, stocky man with powerful shoulders. His head was almost completely bald, and as such he was rarely without his hat. He had been steward for only six months, hired when Mr. Bascombe had retired, and Darcy was not yet convinced this new man would last. If the Howards' barn roof had been badly damaged in the last storm, then it had been left untouched for nearly a fortnight. These repairs had to be conducted promptly so that any materials required could be made or ordered and the work begun. It did not sit right with him that with no pressing crises, this had not been attended within a few days of being reported.

"Harrison," he nodded.

"A nice day for the ride, sir."

"Yes."

Harrison lifted his hat and scratched his head as they rode in silence. He had been steward at Pemberley for nearly six months, but was not entirely comfortable working with its taciturn master. He was more comfortable when left to his own devices to run things, but Mr. Darcy and his new bride seemed to be more interested in staying home than in traveling to participate in the London season or to the homes of other friends. Mrs. Reynolds had mentioned something about her master finally settling down now that he was married, and Harrison cursed his luck to finally fall into a lucrative situation just at the moment when he would have to work twice as hard to earn the money. His employer had seemed displeased when he had been informed about the roof by Mr. Howard. He had not expected that the master would accompany him out to the north fields, so it had not occurred to him to relay the news earlier.

"I expect the repair will be a small one, sir. You need not attend if you have other business." If he could just get the man to go home, the repair would be done quickly and finished.

"Let us judge when we see it, Harrison," Darcy said slowly. He did not appreciate the steward's attempts to turn him back. It made him suspect that the repair would not be small and that Harrison would like to hide that fact. He knew his tenants. Had it been an easy repair, Howard would have seen to it himself.

Half an hour later, he was in the barn, looking up at the cool blue sky through what little was left of the roof. The timbers inside had been soaked from the rains a few days past, and water still dripped intermittently to the ground. The animals were being housed on the far side of the structure where the roof had held. This was the only barn on the property. Clearly this repair should have been addressed immediately to prevent further damage. He stepped outside where Harrison stood.

"Harrison," he said sharply.

"Yes, sir?"

"The repair must be attended to today and completed by the end of the week. I will have Mr. Howard send a note directly to me when the work is finished. Tell Mr. Hall at the mill that he may contact me about payment for an expedited order." He stepped a little closer so that the next part would not be overheard. "This was not well done, Harrison," he growled quietly. "The tenants must make a profit so that I can make a profit. I know you have not worked this far north before, but the weather can turn quickly any time of year, and your delay in attending to the damage might have cost Howard some of his livestock. I am putting you on notice, Harrison. This will not occur again."

Harrison nodded, his jaw clamped shut, the muscles working. What did the man expect? He was not some green boy. He had many things to tend on an estate this size and had taken everything in its order. The weather had not turned from the soft summer rains nor had he heard Howard complain about losing any livestock. There was no harm done here. Certainly no cause for the master to pull caps with him. He said nothing as Mr. Darcy mounted his horse and took his leave, knowing it would do no good, but it chafed. He tugged at his hat and turned to walk to the house to arrange the repair. The master was leaving soon for London, and Harrison could not wait to have him away.

Chapter Three

GRADUALLY, COLONEL FITZWILLIAM became aware that the cannons had gone silent. He forced his eyelids open with a groan and discovered himself in a small stone room with two other men laid out on stretchers. He stared at the ceiling and tried to recall why he was here. His leg ached, and there was a constant whining sound in his ears. The only thing he could hear over it was the screams coming from outside the door. A few candles sputtered weakly on a table nearby. He glanced over at the man next to him, wincing at the pain in his head. Another colonel. He could not see the third man, only a pair of muddy boots. He tried to rise, but his head was still not clear, and the floor pitched unsteadily, so he reluctantly leaned back and remained still.

When he opened his eyes again it was nearly dawn. The door was opening and a short man with broad shoulders and straight dark hair stepped cautiously inside, holding a lit candle. Richard recognized Major Beaufort and weakly raised a hand in greeting.

"Colonel," he said, stepping to Richard. "I came to see how you fared."

"A little the worse for wear, I fear," Richard said weakly and tried to grin. The Major half grinned in response.

"It does me good to hear you speak some sense. You were quite out of your head when we dragged you back here." The lapels of his jacket were smeared with bloody handprints.

"I will not ask what I said, then. What happened?"

"Not sure. Cannon, perhaps even a mine, sir. Most effective. Our losses were heavy indeed. Fortunately you were somewhat protected by the trees."

Colonel Fitzwilliam struggled for a moment. What *had* happened? "Captain Hawke shoved me into the copse." Hawke had done more, too, if he could only remember.

"I do not think I know the man," replied Beaufort.

The Colonel thought a bit more, closing his eyes as the information began to flood back. "He is with the 95th, and I believe he was injured. Would you do me the favor of asking about him? Young. Has blond hair."

"Of course, Colonel. Are you in need of anything else?" Beaufort's face was stoic, but Richard heard the concern in his voice. What the devil had he said earlier? He had no idea, but it seemed to have badly rattled his friend. With some effort, he smiled, a complete smile. "A new head and some quiet country living would suit." *Perhaps William will help me choose a new horse.*

The major chuckled and rubbed his chin thoughtfully. "Aye, you are not alone in that. I will go ask about the captain, and then I must get back to it." He paused before continuing, "The men are not right, Colonel. They are angrier than I have yet seen, even at Roderigo. I fear that once the town is taken, they may not. . . stop."

Richard closed his eyes. "A concern of mine as well. See if you can speak with Sergeant Miller. He knows to whom among the men he may apply for assistance." Beaufort nodded and slipped out of the room. It was nearly another hour complete before

Richard recalled the French soldier, the pistol, and Hawke's timely shot. *I should have died,* he thought grimly. *If there is anything I can do for the boy, I must see to it.* The incessant ringing in his ears had at last begun to subside, so when Beaufort returned, he heard the door swing open gently and opened his eyes.

Beaufort stepped hesitantly over to his side and looked intently at his feet. After an uncomfortable few seconds, the Colonel croaked, "Well?"

"I am sorry to say he is not here, sir. At least, not anymore."

Richard's heart sank. He recalled the bloody jacket, the boy collapsing. Beaufort fidgeted, a folded sheet of paper in his hand.

"What are you holding, Beaufort?"

"A letter. It was in the captain's pocket, sir, at least, that is what the surgeon says." He paused. "The man was busy. Said it was handed to him by another soldier, but could not say who." He rubbed the back of his head tiredly before asking "Were you familiar with the captain, sir?"

"No. We had spoken, but I knew little of him. Why?"

"The letter, sir. It is addressed to you."

Chapter Four

ELIZABETH ENTERED THE breakfast room with a contented air. So many household tasks completed before breakfast! She noted her husband's empty chair, but did not dwell upon it, instead turning her eyes to Georgiana, whose bright complexion immediately lifted her spirits.

"Good morning, Elizabeth," Georgiana said pleasantly, smiling over her teacup. She looked refreshed and was dressed in a sunny yellow dress, her hair in perfect golden ringlets and tied back with a dark blue ribbon. Elizabeth already felt tired and somewhat soiled from her work in the kitchen. Still, she felt lightened by her sister's presence.

"Good morning, Georgiana," she said cheerfully. "I trust you slept well?"

"Indeed. I presume *you* were up quite early?" The shape of Georgiana's eyes and the little line above her nose when she teased were the only physical traits she shared with her brother, but the resemblance was striking, and Elizabeth was still not entirely used to it. She took a plate.

"Yes," Elizabeth replied. "How did you know?"

Georgiana smiled back conspiratorially. "I have spies among the servants," she said with a small laugh.

"Truly?" Elizabeth laughed, "Have you turned French, then?"

"Indeed," Georgiana giggled. "Do not tell Richard."

The two women laughed, and Elizabeth felt a bit of pride in her success at drawing Georgiana out. Even in the short time she had called Pemberley home, Georgiana had begun to open up in a way Fitzwilliam confided she never had before, at least, not since she was quite small. Elizabeth learned more about Georgiana every day, and had made it a point to spend as much time with her as was possible. Her sister was more than accomplished. She was delightful, with a gentle sense of humor and a desire to see the best in everyone. Had it not been for a certain dark event in the recent past, she might also have been a bit naïve, but that characteristic had been forever expunged where men were concerned; Elizabeth was both pleased and distressed that such was the case. They wandered through the gardens, discussed books, played music or sang, but they also spent many happy hours in companionable silence as they followed their own pursuits.

From Elizabeth, Georgiana was learning to sketch the character of those she met, to listen not only to the words they spoke but how and why. The younger girl was also learning to apply all that she had read, to consider her own positions on important topics, and to feel more at ease expressing them. Elizabeth had always loved to sing, and her skills at that art and in playing the pianoforte were steadily improving under Georgiana's kind instruction. From her newest sister she had also gained an appreciation for drawing and painting, though no greater skill in either.

The two conversed pleasantly about the garden, and by the end of the meal Elizabeth had promised to have the gardener plant far more vegetables than she had originally planned. Any excess, Georgiana had explained, would be sent out to tenants or the poor who might have need of them. After Elizabeth had finished eating, Georgiana stood and shook out her skirt. "When would you like to visit the Wrights?"

"Right away, if you please, Georgie. I need to speak to the gardener when I return, and I missed my walk this morning. I thought I would take a short stroll around the lake afterward." It was quite warm, but riding out in the carriage to the Wrights' home would not help the restlessness she felt.

"I thought as much. I am ready now, if you wish."

"Let me fetch the basket from Mrs. Cronk."

Georgiana shook her head. "John will meet us at the carriage with the basket." She nodded at the footman, who stepped outside to relay the message.

"Thank you, Georgie," said Elizabeth with a smile. "I suppose you had anticipated my response? Have I become so predictable?" She loved Georgiana, but noted how running the house seemed to come to her as easily as her proficiency on the pianoforte and could not help feeling just a little lacking in comparison.

As Georgiana laughed, one stray curl escaped its pins, and she tucked it in behind her ear absent-mindedly. "Not at all. However, I see my brother's serious nature has begun to influence you. Fortunately," she spoke more softly, leaning in to Elizabeth, "your influence seems to be changing him as well. I have never seen him happier, Elizabeth."

Elizabeth groaned playfully. "Will you never call me Lizzy, Georgie?" she teased in the same hushed tone.

Georgiana straightened as a blush spread across her fair cheeks.

"I will try, *Lizzy*. For you."

Elizabeth reached out to squeeze the younger girl's hand. "That is all I ask."

***

"Thank you, John," Elizabeth said as they reached the cottage. Georgiana made a move to step out of the carriage, but Elizabeth stopped her, reluctantly fulfilling her husband's request. "Georgie, let me see how the boys are faring before I mention you are here. They may not be well enough for visitors, in which case I shall be out again shortly." Georgiana sat back in her seat with a frown.

Elizabeth almost chuckled, but stopped when she remembered that not that long ago, she too had often been unable to do as she pleased. She had at least had the benefit of nobody to deflect the attention of the sometimes overly solicitous servants or her protective older brother. She patted Georgie's hand and said "I promise I shall call you if a visit is warranted."

John helped her down from the carriage and then reached back into the vehicle for the basket of food. She smiled her thanks and noted his stiff nod. John was nearing forty, she thought, glancing at the sandy hair that had begun to thin on top and his weathered, impassive face. She had heard him laugh in Fitzwilliam's presence, but she could never even get him to smile. She wondered what he really thought of her and then felt her cheeks begin to heat and turned away. Other than his duty, why would she expect him to be thinking about her at all? She was not so foolish as to believe that the Master and Mistress consumed a servant's every thought, even one as loyal to the Darcy family as John Briggs. He was a widower with two sons nearly gown and had more pressing concerns than to tend to her every comfort. *You are becoming quite arrogant, Lizzy*, she told herself sternly. Safely turned away from her companions, she rolled her eyes and had a little laugh at herself. Perhaps she would add this item to her list of challenges. *Keep the merchants from cheating us. Supervise provisions for the poor and the ill. Earn at least one genuine smile from John Briggs.* Then she squared her shoulders and approached the cottage.

The cottage stood in a small, neat clearing in the Pemberley woods, the first in a line of five. There were five more about a mile from the opposite side of the great house. They were comfortable, modern, and relatively large. She knew that Fitzwilliam had spent a good deal of time and money to make them pleasant and accommodating for servants who had families. When she had seen the cottages on one of her walks, she had sought out Fitzwilliam in his study to ask about them. He had nodded for her to sit and explained, "Under servants tend to seek out new situations every two or three years, either heading to the factories looking for better pay or to service with a more prestigious family."

Elizabeth had raised her eyebrow at this statement, and her husband had chuckled. "We are not titled, dear. Even servants seek out the higher ranks, as it reflects well upon their own competence." Clearing his throat, he continued, "Training new servants is disruptive and expensive. Most employers frown on servants with children. Therefore, by allowing for a suitable situation for those who already have children, we gain an advantage. We have more applicants for the positions and those who are hired are more likely to remain." When he paused again, she had prompted him.

"Therefore, over time, you intend to save more money on hiring and training than you spent building the cottages." It was not a question, and he had looked at her with a smile and nodded. "But of course," she had continued slyly, "you never had any thought for the comfort of those servants with children, or indeed, of your family and guests in the pursuit of this scheme."

Fitzwilliam had nodded slowly, thoughtful. "These were also reasons." He paused again and she waited patiently. "Despite the loss of my mother and father here, I have always been happy at Pemberley. It seemed right that those who work for us should at least be as comfortable as possible." He did not add that having children on the property had made it seem less lonely after the death of his own parents, but his wife understood.

With this conversation in mind, Elizabeth reached the Wrights' door and knocked. There was no answer, and she was puzzled. She had sent a message the day before saying that she would arrive around this time. She stood for a moment, and then knocked again. She heard some movement inside and relaxed. Soon, the door opened, revealing a woman a few years older than herself.

Mrs. Wright's long brown hair appeared to have been hastily tucked away in a cap as several long pieces had escaped. She appeared tired and worn.

"A pleasure to see you, Mrs. Darcy," she said softly and swung open the door. "Please come in."

As Elizabeth stepped inside, the other woman curtsied and motioned her to the settee in the small but very clean front room.

"I do not wish to impose, Mrs. Wright. How are the boys?" She handed her basket to Mrs. Wright, who took it with pleasure.

"Oh, many thanks, Mrs. Darcy." She hesitated, glancing back at the boys' room. "I do not know. They seemed to be getting stronger, but it is so slow, and they have not gained much since your last visit."

"What has Mr. Waters to say?"

"Only that they are young and strong and he believes they will recover. But I am afraid, Mrs. Darcy." She looked up at Elizabeth with pleading eyes. "They are still so weak."

"Have they been eating?" Elizabeth asked, feeling great sympathy for the woman. Mrs. Wright's husband was in London completing a task for Fitzwilliam, and other than her two older boys who were just six and eight, she had no other family near. Fitzwilliam had insisted on sending for the apothecary immediately. The Wrights and their four rambunctious boys were great favorites of his, she knew. While he felt responsible that Mr. Wright was away, she believed he would have sent for Mr. Waters in any case.

"No, ma'am. It is terribly difficult even to get them to take some tea." Elizabeth frowned. She did not like this at all. She had come expecting that the boys would be much better, or she would not have brought Georgiana.

Although she knew her husband would not be pleased, she felt she had to see the boys. Perhaps there was something back at the house she could send that would tempt them. If they did not eat or drink anything, they might never recover.

"May I see them, Mrs. Wright?"

Mrs. Wright was shocked at the suggestion. "Oh, no, ma'am, they have been ill. I would not like to see you expose yourself or the family."

"Mrs. Wright," she said softly, "You have been exposed, and I have already seen you several times in the past week or so. You see I am well. Now that there is no fever, I do not believe one quick visit to the boys could harm me." She saw the other woman was considering it, and she added, "Perhaps the boys might be cheered by the promise of some treat for them when they are well?" Mrs. Wright pursed her lips and for a moment seemed on the verge of tears.

"Oh, Mrs. Darcy, you are too kind."

Elizabeth smiled in a way she hoped the other woman would understand. Now that she had such resources, it was a joy to use them in this way. Seeing someone's face light up or hearing the pleasure in an exclamation of surprise was something she dearly loved. She had always adored children, perhaps because, she thought to herself laughingly, she still felt like a child herself at times. There were nearly twenty children who lived in the cottages at last count. She had arrived with a present for each of them when she had first arrived at Pemberley after her wedding, and their squeals of delight were more than enough to buoy Elizabeth's spirits for the somewhat more difficult task of winning over their parents.

She stood for a moment and went to the window to see whether Georgina was still in the carriage. She was, but the two older Wright boys were with her, gleefully kicking up their heels on the seat across from her. She smiled at the tableau. Georgie was delighted with her company, laughing heartily at something one of them had said.

Mrs. Wright gazed at the young mistress with gratitude. The food that had been sent daily from the great house had allowed her to tend to her younger boys without neglecting the older, and the personal interest she had taken in Mr. Wright's absence had been deeply gratifying to the doting, weary mother. She had never had a mistress at Pemberley, and none of them had known what to expect, but Mrs. Wright was only too pleased to tell anyone who would listen that Mrs. Darcy brought sunshine with her. Yet there was more to her than that. Like Mr. Darcy, she did not shrink from real work. Nor, from what the other servants said, did she suffer fools or tolerate those who would cheat her. From experience, she knew what the others were only beginning to comprehend, that, like the master, Mrs. Darcy would not be persuaded from an action she believed to be correct. Mrs. Wright smiled tiredly, and led Elizabeth to the boys' room.

Chapter Five

WHEN ELIZABETH DID NOT return immediately to the carriage, Georgiana sat back with a sigh. What was the point of accompanying her sister if she was not allowed to be of any use? She knew that Lizzy appreciated her presence and companionship, but she longed to be of some real support to her. Georgiana knew what a responsibility Elizabeth had taken on in agreeing to become her brother's wife, and she felt that she had at least some slender knowledge that she could offer. Still, Lizzy seemed determined to do things on her own.

As she sat ruminating, she spied one brown eye peering up at her from just above the door.

"Hello," she said, laughing, as John swung down from his seat to remove the intruder, who was perching on the wheel. "May I ask your name?"

John soon grabbed the child, who squirmed in his grasp. The boy was about eight, thin and wiry, and had closely trimmed brown hair. The day had turned quite warm, and he was barefoot.

"No, no," Georgiana said with a smile, "let him stay. Put him up in the carriage with me." John stood for a moment, hesitant, and Georgiana said to the boy kindly, "You may sit in the carriage with me if you will promise to be a gentleman." The boy gazed at her, clearly smitten.

"Will you behave?" she asked the child with a smile. He stopped struggling and nodded.

John scowled, but Georgiana ignored him.

"What about me?" pleaded a tiny voice from the carriage's other door. A face very similar to the first, but a few years younger, popped into view. Georgiana pretended to look him over seriously before nodding.

"Yes, if you behave as a gentleman, you may also come sit with me while I wait for Mrs. Darcy." The boys sat opposite her, ignoring John's scowl.

When they had introduced themselves as Matthew and Peter Wright, and Georgiana had introduced herself as Miss Darcy, she asked them to explain why they had scaled her carriage. The boys, eager to please such a pretty woman and thrilled to be seated in a real carriage, could not speak fast enough. They were knights come to rescue a beautiful princess who was being held captive by an ogre. Georgiana laughed heartily when she realized that the ogre was John.

John Briggs sat rigid and stoic on his seat at the front of the carriage. He knew his manners were not such to recommend him to the Darcy women, but he was loyal to Mr. Darcy and quite anxious to return both ladies safely to the house. He had always felt a bit of an older brother to Mr. Darcy, who had been born the year John had turned twelve, and was comfortable in the master's company. Knowing how protective the man had always been of his sister, and judging from his changed character how fiercely he loved his wife, John was always a little on edge when the women traveled with him alone. He felt the great weight of the trust that had been placed in him, and he would do all that he could to prove that trust justified. He glanced back at the carriage to be sure the boys who had wormed their way into the carriage were not causing trouble, but Miss Darcy's smile indicated that she was pleased with them. He turned back to face forward, not at all mollified.

With the boys both balanced precariously on the rear-facing seat, their small legs swinging in delight over finding themselves the center of attention, Georgiana thought with some pleasure that she had found an indirect way to help Elizabeth. At least she could entertain the older Wright boys so they would not disturb her sister's visit. Besides, the boys were truly charming if a bit grimy from their adventures. The older boy clapped a hand to his stomach as he spoke, lifting a small dust cloud and causing his to sneeze several times, his little legs swinging up together with each whoosh of air.

She smiled at them both and they began to chatter at an even greater speed, making it difficult to understand them. *Adorable*, she thought, as she nodded in what she hoped were the right places, and smiled when they had exhausted themselves. By the time Elizabeth returned to the carriage, they were both fast asleep.

"My goodness," cried Elizabeth in mock astonishment. "Who is sleeping in my seat?" John swung down to grab the boys, but Elizabeth put a gentle hand on his arm when she saw that they were sleeping deeply.

"It is all right, John. Would you perhaps carry them inside? I am sure Mrs. Wright would be happy for them to nap while she takes some rest herself."

John nodded silently and with the women's help soon had one boy's sleepy head on each shoulder. He turned slowly to take them to the house, and Elizabeth turned tiredly to Georgiana and tried to smile.

"Thank you, Georgiana, for entertaining the boys while I spoke with their mother."

Georgie sighed happily. "I am pleased to have been of help. How are the younger Wrights?"

Elizabeth began to answer, but a movement on the path below the cottages drew her attention. It was Mr. Waters. He did not see them at first, lost in thought, his hat pulled down over his forehead. When his eyes met Elizabeth's, he strode over to the carriage with purpose.

"Mrs. Darcy, Miss Darcy," he said with a bow. "How do you find my young patients today?"

Georgiana thought Mr. Waters quite handsome in his blue coat, though the sleeves were a bit frayed and his boots worn. She knew he was almost as fond of walking as Elizabeth, and as there had been no physician in Lambton since the death of old Mr. Gordon a year ago, he was much in demand. She determined to practice putting herself forward a bit more rather than shrinking into the seat cushions as she was wont to do. She briefly forgot that as Mrs. Darcy, Elizabeth should have offered the first greeting and answered his question.

"Have you walked all the way from Lambton this day, sir?" she asked politely. Elizabeth turned to look at her with a merry twinkle in her eye. Georgiana cast her eyes down, unsure what she had done to excite Elizabeth's mirth. When she realized, her cheeks grew rosy with embarrassment. At least her sister did not seem to be offended. So chagrined was she that she barely heard Mr. Water's response.

"No, ma'am," he said. "I tied up my horse at the edge of the Pemberley road and walked from there. I have other patients to visit today and must travel more expeditiously."

Elizabeth answered Mr. Waters' question. "They are not as ill as they were, but Mrs. Wright is still worried that they do not seem to wish to eat or drink."

Mr. Waters smiled. "I think she has not yet offered them something they would like. They have been days without fever, and I fear they have become accustomed to being waited upon by their devoted mother."

Elizabeth nodded. "I hope that is the truth, Mr. Waters."

Mr. Waters tilted his head amiably. This was not his first conversation with the young Mrs. Darcy, and he waited politely for the question he knew would soon follow.

"Mr. Waters," she asked, "what was your treatment in this case?"

Georgiana looked out across the wooded lane as the two discussed the stages of the illness and what he had done to care for the Wright boys. Mr. Waters was something of a radical, she knew. He believed that the patient could, in most cases, do well without many of the old cures. Although not a surgeon, he had many opinions on the uselessness, even danger of bloodletting and used laudanum only sparingly, often only when the patient's family demanded it. He preferred to come up with his own remedies whenever possible and was often to be found reading up on new cures. Mr. Gordon had not thought much of him.

However, Fitzwilliam had spoken with Mr. Waters at length about his theories. In the absence of a truly local physician and not impressed with the available surgeons, he had invested in the young man's training and allowed him the use of whatever books from the Pemberley library he thought might be of use. He had even ordered some written by French doctors, which had raised some eyebrows in Lambton. She knew that her brother was thinking of the care of his own family, but having Mr. Waters well trained was good for the townspeople as well. She smiled. There was no denying that her brother had taken a liking to Mr. Waters. In fact, Fitzwilliam seemed to really trust him, and so, it appeared, did Elizabeth.

As they finished their recounting of the steps and treatment of the illness, which Mr. Waters believed to be influenza, he glanced at the cottage and then back at Elizabeth.

"When does Mr. Wright return?" he asked.

"I do not know. He is still in London. I do not believe he knows the boys have been so ill, as when Mrs. Wright first wrote, she thought they would soon be well. She plans to take them to her sister in Cardiff for their recuperation. The older boys will wait here for their father's return."

Mr. Waters nodded. "I expect she will be able to take the boys in another few days."

"My brother makes for London shortly," Georgiana interjected softly. "Perhaps he will send Mr. Wright home."

"Perhaps." Elizabeth did not wish to think about Fitzwilliam's impending trip. She knew he needed to conduct important business with the solicitors that had been neglected. She also knew that he would not stay long, perhaps two or three weeks, but the time apart, the first since their marriage, made her apprehensive. She had grown accustomed to always having him near.

The two said goodbye to Mr. Waters, who handed Elizabeth into the carriage before turning back to the cottage. Elizabeth shook her head at some of his notions. Still, he spoke with quiet authority, and the Wright boys had been brought through a frightening illness and did look to be recovering. She would not, nay could not argue with the outcome of his treatment.

Her mind wandered back to Fitzwilliam. He had promised that he would not even bother to open Darcy House, as it would signal to the *haut ton* still in town that he was available for social calls and delay his return. Instead, Fitzwilliam would stay with Charles and Jane. Elizabeth had hinted, and had hopes, that Mr. and Mrs. Bingley would eventually find an estate to purchase somewhere closer to Pemberley. Elizabeth was sure it was only a matter of time before the two would wish to remove from Netherfield, and Bingley had been interested when she had mentioned it. Jane would never admit that they lived too close to their mother, but if Bingley could be persuaded there was hope. Elizabeth loved to think about it. Jane and Georgiana would get along very well, and she missed having Jane near. Of course, this was not the time for her to accompany Fitzwilliam to London, the weather being so warm in the city and there still so much to accomplish at Pemberley.

Elizabeth returned to thoughts of her visit. Despite Mr. Water's assurances, she was concerned about the Wright boys. Georgiana carefully moved to the opposite seat and perched next to Elizabeth. She squeezed her hand sympathetically and was silent. Elizabeth saw in her sister's face that she knew the source of her dismay.

Another of the joys of her marriage, Elizabeth thought gratefully, was that so many of those who surrounded her knew when there was nothing more that could be said.

Chapter Six

FITZWILLIAM CLEARED HIS THROAT. "Elizabeth?" he asked, bemused to find her so distracted. She had asked him to relate the details of the repairs that he had authorized should she be consulted while he was away, but now she did not seem to be listening to his response. She glanced up from her plate and he was concerned to see that she had not been eating.

"Oh, I am sorry, William," she said quietly. "I know I asked a question, and it is quite rude of me to ignore your answer. I am afraid I am a little out of sorts this evening." While her mind was still on the Wright boys, she was also dreading Fitzwilliam's trip. Perhaps she should have asked to go with him after all.

Not only would she miss him, for the first time she would be left in charge of the entire estate. She was sure she could run the house well enough for the few weeks he planned to be gone. Mrs. Reynolds was always thoughtful and thorough in her assistance. In many ways, though, she would need to take over his duties as well. Of course, she would have Mr. Harrison to assist her, but the steward, a short, thick man with little hair, heavy eyebrows, and a coarse manner did not trust her yet, and might never. She did not wish to admit it openly, but she did not feel as though she could trust him, either. He never looked her in the eye when he spoke, and she was wary about the way he glanced about the house when he was inside, almost as though he was memorizing everything and everyone in it. She noticed that he did not do this in William's presence, but he did not hesitate to do so in hers. He was superficially flattering, but she detected a harshness in his words that concerned her, and although she knew herself able, she did not anticipate with pleasure any need to navigate a difference of opinion with him.

She chastised herself silently, realizing she was wasting the private time she had left with Fitzwilliam, time Georgiana had kindly given her by requesting her meal above stairs tonight.

"Elizabeth," Fitzwilliam said softly, putting a finger under her chin gently and tilting her face to meet his gaze. "Are you well?" She blushed a little under his gaze. This was ridiculous. She must not worry him.

"Yes, dearest," she said, looking up. "I am well. It is just that I will miss you terribly." She raised her chin a bit more. "However, I shall rally," she said stubbornly, forcing a smile that was not reflected in her eyes, "and you will be quite proud of me when you return."

Fitzwilliam lowered his hand but continued to silently consider his wife's countenance. His heart beat a little harder at the expression of loss she was attempting to conceal. As much as he had loved her before their marriage, every day they spent together only increased his esteem. He had not thought it possible that he could love any woman this much. He reached out to take her hand.

"As you are quite aware, I am already very proud of you," he said evenly. He met her gaze, coaxing from her a small but sincere smile. "I will miss you as well, my dear," he said quietly. "You have no idea how much."

"I beg your pardon, *Mr*. Darcy," she retorted haughtily, "I do know. I feel it myself." He took her hand and smiled rather bashfully at her, and she smiled back, truly pleased.

"William," she said firmly, "please make sure that you send Mr. Wright home as soon as you arrive." She looked so suddenly dejected at the reminder of the Wright boys that Fitzwilliam's heart twisted in his chest.

"I shall not forget, Elizabeth," he promised, but then teased, "It is the third time you have asked."

She laughed, realizing that he was correct, and shook her head at him. Fitzwilliam removed his hand from hers and gestured to her plate.

"Elizabeth, please. You must eat something or I shall have to feed you myself. I do not want a skinny wife." His eyes were teasing, but she could detect the seriousness behind them. He would not leave her behind if she did not show that she would be well in his absence. She realized suddenly that if she was to convince him that he could depend upon her, she must make a better show than this. She nodded and began to eat, though she tasted nothing. He finished his own food, but watched until hers was nearly gone, and then nodded once, satisfied. A lock of his hair fell over his forehead and she reached to brush it back.

He looked at his wife again, but her eyes were on her plate. He began to speak but thought better of it and bit off the words. Instead, he said, haltingly, "I have heard from Richard. He is in town."

"Oh," she said, looking up, her brown eyes alight with pleasure and relief. "Will he be in London for long? Will you have an opportunity to see him while you are in town?"

"I believe so," he replied, pleased to see her spirits revived.

"What did his letter say?"

Fitzwilliam looked at her for a moment, searching her face carefully, then smiled and said. "As much as it ever does. He is in town and if I am available, he will come to visit."

Elizabeth noticed the hesitation, and briefly waited for an explanation. When none was forthcoming, she laughed lightly in response and replied, "Please give him regards from the Darcy ladies. Oh, it has not been so very long, but it seems an age since we have seen him. Especially since. . ." she stopped suddenly and glanced at her husband. They had both read the accounts of Vitoria in the London papers.

"Indeed," was his only reply. He sipped his wine and she picked up her own glass. When she set it down, she looked up at Fitzwilliam.

"I promise to return as soon as I am able," he said seriously, his dark eyes refusing to relinquish hers. "I certainly have no desire to be gone one moment longer than necessary." He stood, tossed his napkin on the table, and held out his hand. "Now, Mrs. Darcy, shall we repair upstairs?"

Elizabeth stood to take his hand, and they walked upstairs to share the night together.

***

The early morning sky was still gray when she walked down the stairs with Fitzwilliam to say goodbye. His trunk was already in the front hall as he tucked her letter for Jane into the inside pocket of his greatcoat. She held his arm while the coach was loaded, and too soon, it was time. Elizabeth stood on her tiptoes to kiss her husband goodbye. She hugged him tightly and he buried his face in her hair. Finally, he bent down to look her in the eye. The solemn gaze was broken suddenly as he grinned mischievously and winked at her. She was so shocked she laughed out loud, which had, no doubt, been his intention. With one last kiss, he murmured "I will return soon, my love." Then he was down the stairs and in the coach, pulling away. She watched until he was out of sight, and then took a deep breath and turned to the footman.

"May I have my pelisse, James?" she asked pleasantly. "I wish to go for a long walk before breakfast this morning." She could see the conflict on his face and tilted her head at him, raising her eyebrows.

"What is it, James?" she asked, though she thought she might already know.

"If you please, ma'am, I will get a footman to accompany you. Mr. Darcy asked that you not walk alone while he is gone." She shook her head. Of course he had.

"Mr. Darcy is not here, James, and I shall never tell. If he truly did not wish me to walk alone in his absence, he should have spoken to me about it himself." James still looked reluctant, but Elizabeth shook her head, more amused than annoyed. "I do know where my pelisse is, James, and can fetch it myself," she teased. Elizabeth looked outside, where the sun was beginning to flood the grounds. Soon the dew would be dry on the grass, but it would still be cool for a few hours, a wonderful time of the day for a stroll around the grounds.

"Of course," she mused aloud, her lips quirking up at the corners, "I could simply go without it." James' defeated footsteps echoed in the entry as he moved to fetch the pelisse. Worse than failing to persuade her to take a companion would be his stubborn mistress walking out of doors both alone *and* unprepared for the damp.

"Thank you, James," she said sweetly as he held it out and she slipped her arms into the sleeves.

"Yes, ma'am," he said, resigned, and she walked down the stairs into the morning. The sun was soon warming her steps and Elizabeth was feeling far better than she had when she watched the carriage carry Fitzwilliam away. Now the worst was over and she had only to fill the time until his return. She was surprised to find that once the dreaded farewell was over she could pull herself together tolerably well over the course of a single walk. A long walk, to be sure, but by the time she returned several hours later to break her fast with Georgiana, she was feeling inordinately improved and actually looked forward to all she would have to show her husband she had accomplished in his absence.

As the young mistress finally emerged from the walking path around the lake, John Briggs moved away from his vantage point on the hill behind the stables, where he had stood on watch, arms folded across his chest, ever since he spoken with James. He shook his head. Not enough that he had not been asked to accompany Mr. Darcy to town to see to the horses, as he normally would, but had been asked, very particularly, to remain at Pemberley to be charged not with training the new stallion, but with keeping an eye on both Darcy women whenever they were out of doors. Knowing his master as he did, he was both honored and apprehensive. The responsibility weighed far more heavily upon him than his typical duties, and the mistress seemed determined to make his position even more difficult. *Stubborn woman*, he thought, irritated. If she would not follow her husband's wishes, what chance did he have? No, his only real hope now was that Mr. Darcy would not be away long.

Chapter Seven

Fitzwilliam Darcy watched the lithe form of his young wife disappear behind the trees and sighed. He tossed his hat on the seat beside him and ran his hand through his hair. Opening his valise, he pulled out some letters of business he thought to concentrate on during the trip. With any luck, he could prepare much of his work before he arrived, as he would now have to attend to the additional task his cousin meant to set for him.

His own business could normally be completed within a few weeks, but yesterday, an express from Richard had arrived while Elizabeth was out. He had intended to mention the entire message to his wife, but he had changed his mind. She was already dreading the separation. How could he add this to her worries? Richard had summoned him in an unsettling manner, but he did not know exactly what awaited, so he was also unable to reassure her all would be well. Surely there was no need to add to her burden without cause. Setting his business aside, he removed the letter from his pocket and reread the cryptic message:

Darcy,
Your man Wright tells me you will be in town shortly. I require your assistance on a matter of some urgency. No need to write. I will know when you have arrived.
Alea iacta est,
Richard

Richard was not a reliable correspondent, and his notes from town were often brief, but this missive was more from the Colonel than his cousin. The Latin phrase Darcy recognized immediately from their boyhood lessons. It meant "The die is cast," but to the two men it meant much more. It had begun as a phrase shouted cheerfully as they adventured or played at soldiers in the woods at Pemberley and Matlock, had become a complaint accompanied by a shrug and a drink at Cambridge after an exam or other trial. The last time Richard had used the phrase was when he took his leave as a young lieutenant off to the wars. It had been poignant then, but not yet bitter.

Though his cousin had maintained his easy manners in company and was the first to turn serious matters into jests, Darcy knew Richard had not come back from the wars unchanged. There was a hollowness under the gentlemanly façade that very few saw, though he sometimes suspected that Elizabeth had glimpsed it, too. While Richard was friendly with all, he was friend to very few. Other than Darcy, most of Richard's friends were also men who had served. Darcy grimaced. Despite his wish to help his cousin in any way in his power, he knew he could never truly understand what Richard had experienced. *Perhaps,* he thought, *whatever this is requires skills other than those of a soldier.*

The Latin made it clear. It was not just business. It was personal. Richard was already involved in something, possibly deeply involved, and he needed help. He refolded the letter and replaced it in his coat pocket. The heel of his boot gently tapped the wooden case under the bench, where he had stored his pistol. Whatever it might be, he would not deny his cousin the aid he requested.

Chapter Eight

TWO DAYS FOLLOWING Fitzwilliam's departure, the warm summer air began to chill and the skies turned dark. Then it started to rain, the water falling to the ground in heavy sheets, turning the roads into muddy rivers and making it impossible to venture outside. Elizabeth watched from the windows in her study, hoping that Fitzwilliam was not encountering the same wretched weather. It took three or even four days of travel to reach London depending upon the state of the roads, and she hated to think of him stranded at an inn unable to make progress. She turned to her desk where a neat pile of correspondence awaited. She would not have a servant take her letters to town to post today. Perhaps she might leave answering it until tomorrow, but finally admitted to herself that she required the distraction.

Mrs. Wright had sent word directly after Mr. Waters' visit that the boys were accepting tea and some food. She planned to take her youngest boys to her sister's home in Cardiff to recover more fully. Elizabeth had quietly supplemented Mrs. Wright's purse from her pin money so that they might have a more comfortable journey, and the three of them had left the day after Mr. Darcy's departure. Mrs. Wright's sister was an experienced nurse and they would stay with her perhaps until the fall. Elizabeth thought this a sound plan, as Mrs. Wright was worn down and would benefit from a bit of rest nearly as much as the children. The older boys had been left with a neighboring family to await Mr. Wright's return from London.

She glanced out the window again and offered a short prayer for Fitzwilliam's safe journey. He would write when he arrived, but with the state of the roads it was entirely possible she would not receive his message with any speed. She sorted through the stack of letters and began to write her replies while thunder cracked and lighting flashed outside.

In the days since her husband took his leave, Elizabeth had answered all her letters, reconciled the house accounts, and read through the following week's menus. She wondered, not for the first time, whether Fitzwilliam could have reached London yet when Mrs. Reynolds knocked softly on the door. Elizabeth looked up to see the housekeeper step inside.

"Would you like a tray, ma'am, or will you dine with Miss Darcy this morning?"

Elizabeth sprinkled her final letter with sand and stood. "In the breakfast room, if you please, Mrs. Reynolds. Is Miss Darcy downstairs yet?"

The housekeeper shook her head. That was unusual, Elizabeth thought. Georgie was always up and dressed by this time. She nodded at Mrs. Reynolds and said, "I shall go seek her."

"Very good, ma'am." The older woman nodded and quietly retreated from the room.

Elizabeth paused for a moment to fold up the final letter, wrote the direction, and sealed it. She glanced at her completed pile of letters and nodded, mentally crossing this task off of her list. She was quite proud of how methodical she had become. The rhythm of her days at Pemberley had eventually settled over the last four months into patterns she could now better recognize, and she was becoming more adept at anticipating and completing those tasks requiring her management. There were fewer whispers among the staff, though she had heard a few more comments about her being far below her husband only a few weeks before, and one about her unladylike insistence on walking alone in the mornings just yesterday, though not from James. She did not directly confront those who spoke thus, afraid it would serve only to make the staff more secretive. She felt better knowing what the rumors were. If the worst of it was that she had, as had once been charged, a sort of conceited independence, then she would live with that. She still had enough of Lizzy Bennet in her to lift her chin at such dismissals.

No, Elizabeth was determined to silence her naysayers with kindness and compassion, though she had to admit that her temper was often tried, and therefore sometimes difficult to regulate. Still, she had managed thus far to convince herself that once they knew her, they would find little to reprove. Shaking off the unhappy memories, she thought with some pleasure that by the time Fitzwilliam returned she would able to finish her work by the end of each morning and would then have time for other, more pleasurable pursuits. She flushed briefly when she considered the smile Fitzwilliam might have given her had she said that to him.

She was doing her best, trying to remain occupied much of the day, but oh, how she missed him. The nights in particular were terribly lonely.

Elizabeth sighed just a little as she dropped her letters on the silver tray next to the desk and stepped out into the hall to search for Georgiana. Perhaps she was busy in the music room. Just as she put her foot on the first stair, there was a commotion behind her, most likely at the front door. Someone was speaking urgently. She hesitated a moment. It sounded like Mr. Harrison. Surely he would wait. She stood still for a moment, one foot still on the first stair, trying to discern his words. She could not make them out though he was certainly making no attempt to speak quietly. Ultimately, her curiosity would not allow her to delay, and she turned back towards the entry.

"Mrs. Darcy!" called Mr. Harrison as she approached. He was removing his coat and hat, water rolling off both articles of clothing and pooling on the tiled floor. Whatever could cause him to travel through this kind of storm?

"Forgive my appearance, ma'am, but I must speak with you immediately." Elizabeth nodded. As he started towards her study, she turned to the housekeeper.

"Mrs. Reynolds," she said quietly but firmly, "would you please seek Miss Darcy and inform her that I am occupied? She need not wait on me this morning." Mrs. Reynolds nodded and moved towards the stairs.

Mr. Harrison looked agitated as Elizabeth walked into the room and sat behind her desk, as she had seen Fitzwilliam do. She studied the man's face as he struggled to begin. There was more than agitation there. He was breathing heavily, and his face was pale. He was afraid. She stood quickly.

"What is it, Mr. Harrison?" she asked, pushing down the panic that threatened to rise.

"One of the servants came to my door quite early this morning, ma'am." He met her gaze. "Fever, ma'am." Elizabeth froze as he looked up to meet her gaze. "Mostly the children at the cottages, but almost all of them are down with it." He looked at his boots. "Mrs. Wright took her youngest out of town to her sister in Cardiff, but left the older two with Mrs. Porter, and the boys were taken ill yesterday. By this morning, nearly every child. . ." his voice trailed off.

Elizabeth's mind was reeling. The older Wright boys were everywhere on the estate, instrumental in every act of childish mischief, and they were uncommonly charming. Every child in the cottages followed their lead. If the Wright boys were ill, it was no wonder they all were. She drew in a deep breath to steady herself. She had to think. What was to be done, and in what order? She looked at Mr. Harrison. He was not a father, but he looked as stricken as though he were. No, she corrected herself, studying him more closely. He was shifting his weight from one foot to the other, his breaths still coming in quick huffs, his eyes glassy with panic. He was unsteady, uncertain. He did not have his fear under control. How could she trust him to lead the servants in this state? Perhaps once there was a plan in place he would settle.

Elizabeth's voice was firm, clipped. "Is anyone else ill or just the children?"

"As far as I know, ma'am, just the children." Harrison shuffled his feet and added, "Thus far."

"How many?"

His jaw tightened. "I have not seen them myself ma'am, but the servant told me as many as thirteen, fourteen maybe."

Elizabeth felt rooted to the spot where she stood, but reached out to hold the back of the sofa for support. So many? All of them at once? She let out the breath she did not realize she had been holding.

"Have you sent for Mr. Waters?"

"Yes ma'am. I knew it was what you and Mr. Darcy would want."

"You are quite correct. Has he arrived?"

"No ma'am, not yet."

Elizabeth frowned. The young apothecary had always been very prompt. "When was he called?"

"Several hours ago, ma'am."

Elizabeth felt something close to the panic she had seen in Harrison's face. There were only a few reasons she could believe that Mr. Waters would not have come directly at such a summons. Either he was tending to others, indicating a larger outbreak, or he was himself taken ill. *No,* she chided herself. *He could be tending someone for a different reason altogether.* She tried to believe it, but she squeezed her eyes shut when she recalled how often he had been in the Wright's home caring for the boys.

"Are you all right, ma'am?" Mr. Harrison asked, staring at her, clearly still uncomfortable. "Shall I call Mrs. Reynolds?"

"No," Elizabeth said resolutely, holding up a hand to stay him. "I am well. A moment, if you will." She opened her eyes and began to pace. Five steps forward, turn, five steps back. *Think, Lizzy,* she scolded herself. *Think.* She had discussed Mr. Waters' treatment for the boys both with Mrs. Wright and with the apothecary himself at some length in the hopes that she might be able to provide assistance. She knew Mr. Waters was young and his treatments considered rather odd, but Fitzwilliam believed him to be well read and unusually well trained. He trusted Mr. Waters, and Fitzwilliam trusted so few people. . .

Finally, she turned to face Mr. Harrison. He waited expectantly.

"Mr. Harrison, please relay my sympathies to the parents. Ask that they follow my directions exactly." He nodded as she ticked them off each item on her fingers. Bring down the fever with cold compresses, keep the children cool if fevered and air out the rooms every so often, even if the weather remained damp. Make them drink. Finally, try to keep the sickroom as clean as possible. Mr. Harrison's eyebrows lifted at the advice he had not expected, but he said nothing. She ended with a grim smile.

"Mr. Harrison," she said evenly, "these are the instructions. It is how Mr. Waters treated the younger Wright boys, and they are clearly well enough to travel." He nodded, unconvinced, but unwilling to argue with her. "I will have someone deliver food and medicine for the families by this afternoon, but I cannot ask anyone to take these things into the homes, so the families should know to expect a delivery outside. When you have relayed the message, please return to the house as I may have need of you." She noticed the scowl on his face, but did not turn away. It was not necessary for him to be pleased with her. He could take his complaints to Fitzwilliam upon his return. She glanced outside. The thunder and lightning had eased, but the rain continued. It would be a miserable ride.

"I am sorry to send you back out in this weather," she said softly. "Have Mrs. Cronk make you something to eat and drink some tea before you go." He bowed stiffly, but when he straightened, while his face was still fearful, it was also set, grim, angry. It was a momentary flash, gone so quickly she could not be sure it had ever been there. Then he turned and was gone. She let out a breath. How was she to work with this man?

Mrs. Reynolds stepped inside, dismissing the footman, and shut the door with a click. Her face was ashen.

"Mrs. Reynolds? Has Mr. Harrison spoken with you?"

"No, ma'am." She looked imploringly at Elizabeth. "Miss Darcy is unwell."

The lines on the housekeeper's face seemed to deepen, and though she stood as straight as always, she seemed smaller, somehow. It took a moment for Elizabeth to allow the words to register.

No, Elizabeth thought. *No, not Georgie.*

"Mrs. Reynolds," she said, her clear voice penetrating the older woman's fear and masking her own, "The children in the cottages are ill as well. Miss Darcy was visiting with the elder Wright boys a few days ago and may have been exposed then."

"How would she have come in contact with the Wright children?" asked Mrs. Reynolds, astonished. "Mr. Darcy would never have allowed it."

"With Mr. Darcy's permission, she accompanied me on a visit to Mrs. Wright. She remained in the carriage, but apparently the older boys were invited by Miss Darcy to sit with her while she waited." She knew Mrs. Reynolds was not blaming her, but Elizabeth felt her guilt. *Another time,* she thought. *I cannot focus on this now.*

"Please go to the kitchen, Mrs. Reynolds. Tell Mrs. Cronk that Miss Darcy is ill and ask her to prepare a quantity of willow bark tea, saline draughts, and barley water. We will be sending some out to the cottages as well. We have summoned Mr. Waters and he may have additional instructions, but for now, inform Mrs. Cronk that I will be there to consult with her shortly. I need you to check in with each of the house servants to see if anyone else is ill."

"Yes, ma'am." The woman said quietly, her face drawn.

"Mrs. Reynolds," Elizabeth said gently. "I know that Mr. Darcy has long relied on your fortitude. Miss Darcy is depending upon it, and the servants will look to you to see how they should respond." *Heaven knows they will not be able to look to Mr. Harrison.*

Mrs. Reynolds squared her slight shoulders and lifted her chin. "Have no fear of me, ma'am."

Elizabeth met her gaze gratefully. "Never for a moment." The housekeeper nodded once and moved down the hall towards the kitchen.

Now she must take her own advice. Elizabeth paused for a moment to feel her fear, then took a deep breath and carefully tucked it away. She could not allow her distress to show. Instead, she opened the door and strode out into the hallway with purpose. By the time she arrived at the top of the stairs, she was reviewing the stages of the Wright boys' illness. First chills, then fever, and, for one boy, delirium. The fever had finally broken after several days, first one boy, then the other, leaving them indolent and wan. It had taken nearly a fortnight for them to recover enough to leave bed, and the fever had come and gone several times, though never as hot as at the beginning. Mr. Waters had forced the boys to drink saline draughts and barley water before starting them on heartier fare. Elizabeth had taken the boys some beef tea on her last visit, which they had reportedly enjoyed enough that they were feeling somewhat improved the next day. During their illness, the boys had resisted eating or drinking anything, but their mother had been persistent, even forceful. Elizabeth realized that she would need to be the same. This was no longer a matter of hoping the staff would trust her. They needed someone to be in charge, and that someone, at least for the moment, was her.

She reached Georgiana's room and entered. Georgie was sitting up in bed, blankets twisted uncomfortably about her yet still shivering. Her normally lustrous golden hair was dull and plaited plainly down her back. She half smiled when Elizabeth arrived and made a face.

"I am so sorry, Elizabeth," she said, shaking so hard that her teeth nearly chattered, "I meant to be such a help to you and here I am just another burden."

Elizabeth forced herself to smile and busied herself with the bedclothes.

"You are being silly, dearest," she replied with a smile. "You could never be a burden to me." She carefully unwound the blankets and set them to the side. Then she pulled the bedsheets straight, took the warming bricks from their place by the fire and positioned them at the foot of the bed. Finally, she unfurled the blanket and tucked it in securely at the foot of the mattress, pulling the rest of it snugly over Georgiana.

"I will have some tea brought up," Elizabeth said quietly, kissing her sister on the forehead. Although

Georgiana was shivering, Elizabeth's lips burned with the heat from the girl's forehead. "Please try to drink it and then get some sleep."

"Oh, Lizzy," the girl moaned, burrowing into the covers, "I do not think I can drink anything."

Elizabeth sat on the side of the bed and leaned in to look Georgie in the eyes. Slowly and seriously, she said, "Georgie, I know you do not feel as though you can, but you must. Do you understand me? You are not the only one taken ill, and you must do your part to get well. If you would ease my anxiety, you must drink." Georgiana's eyes widened, and she nodded silently.

Elizabeth felt a weight settle on her shoulders. She hated to speak to Georgiana in this way. Her young sister was so patient and kind that any harsh word fell heavily on her. In this way, she had always reminded Elizabeth of her sister Jane. However, she knew the one way to ensure Georgie's acquiescence was to appeal to the Darcy sense of duty. If she thought being a compliant patient would lighten Elizabeth's load, she would do so faithfully, no matter how ill she felt.

"I must see to the others," she said gently. "I will send Mrs. Reynolds up shortly and will come to sit with you later. Please Georgie, I need you to do everything we ask without argument so that you will be well when your brother returns. Will you promise me this?"

A silent, shivery nod was her only answer.

Chapter Nine

DARCY PACED THE LENGTH of his tiny room at an inn fifty miles outside of London. He had awakened very early in the hopes of speaking to his cousin before the day was out, but the thick, black clouds that had been threatening the previous day had finally overtaken them, blowing in from the north while he slept. Now there was a heavy rain pelting down, coming in nearly sideways in a howling wind that had forced him to send the carriage back to the mews. There was no way to travel in this squall. He hoped it would not set him back much longer, as he was exhausted from speculation.

Richard had issued such a summons only once before. It had been while Darcy was still attending university. Richard had completed his own studies and his father, the Earl of Matlock, had purchased a commission for his son in the regulars. When Darcy received Richard's message, he left Cambridge within the hour, riding directly to his cousin's quarters in London where he had found Richard agitated and angry over some long-standing thievery on the part of his captain, who was skimming money sent from his men to their families.

Due to his position as the junior officer, for the first time in his life, Lieutenant Fitzwilliam had found himself unable to act openly. His genuine affability had been materially damaged by a full understanding of his new position; the need for a profession would likely require the compromise of his integrity. He was desperate for a plan to thwart the man, but he could not employ his typical direct, forward assault. Darcy knew his cousin could best him in contests of brute strength, but in this he needed a more subtle partner, and Darcy had been honored to be asked. Together, they had manage to leave evidence in the path of the man's colonel without drawing any attention back to Richard. Darcy had never breathed a word of it, especially not to his father, who would not have been pleased to hear that his son had left his studies, even temporarily, for such a reason. But Darcy had never been able to deny his cousin anything he genuinely needed, not even to please his father. Darcy smiled at the memory. They had both been so young then.

"You are an excellent chess player," Richard had said triumphantly, clapping him on the back and offering Darcy a drink. It had been true then and was still, despite his uncharacteristic disaster in the courtship of Elizabeth. Thank God that had worked itself out in spite of his stupid blundering. He still blushed to recall his dismissive words at the Meryton assembly, though for Elizabeth they had become no more than something to tease him with. Once she had understood how much the reminder pained him, she had apologized and stopped, but he had never been able to forgive himself. Even Elizabeth, though, had never teased him about his insufferable first proposal, as it brought so much pain to them both. He might have driven her away forever. He might have lost her. Unthinkable.

When had he become the man who insulted Elizabeth Bennet without a thought? He had not been that man when Richard called for help. Darcy returned to the days following his sudden ride to London. He had finished his schooling at Cambridge with, he believed, a reputation for being quiet and serious but not severe. He was willing to be teased and his sense of humor though dry, was yet intact. Nobody appeared shocked when he smiled. He had enjoyed himself as much as any man careful of his family name was able. It was only several years after the escapade with Richard, after his abbreviated wartime tour of the Continent and subsequent return to England that his life had taken this turn. He had received an express at Darcy House not long after his return, summoning him immediately to Pemberley. One look at Mrs. Reynolds' pale face as he alighted from the carriage had told him everything. Two sleepless and agonizing nights later, George Darcy died while his son held his hand and prayed.

Richard had arrived hard on Fitzwilliam's heels, having seen the express in London and taking the time only to inform his commanding officer that he would be taking a month's leave. He did not wait for a response. Even the Earl and the Viscount, both in town for Parliament's session, had not reached Pemberley so quickly.

Darcy had become a different man in the aftermath of his father's early death, and Richard had watched that transformation with ill-concealed dismay. He could do nothing to alleviate his cousin's concerns for him, as he had been entirely adrift. George Darcy had taught his son well, but had not yet had the time to truly work as partners side by side with his son, to teach him the intricacies of managing an estate as vast as Pemberley. He knew, in general, how things ought to be managed, he had some knowledge of the family's investments, but he had less experience dealing with people than he should have had. Most of the tenants and merchants who had known his father were honest and decent, but they had not always been above trying to take advantage of the younger Darcy's inexperience to improve their own situations. Negotiating rents, mediating tenant disputes, reviewing and renewing contracts from the village for everything the estate required to keep running, it had all taken a toll. Darcy stretched his arms high above his head, trying to work out the stiffness from the interminable carriage ride that had stranded him here, unable to move forward or to head back.

Truth be told, even the Earl and the Viscount had been interested in helping advise him on the management of the estate. Young as he was, Darcy knew the offers, though not entirely self-serving, had also not been completely altruistic. His Matlock relations had their own ideas about the investments he should make and with whom, hoping, perhaps, to forge or maintain advantageous political alliances. Aunt Catherine had begun to cluck about his parents' wish that he marry his cousin Anne, as though taking over Pemberley was not daunting enough a task without taking a wife. Both aunts pressured him to hand Georgiana's care over to them. Everywhere he turned were people with their hands out, recommending, cajoling, demanding. Except Richard.

Instead, Richard, Major Fitzwilliam by that time, had put his military training to good use. He had bundled his father and older brother off in a carriage to London the day after the funeral, citing his father's duty to Parliament and Viscount's duty to learn the business of politics. He had unceremoniously lied to Aunt Catherine about George Darcy's final instructions including a moratorium on marriage for at least two years while his son became accustomed to his new duties, commenting with a laugh that one lie deserved another. He had asked Mrs. Reynolds to oversee mourning clothing for Georgiana and armbands for the men. Most importantly, he had talked with Darcy for hours, sometimes all night, about what lay ahead for him and what they meant to do for Georgiana.

Richard was to share guardianship, a tremendous relief, with both aunts clamoring to take custody and his ten-year-old sister adamant that she would not leave her brother. He had even acted as a secretary, writing out lists of meetings as Darcy spoke haphazardly about needing to understand the full state of the accounts. He and Darcy had discussed refusing or buying out the living his father had recommended for George Wickham so as to rid himself of the man, and Wickham had made it simple when he requested money rather than the living, showing up precisely one day following Richard's departure for his regiment. There was no doubt that everything necessary was accomplished in better time and in stricter order because Richard had been there to support him when he had been bowed down by grief.

The shock of his sudden responsibilities and his driving need to live up to George Darcy's example had, he acknowledged, affected him deeply. He had become reticent, distrustful, grim around everyone except Richard and Georgie. It was one of the reasons Charles Bingley had become such a good friend. The easy, unaffected affability of the man had been like an oasis in the middle of a desert. He had not been influenced by the grasping nature of town, despite his sisters' desire to improve their station. With Richard away on the Continent, Bingley alone could occasionally lighten his mood, at least when they were on their own. He forced Darcy to attend balls where every woman thought of him as something to be caught and parties where every man wanted to connect himself to Pemberley's wealth and consequence, yet had never once sought to use that influence for his own benefit. Dodging his social obligations entirely, as Darcy was tempted to do, would have made it difficult for Georgiana in her first season, though that was still a few years away. Bingley's open desire to enjoy himself by dancing and conversing with pretty women had saved him from becoming a recluse. Like Richard, Bingley was not interested in what his friends had, but who they were. Neither man seemed to fully comprehend, even now, how exceptional they were, how necessary to his state of mind.

Though now he understood that even his excellent father had not been the perfect master of Pemberley, at barely three and twenty, he had not. He had spent entirely too much time trying to reach an impossible standard, and that dark time had left an indelible mark on his personality, one he believed would never be altered. Until Elizabeth.

Fitzwilliam's thoughts lingered more pleasantly now, on his wife, particularly the way in which she had taken to her new role as mistress of Pemberley. The day following their return from the wedding tour she had made the unusual request to visit the children of the servants to distribute presents and learn their names. She had made a sweet picture, removing her bonnet and bending down to speak to each of them in turn as she handed each a gift, laughing at the things they whispered to her, smiling at a few of the boys who had clearly been taken with her charms. He thought of her practicing a duet on the pianoforte with Georgiana, stopping with a laugh to ask about the fingering of a certain passage, bending her head next to Mrs. Reynolds at the desk in her study as they reviewed the weekly menus or went over the tenant visits, her sweet scolding face when she opened the door of his study to tell him he had worked too long and it was time to dress for dinner.

He smiled in spite of his frustration. It was still less than two years since he had met Elizabeth, less than a year since she had accepted his hand—but already he could not imagine being without her. His wife had brought light, cheer, and grace back to his life, though she also possessed a rather clear, if not detailed understanding of the world and its evils. Her goodness was not inherent. Instead, it was a choice, a decision she made each day, to act with integrity but also with compassion and kindness. He reflected, briefly, on how that might require a good deal of bravery, a kind of courage he did not believe himself to possess. He had been away for only three days yet already desperately missed the curve of her hip, the blush in her cheeks, the fire in her eyes when she was scolding him about something. He missed her just being near.

As his thoughts turned to his current journey he scowled, thinking about how he had kept Richard's message a secret even from her. It had gone sorely against the grain, but the Latin, he knew, was a warning, and she had been so upset at dinner the night before he departed. He rubbed his forehead. Elizabeth would have his hide when he finally told her, and she would be in the right. Well, it could not be helped now. The roads were in such a state he would never be able to send a letter. If only this damned rain would stop.

Darcy tapped a fist on the window frame as he watched the water cascading from the roof of the inn to the ground, creating a swift stream that ran along the back wall and down the hill outside. He cursed, cursed again, and then let out a soft but energetic burst of invective aimed at the weather. By the time the rain finally tapered off and the clouds began to clear, it was late afternoon, too late to reach London before dark. He would have to wait and try again in the morning.

***

It was almost noon before the carriage rattled to a stop in front of the Bingleys' townhome and Darcy swung out nearly before the steps were placed. He gave quick orders to the coachman and the men unloading his trunk and thought briefly about sending for Richard, but remembered that his cousin had said there was no need. The front door opened and Bingley strode past the butler to shake hands with him.

Charles, truly his brother now, was all smiles, and he tried to smile back.

"Darcy! It is very good to see you. I can see that you are well. How is your lovely bride?"

A genuine smile broke through his worry, and he assured Bingley that his bride was very well, indeed. *The making of me*, he added silently, something his friend would understand. They were very fortunate men. His thoughts briefly ran to Richard, who had not been as fortunate, returning to Spain a few days after the wedding, fighting a war while he and his lovely young wife had taken an extended wedding tour. He forced himself to return his attentions to the present, and the two men entered the house.

While Bingley called for tea and led him toward the drawing room, Darcy considered what he ought to do. It was likely, knowing Richard, that he would make his appearance within the hour. As Bingley reached for the door's handle, Darcy put his hand out to stall their entry.

"Charles, before we go in, I must inform you that my cousin Colonel Fitzwilliam has a matter of some importance to discuss with me. He will likely be here shortly, and I would beg the use of your study when he does."

"Is the Colonel back in town? That is marvelous news, Darcy. I had not known it.

"He is welcome join us for tea."

"Perhaps. It will likely depend upon the business he has come to discuss."

"Certainly, Darcy. The study is yours as long as need be," Charles said, the lines of his face straightening into a more serious expression. "If I may be of any assistance, you will of course inform me."

"I thank you, yes."

Bingley silently examined his brother's face. He had believed that he knew all of the man's expressions. He had seen the man happy, angry, stoic, in pain, in a deep, agonizing love. He had seen him weep for his father. He had even witnessed rage, the flames smothered but the embers still glowing. This was new. The man before him was something different—apologetic, restless, worried. He could not quite put his finger on it. Clearly, something serious was afoot, and he planned to have the truth of it. Now was not the time, he thought, as he waved Darcy into the drawing room, where Mrs. Bingley awaited them.

He opened the door and stepped inside where his wife was waiting.

"My dear," he said, with just a bit less enthusiasm than he had shown outside, "our brother has arrived."

Jane Bingley rose with a genuine smile that reminded Darcy of her sister, and he answered her with one of his own.

"You are very welcome, *brother*," she said, her blue eyes sparkling as she spoke the word. "I know your trip was a long one. I hope it was not too inconvenient."

He took her in, knowing Elizabeth would want all the details he could muster. She was dressed in a lovely deep blue silk dress, her hair done simply but stylishly. Her face was no longer serene, he observed, but fully happy, content. She tilted her head slightly, waiting for him to speak. He exerted himself.

"My trip was indeed far too long, but otherwise uneventful, thank you, Jane. It is very good to see you looking so well."

Jane smiled again as she glanced at her husband.

"Yes," she said without a trace of shyness. "I am very well indeed." Bingley flushed a little, and then Jane began to pour the tea as they all sat down.

In the middle of a conversation about their tour, details about their engagements in London, and a second pot of tea, there was a knock at the door and Darcy, not Bingley, was presented with Richard's card. He stood and made his excuses. Jane was a little surprised, but after glance at her husband the expression disappeared.

"Let me show you to the study, Darcy." Bingley rose to escort him out. As they stepped into the hallway, they saw the Colonel approaching. Both men noticed that the Colonel was walking with a slight limp. Bingley shook his hand, watching as he turned to his cousin for a brief handshake and a nod.

"May we speak, cousin?" Richard's face was drawn.

"This way, Colonel, Darcy," said Bingley and led them down one hall to another. "Second door on the right. I will let the staff know not to disturb you. Shall I send for tea?"

"I thank you, no." The Colonel's normally affable manners had deserted him. The man before them was grim, every bit the soldier. Bingley stopped them for a moment with an outstretched hand. He took a breath to repeat the offer he had made to Darcy.

"Gentlemen, I appreciate your need for privacy and will leave you to it. However, I am now Darcy's brother and therefore count you as family, Colonel. I have offered my help to Darcy, but let me do the same with you. If I am able to offer assistance in any way, I must insist you inform me."

The Colonel's grimace twisted up for a moment into a ghostly approximation of a grin. While he knew the gesture well meant, the expression chilled Darcy to the bone.

"Thank you, Bingley. If we have need, we shall indeed inform you."

Clearly dismissed, Bingley nodded once and turned to return to his wife. He heard the two men muttering something and then the door shut with a soft click. He hoped this discussion would not be as bleak as it appeared. He did not know the Colonel as well as Darcy, but he knew that both men deserved fewer burdens than they carried. Good to his word, he approached the butler to explain that no one was to interrupt the meeting.

"Now cousin," Darcy said firmly as he followed Richard into the study, "What is this all about?"

Richard sighed and took a chair. Darcy frowned. His cousin did not often sit to deliver news. He preferred to stand, to move.

"Are you well, Richard?"

"I was slightly wounded at Vitoria. I returned to town about a fortnight ago."

"You are recovering." It was a statement, but also an invitation to elaborate.

"I am." Richard looked around and waved his hand at a bottle. "If Bingley wishes to be of service, he can allow me a glass or two of his port."

Darcy grinned a little and poured two glasses. As Richard took one, Darcy took his and began again. "Now cousin, out with it. Why the secrecy?"

"Darcy, I hardly know. I had thought this would be easier, but I find myself quite. . . perplexed." Richard gulped the liquid from his glass, draining it and setting the glass down gently but with precision. He looked up at his cousin, and Darcy saw the hollow man lurking behind Richard's green eyes.

"Cousin," said the Colonel finally, "I should have died at Vitoria."

Darcy felt cold, sick. He drank the port in a gulp and felt the alcohol burn its way to his stomach. "Indeed?" he forced himself to ask, absently turning the empty glass in his hands.

"Yes." He looked at Darcy appraisingly. "I hardly know what it is I have stumbled into, but I know I am not up to the task. Not on my own."

Darcy waited. He had heard such an admission from Richard only once before, but that had been a young man's problem. If Colonel Fitzwilliam was admitting he needed help, the problem was likely to be far more difficult.

Richard gestured to the bottle, and Darcy refilled his glass. This time his cousin sipped the wine.

"When I returned to my regiment after your wedding, I happened to meet a young man from the 95th, a Captain Oliver Hawke. We struck up a conversation, as his regiment was out of Kent. He had heard of Aunt Catherine." He chuckled softly, but the sound was strained.

Darcy nodded once and frowned. "Hawke? Was he related to the Hawkes of Staffordshire?" There had been a Hawke family in the neighboring county some years back with a fairly large estate. The main house had burned to the ground and he thought he recalled that the entire family had been killed. When had that been? Ten, perhaps twelve years ago? He had been away at school then, preparing for Cambridge. The servants at Pemberley had still been gossiping about it when he returned home for the holidays. The tenant farms were flourishing and a steward collected rents and managed the land, but the main house had never been rebuilt. He had considered offering to purchase the property a few years back but had decided against the outlay of funds.

The Colonel shrugged. "I do not know," he admitted, surprised.

"I beg your pardon for the interruption," Darcy said seriously. "Pray proceed."

Richard swirled the port remaining in his glass. After some time had passed, he said "We were finishing off the French at Vitoria. We were able to take the bridge with little resistance, but once across, there was fierce fighting. We were to flood across a narrow bridge and overwhelm them with numbers. They were defending with artillery, William. Defending with vigor." He paused and rubbed his eyes tiredly. "We were all exhausted. The men were bitter. They wanted to break the enemy's back, and I believe we accomplished that." He faltered a bit, but recovered. "I lost my mount, and was behind my regiment as a result. I could see Hawke ahead of me on the other side of the bridge, trying to organize the rifles and target the French officers in order to cause panic. They were instead rushing the enemy, against their orders." He shook his head and met Darcy's worried gaze. "Who would purchase a commission for a boy, particularly in such a regiment? They seek out conflict, they relish it, and he was so damn *young.*"

Darcy noted Richard's use of the past tense but said nothing, just waited for his cousin to resume. He closed his eyes. "As I tried to get into position, he was shouting something about another cannon." He finished the drink with a practiced flick of his wrist. "He was trying to wave everyone out of the line of fire, and before I knew it, he had shoved me away. I smelled the gunpowder, felt the ground shake, and was thrown back by the blast. I do not understand how he realized what was happening, how he reacted so quickly, but instead of fleeing or seeking shelter himself, he knocked me out of the way." He looked up at Darcy again. "The boy took the brunt and I am left with only the smallest limp. But that is not yet the whole of it."

Darcy waited patiently for Richard to continue. The silence was difficult to bear. Richard's eyes clouded over. He was far away. Finally, he spoke again.

"I hit the ground quite hard and for a time could not move. I could only see him crawling away, though for what I could not have said. I was not thinking clearly. Now I realize he must have been trying to reach his rifle, which he had lost in the blast." He grimaced, the words coming slower and with more difficulty. "When I turned away from watching him, there was a French soldier pointing a pistol at my heart."

Darcy's breath caught, though he tried to hide it by taking a drink. Richard was not fooled, and a wistful smile flickered on his face.

"I was ready, William. I could barely move. I was tired, I was hurt. I was ready. I was fully willing to watch him deliver me to the devil. I do not know why he hesitated. It was only a matter of seconds before I heard the shot. But instead of my own death, I watched his. Captain Hawke was sitting about twenty feet away. He shot first and the shot was true. He saved me not once, but twice."

Darcy shut his eyes for a moment, grieved yet profoundly grateful. "The boy?"

The Colonel shook his head. "By the time I came back to myself, I had been carried off. One of my men sought him out at my direction but could not locate him. One of the surgeons offered him a letter that had been in the boy's pocket." Darcy knew what that meant. There was no room for the dead, only the wounded.

"I am sorry, Richard." Darcy said. *He will never forgive himself.* "What did the letter say?"

Richard blew out a heavy breath and set his empty glass down. "Well, now, we come to the point. He has asked me to find his sister and be sure she is safe and cared for. It is a debt of honor, and I am bound to fulfill it. Not," he added, "that I would wish to avoid it." He growled as he dropped his head to stare at his boots, his hand rubbing the back of his neck. "Damn waste."

"You said you needed my assistance," Darcy prompted. He was determined to shake Richard's self-recriminations. He knew that this was a debt that would drive his cousin mad until it was completed. Clearly it was already beginning to do so.

"Indeed I do, cousin. As I said, we had spoken previously. But why did he address this request to me? Why not one of his own?"

"Were you well acquainted?" Darcy asked gently.

Richard shook his head. When he spoke, he seemed to be giving voice to a list he had already compiled. "We spoke a few times. We discussed Kent. He had taken orders from me back to his colonel. I recognized early on that his men not only admired him, for he was a crack shot, but were truly loyal to him. He had a respect for command. I admired that. I would say he was a regular out and outer, William, but that there was a seriousness there. It is usual in the 95th to earn promotions on merit, not purchase, and I have since learned this was the case for him, though he had been with them less than a year. His reputation was that his men were always foremost in his mind, though he was not particularly friendly with them. Indeed, they would never have followed such a young man if he was not proven in battle and devoted to them." He shook the memory away and continued. "Why me, William?" he spoke hardly above a whisper. "I was not even in his regiment. Even compared to his fellows in the 95th, I barely knew him."

Darcy shook his head. "I cannot say, Richard. Perhaps his sister will know."

"And this is where I need your assistance, cousin." The Colonel sighed, opened his eyes, and met Darcy's troubled gaze. "For I cannot find her. She has disappeared."

Chapter Ten

THE STATEMENT HUNG in the air for several long moments, heavy with Richard's misery. Finally, Darcy cleared his throat to ask, "What do you mean, disappeared?"

Richard moved as though he would stand, but winced and remained seated. He shook his head. "I am afraid I do not know much for all the work I have done. I took Miss Hawke's direction from her brother's letter, but it led me to a rather fine townhome near Savile Row, not all that far, in fact, from your own."

"Then why. . ." began Darcy, but Richard shook his head and interrupted, tossing his hands up in the air, clearly agitated.

"I wondered myself, but when I inquired of the servants, all they would tell me was Miss Evelyn Hawke had left the home quite suddenly some weeks before and that they did not know her current whereabouts."

Darcy frowned. "I presume you have made inquiries."

"I have. What I learned led me to rooms in a home in Seven Dials." Darcy's face must have expressed his distaste, for the Colonel actually chuckled. "Do not concern yourself, cousin. I have no need to drag you to that part of town. She had been in residence, but removed, apparently with two other people, a few days before I arrived."

"This is curious, Richard, but surely your efforts are enough to satisfy. Her brother could not have expected that you would track her throughout the city."

Richard nodded. "No, I expect not. However, I do not *feel* satisfied, cousin. I fear she is in some difficulty. The neighbors indicated she had been removed under some duress. If she is in some sort of trouble, I would feel honor bound to assist her however I am able. The rooms in Seven Dials, I admit, concern me." He was quiet for a time, leaning forward, his arms on his knees, his hands clasped together. "One thing of which I am certain is that I should like to see and speak with her. If she wishes to hear it, she should know how her brother died."

Darcy nodded. He had expected such an answer from Richard, whose sense of honor was highly developed and deeply personal. Indeed, he was listening to the answer while already considering what might be accomplished, silently reviewing those in his employ upon whom he might call. Richard's military connections could only get him so far without additional resources, and many of the men upon whom he had relied here in town were likely wanted in Spain.

He had hired investigators a few years ago, after George Wickham returned to Pemberley to demand the living to which the blackguard had previously relinquished all claim. Wickham had smoothly threatened him with revenge, and while Richard had offered to handle the problem, Darcy had preferred his cousin not be hanged for murder. Instead, he had hired men to have Wickham watched. He had regretted that decision, as the information they had provided led to a frantic ride to Ramsgate just in time to foil an elopement with a very young Georgiana. He wished to continue his surveillance of the man once it was clear he would have to bury the entire incident, so as far as anyone else knew, his arrival had been coincidental.

After the hasty marriage of George Wickham to Lydia Bennet, Fitzwilliam had maintained the employment of the two best men, one a former Bow Street Runner and another who had been in service for the Prince, but had chosen not to continue in his Majesty's service once he became the Prince Regent. He had hired more men in Newcastle to ensure that George was treating his wife well, leaving these two men free to attend Richard's task. Should they need additional support, he believed they would have their own contacts. Richard studied Darcy's intense, distant countenance and sighed in relief.

"I knew I could count on you, cousin," he said with something like his former cheer.

"Always, Richard. You need never doubt," Darcy said gruffly. "May I ask what else you learned from those who located the Seven Dials residence?"

"Not much. Miss Hawke was with a female companion, and they meant to remove to the country with an older gentleman, perhaps her uncle. The gentleman did not stay with them, he rather came to collect them. Miss Hawke and the uncle were dressed in fine clothing. However, no one was able to tell me about the companion, the uncle, how they had been transported, or precisely where they were headed."

Darcy nodded without comment. He knew that Richard would have already spoken to any hackney drivers who frequented the area or any other carriages for hire within a reasonable distance, but it would be difficult to gain information in a neighborhood like Seven Dials without adequate contacts, and that required funds.

What had a young woman who lived in Mayfair be doing in Seven Dials? Why had the man spirited them away? Had she fled from him to meet this friend? Had he found her? Why had he not then simply taken her home? He shook his head.

"I am afraid I find this quite as puzzling as you, Richard. Before we begin, I must ask." He met his cousin's brooding gaze and spoke slowly and very clearly. "We do not know what is happening with Captain Hawke's sister. We may be simply interfering in family affairs, which should be enough to give us pause, but it is also possible that there is something more significant being played out. Are you absolutely set on this?"

Richard smiled grimly and replied, just as carefully, "I have an obligation, Darcy. My honor is engaged."

Darcy nodded once, brusquely. He had expected no less. "Then let us commence. I will send out some inquires today and we will meet again tomorrow afternoon. Are you staying at Matlock House?"

"No. My parents are not aware I am in town."

"Richard, you have been in town for more than a fortnight. Do you leave your parents to worry about your welfare when they might know you are safe?" Darcy asked with surprise. An idea flashed through his mind: *He is not certain he **is** safe. He will not know until he can discover her.* It made sense. Richard always went straight to see his parents when he was fortunate enough to be home.

"I could not do what was required were my presence known to my parents," Richard said with a shrug. "Father is busy with his politics and my mother would wish to monitor my movements, like any good general. Now that I have called here, I will visit them. They shall be removing to the country soon in any case. Most of his colleagues are already gone."

Darcy shook his head. "In other words, now that you have revealed yourself in a neighborhood where you might be recognized, you will tell them you are here before someone else does."

Richard shrugged. It ought to bother him that his cousin could read him so well, but it did not.

"Indeed. On that, I will depart. I shall meet you tomorrow afternoon, Darcy. Please send the time around to Matlock House when you know it." With a grimace, Richard stood and grasped Darcy's hand to shake it, his other hand clapping Darcy on the shoulder.

"I could not be more grateful, Cousin. I will see you tomorrow."

"I will do everything I can, Richard, you know that. Have I your consent to inform Bingley? His contacts may also be of use."

Richard considered the request. "Not yet, William, if you please. This is a delicate matter, and I fear using too many beaters, lest the pheasants fly before we are prepared."

"Very well," Darcy said and stood to open the door. He followed Richard into the hall. "Until tomorrow. And Richard?" His cousin turned back to face him. "I beg you. . . bathe, man."

Richard laughed at that, a genuine laugh, and it eased Fitzwilliam's heart a bit to hear it. He followed his cousin out and watched the Colonel's carriage until it rattled around the corner on its way to Matlock House. It was entirely unlike Richard to have left his family ignorant of his presence for so long. Lady Matlock, in particular, was anxious for her son to sell his commission and settle in England, but Richard was both determined to live as independently as possible and loath to leave his men while Napoleon was still in power. It was one of the most essential parts of his character, to protect what he loved—and, once committed, he could not be swayed without good reason. Darcy was witnessing that now. They were not so different, after all. His own devotion to those he loved generally did not require putting himself at physical risk, he thought ruefully, but he would not hesitate, should it be required of him. How his life would have been different had he not the means to protect those he loved, he could not say. He did not wish to think of it.

For now, he would return to the drawing room, but after tea, he would need to write several letters. He would call for Wright and send him home to fulfill his promise to Elizabeth, then he would write to his solicitor and make sure the documents he had drawn up before the wedding were signed and complete in every way. Darcy was unsure why he should feel so entirely unsettled at this business of Richard's, but he was, and he would not disregard those feelings. He would put his new life in meticulous order. He squared his shoulders, ran a hand through his hair to make sure he was presentable, and then strode through the drawing room door. Two faces looked up at him, one questioning, the other pleased.

"Now," he said almost gaily, "Jane, where were we?"

Chapter Eleven

RICHARD TOOK THE STAIRS in front of Matlock House more carefully than normal, not so much from the ache in his leg as a reluctance to face his parents without his work completed. He knew he had been pushing too hard since his return to England, but the gnawing unease he felt was affecting his temper as much as his leg and the headaches that still plagued him. He still did not recall the entire incident at Vitoria, though he did recall losing his mount and being saved by Hawke. He did not remember being hauled away from the field, or anything else that happened before waking up in the darkened room. Whenever he attempted to work through a difficult problem, his head began to pound, though it was improving somewhat. He was a bit battered, he thought drily, but rather grateful to be in one piece.

He had been surprised to learn that his parents were in London, believing that at this time of year they would have left the heat and stench of the city for the family estate in the north. He should have contacted his parents immediately upon learning that they were in residence, but there was just not enough emotion left in him to face them. His mother loved him, and he felt vaguely guilty that she did not know he was home. She was always trying to discover a woman with whom he would fall in love, believing that this was the best way to convince him not to return to the war.

His father, on the other hand, was not sentimental. He loved his younger son, in his own way, but the two of them did not understand one another. The Earl thought Richard was wasting his life in the regulars when he could be helping create real change through the wielding of the family's significant political power, and Richard found the nuances and continual compromises required by this kind of maneuvering distasteful. While there was political posturing in the military, of course, at least the real work Richard performed was straightforward, direct. Do not allow the enemy to reach England. Do what is necessary to protect the country and its citizens. This was the kind of work at which Richard had always excelled.

The Earl of Matlock was a beloved politician, one who fought to improve the lives of the poor and destitute despite his own position of privilege. Richard respected the politician, but as a father, Henry Fitzwilliam had always been distant and distracted, more interested in changing the world than tending to his second son, more invested in grooming his heir as his successor in Parliament than in even speaking to his other son much at all. Richard had always been very much the spare in a family with a hale and hearty heir. Since Richard's older brother Philip had turned twelve and began spending all of his time either at school or with his father, Darcy had been more a brother to him. He knew that Darcy would never turn him away, no matter how difficult or incoherent his need. He had the proof of that again today. With his father, he had no such assurance.

He arrived in his father's study three long strides ahead of Broome, the staid butler who had been a part of Matlock house longer than Richard had been alive. His father stood as he entered.

"Richard," he said, clearly pleased. "I heard about an hour ago that you were in town. Are you on leave?"

The Earl was not quite as tall as his son, but he was broad shouldered and muscular, a well-built man. Like both his sons, he had sandy brown hair that looked auburn in the sun, though, nearing his sixtieth year, it was giving way to silver. His face was lined, but not weathered, and a pair of spectacles, balanced precariously at the end of his nose, only served to make him appear more distinguished. Next to his handsome father, Richard felt every bit the weather-beaten, sunburnt wreck of a soldier he saw in the entryway mirror.

Of course he knew I was here, Richard thought. *The moment I surfaced near Piccadilly, he was informed.* He felt the old flicker of annoyance, but forced himself to respond civilly.

"I am, father. I was surprised to learn that you are still in town. You and mother normally travel north as soon as the session is complete."

"Yes, I had some additional business in town, but we will be leaving within a few days. Are you able to join us?" The Earl motioned to a chair and Richard walked in and sank into the cushions.

"No," he said quietly. "I am afraid I do have a commission to complete. Perhaps I shall join you after."

The Earl frowned. "I thought you were on leave."

Richard shook his head. "I am on leave, but I am not at liberty."

His father lowered himself into the chair behind his desk with a small grunt. "Must you always speak in riddles, Richard?"

Richard grimaced. Must his father always demand details to which he had no right?

"I have to deliver the news of a fallen officer to his sister. Therefore, I am not available to remove with you to Matlock."

"Are you the only man available for that job?" The Earl was already reaching for ink and paper, planning, no doubt, to ask one of his contacts at the War Office to relieve him of his duty. Richard rubbed his palms along his trousers and tried not to lose his temper.

"I am the one charged with it by the man who fell." He paused, and then decided that the Earl would likely know soon enough anyway. "He saved my life, father. I will not allow anyone to take my place."

The Earl was still, though he did not look up. "He saved your life?"

"He did." Richard gave his father an abbreviated version of the story.

His father's only reaction was to briefly close his eyes. When he opened them, he asked in an off-handed manner, "What was the man's name? If I can offer any additional assistance to his sister, I would be pleased to be of service."

Richard was startled by his father's statement. He had expected a lecture about the dangers of the battlefield and the idiocy of choosing to put himself at risk when he could do more to help England by assisting his father and brother with their political work. He had heard the lecture many times before.

"Thank you, father. He was a boy, really. Captain Oliver Hawke."

The Earl blinked, and Richard thought he saw a muscle twitch in the old man's cheek, but his face settled so quickly into its accustomed placid inscrutability that he could not be certain. He pressed on. "Did you know him, father?"

The Earl did not answer right away, gazing as he was at something above and beyond Richard's left shoulder. Finally he focused on his son, who was awaiting a response.

"No," he replied slowly. "I did not know Oliver Hawke." Richard stood, unconvinced but knowing he would learn nothing more.

"Well, sir, I should say hello to mother, then."

"You will stay with us until your commission draws you away?" The Earl asked, and then abruptly added, "I know your mother would appreciate it."

"Yes, father, thank you. I shall seek out mother and then change. I will see you for dinner."

"Until then, son."

The Earl watched his son leave the study. He stood very still for a few moments, and then locked the door. He crossed the room to a cabinet sitting on the floor behind his desk. Inserting a small key and opening the door, he drew out a bottle of very fine, very illegal French brandy, and poured himself a generous drink.

"Captain Hawke," he said, lifting his glass in salute. He sipped the brandy until it was gone, then turned to the window and silently refilled his glass.

***

Richard knocked softly on the door to the drawing room and quietly slipped inside. His mother was perched on a settee completing some needlework. She looked up as he entered and gasped with delight.

"Richard!" she called happily, and stood to greet him, arms thrown wide. He smiled and leaned down to embrace her.

Lady Matlock was not a tall woman. She was squarely built, buxom and curvy, her light brown hair gathered into a bun with curls falling gracefully over her ears. Her green eyes danced joyfully as her son released her and straightened to his full height.

"I thought you still abroad," she said breathlessly, patting down the silk skirt of her violet gown. "Are you well? Are you able to stay? How long are you here?"

Richard smiled and answered her questions in order. "I am clearly not abroad, I am well now, and I will be in England for a short period, though I do not know how long, precisely. I do have work to do that will prevent me from accompanying you to Matlock, but I may be able to join you there when my commission is complete. Is that all, madam?"

Lady Matlock closed her fan and lightly hit her son's arm with it. "Do not tease me, boy. I have missed you dreadfully." Richard ducked his head and kissed his mother's cheek.

"I apologize, mother. I know you worry. I have missed you as well."

"Have you seen your father?"

"I have, yes."

When Lady Matlock realized that this was all her son was to say about his meeting, she glanced at him reprovingly. "He only wants what is best for you, my dear."

"No, mother. I think we both know that he wants what is best for him."

She shook her head. "I will not engage in this today. I am too happy that you are here to spoil it by trying to play interpreter for either of you. Promise you will be kind to your father."

"I shall be as kind as he, mother."

"Richard," she said beseechingly, "please, be kinder. He means well."

Richard sighed and gave his mother another hug. "I will try, mother, to please you."

She reached up to pat him on the cheek, and then took him by the arm and led him to the door.

"Broome," she called. Broome was suddenly at her elbow, looking dour and unflappable.

"Yes, madam?"

"Please see that my son's room is readied for him and a bath drawn."

"Very good, madam." Broome bowed and left the room.

Richard laughed, recalling Darcy's command. "Am I pungent, mother?"

"Richard," she said with a wide, loving smile and a mischievous glint in her eyes, "you boys are always pungent. Take your bath and I shall speak with you at dinner."

Richard moved towards the stairs when he heard his mother call his name. He turned back at her summons.

"Thank you for coming, Richard. You have no idea how happy you have just made me."

Richard felt a blanket of guilt settle over his shoulders, but he simply smiled at her and moved upstairs. *A bath would feel like heaven*, he thought. *It is not so bad to be home.*

Chapter Twelve

AFTER SENDING MRS. REYNOLDS upstairs, Elizabeth entered the kitchen. The staff looked up from their tasks as she entered. At least twenty anxious faces turned to greet her when she entered. Even Mrs. Cronk, who hid it well, seemed to hold her breath. She cleared her throat.

"The news from Mr. Harrison is that the children of the cottages are ill. Is anyone else absent from their work today?"

A small woman with chestnut brown hair tied back from her face and wound into a bun replied quietly, "Robert Winton is missing. I thought perhaps he was just late, but it is not like him."

"Thank you. . ." Elizabeth hesitated. She had not met this girl yet.

"Marta, missus."

"Thank you, Marta." Robert Winton was an elderly groom who had moved to help out in the kitchen when his knee no longer allowed him to be of use in the stables. Elizabeth had met him in her first week and liked him immediately, though the other servants thought him a curmudgeon. He did not have children. She turned to the others. "Anyone else?"

It took only a few minutes for Elizabeth to realize that not only were there another five servants missing, but that while a few lived below stairs, three others lived in different places across the estate. She maintained a stoic expression. This was not confined to the cottages. She would have to keep a list. She reviewed the names silently. It seemed the illness was primarily affecting the young and the old, but she did not trust it would remain so. She shook her head. With no apothecary to travel between them, this was an impossible task. Had Fitzwilliam been here, he could have accompanied her to each home. No, he would have refused to allow it, fearful for her health. Well, he was not here and she would not hide.

"Very well," she said without emotion. "I will keep a list. In the meantime, we must try to locate Mr. Waters and discover whether he is well and able to assist." She spied John standing near the back door with his arms crossed across his chest and caught his eye. He nodded curtly and began to move around the side of the room towards the inner doorway.

"Mrs. Cronk, Mr. Waters asked that everything in the Wrights' home be kept very clean while the boys were ill. I intend to follow that advice. We will need to keep water boiling at all times for cleaning and laundry. In addition, he recommended that the boys drink as much as possible, even if they could not eat. He had some saline draughts and infusions for the tea, which I will discuss with you, as we should all drink them. I would also like to have some gooseberry wine brought up. I will otherwise leave the kitchen staff to your management." Mrs. Cronk nodded vigorously, and Elizabeth turned to address the others. She took a breath and stood as tall as she could, her chin tilted up ever so slightly.

"Today will not be the day we anticipated when we woke. However, if we can count on one another to perform the work we must, I have no doubt that we will prevail." She cleared her throat. "Mrs. Cronk and I will speak about what is to be done, and in the kitchen, she will have ultimate authority as always. Please do as she asks, even if it is not your normal task or you feel it below your station. Believe me," she said with a command in her voice she knew she was borrowing from her husband, "at the moment, there is no task below any of us." She motioned to John and nodded at Mrs. Cronk.

"Mrs. Cronk, I will return shortly so that we may consult."

John followed Mrs. Darcy out into the hallway. Her words were fine, and they had offered the others a sense of purpose and hope. Of them all, only he had seen the quick blaze of something in her eyes before the mask was firmly in place. He thought it might have been fear. He had been reminded with a jolt in that moment just how young she still was, and he felt a sudden rush of sympathy for her. The timing of this could not have been worse, with Mr. Darcy in London, or nearly, and the roads too wet to send for him by post. The mistress was on her own. He would do what he could to help her in the master's absence, but he was no nurse. He realized with a start that she was already speaking.

"John," she was saying calmly. "I will need you to locate Mr. Waters. When you find him, I need you to send him here, to the house."

He narrowed his eyes. "Here? Why not directly to the cottages?" She pursed her lips, met his gaze, and raised her eyebrows.

"No," he whispered, the air escaping in a moan. Not Miss Georgiana. He immediately recalled the boys in the carriage. "Those damned little. . ."

"John," she said, irritating him with an uncharacteristic reserve, "nobody knew they were ill, not even the boys themselves. This was several days ago. It may be that she was exposed later, by a servant who was already ill. We do not know for sure. Mrs. Reynolds is sitting with Miss Darcy now. The sooner I can dispatch you, the sooner I can go upstairs to help her."

John stopped at that and nodded. "I will find him, Mrs. Darcy."

"Once you do, it would also be helpful to know whether the outbreak is confined to Pemberley or has also appeared in Lambton. Make sure you do not approach anyone from town too closely." He nodded, anxious to be gone, and she released him with her thanks. He strode quickly down the hall towards the entrance to the stables.

She thought it fortuitous that they had already received several large orders of food for the week and that Mrs. Cronk always kept extra provisions on hand for unexpected guests. There would likely be no more deliveries from town until the illness had abated. How long had that taken with the boys? She tried to recall. Four or five days for the fever to break, and then another week to recover. She would not consider the possibility that anyone would not recover. She turned back to the kitchen to work out a schedule with Mrs. Cronk.

***

After checking on Georgiana and an hour in the kitchen conferring with Mrs. Cronk, Elizabeth returned to her study to compile a list of the afflicted. She sat quietly as the rain poured down outside and the pen scratched across the paper. When she finished, she counted the names. Twenty-two in all. Hopefully this list was complete. She stared at the page, particularly the first name: *Miss Georgiana Darcy*. Not even noon, and how the day had changed. She sanded the page and turned to the next. After a moment to think, she began.

Dearest William,

You have been gone but two days and are likely not yet in London. The weather has been very wet, and the roads are not passable. I therefore do not expect that you will receive this message before the end of our current trial, indeed I have no idea who might dare to take the paper from my hands. However, I have much to do and so must write you now, as I can.

There is fever here, William. I believe it to be the influenza that sickened the Wright boys. The children at the cottages are ill, as well as several of our elderly staff and pensioners. William, I can hardly write the words, but Georgiana is also ill.

At the moment, we cannot locate Mr. Waters, but John has gone in search. I recall Mr. Water's instructions for the Wrights very well and we have begun to follow them.

I must take leave, my dear, but before I do, I beg of you one thing—do not return to Pemberley until the danger has passed and I have written. I have enough to do, I could not bear it if you were taken ill when you are now safely away. For the present, the rest of us are well and focused on the task before us.

Until we meet again, my love.
Elizabeth

Elizabeth read the last paragraph with a sad laugh at her own boldness. She knew Fitzwilliam Darcy would never heed a request to remain in safety when his family was in danger, but he would realize that she must ask nonetheless. She thought how she had once hoped that his travel would be swift and the days dry. In one morning, everything had changed.

Keep him in London, Lord, she prayed. *Please, just keep him safe.*

Chapter Thirteen

ELIZABETH COMPLETED her preparations with Mrs. Cronk and relieved Mrs. Reynolds before dinner. As much as she trusted the upper servants, there was nobody she felt could nurse Georgiana as well as Mrs. Reynolds and herself. Georgie was sleeping restlessly, shaking with cold yet flush with fever. Elizabeth stroked the girl's cheek gently and sighed.

"Oh, Georgie, I am so sorry you are ill," she said softly. She touched the water in the basin with her finger to check whether it might need to be replaced and smiled when she saw a small misshapen piece of ice floating in it. Having access to an ice house on the property had never felt so propitious. Here it was July, and there was still ice. Mr. Waters insisted that a roaring fire in the summer was not necessary for a sickroom, and for this, Elizabeth was grateful. She recalled illnesses of her own as a child when she had become so overheated she would stagger to her window to gulp down some fresh air. What good would a fire do other than to make Georgiana even warmer?

There was a light knock on the door, and she rose to take the barley water sent up from the kitchen. Elizabeth gently woke Georgiana to get her to drink it. The young woman groaned and tried to refuse, but Elizabeth coaxed her persistently.

"You promised, Georgie," she said sternly. "You said that you would set the example. You must drink something." Over a few hours she was able to get her sister to drink an entire cup. She was not entirely satisfied, but it was better than nothing. She would let Georgie sleep and try again later.

Elizabeth stood and walked to the window. She sat on the sill and focused on the pattern: chills, fever, broken fever, possible relapse, recovery. She did not want to list delirium, but she knew if she could not get Georgie's fever down, that would follow. Her stomach churned relentlessly with worry, and she absently rubbed at it with her hand closed in a fist. She forced her mind to concentrate. By focusing on what to expect, she should be able to contain her anxiety. She dipped a clean cloth in the cold water, wrung it out, and placed it on Georgiana's forehead. Then she took another and began to carefully run the damp cloth along the back of Georgie's neck, her arms, her legs. *You will drive this fever into pneumonia,* a shrill voice whispered in her head. *Where is Mr. Waters now, when you need him? Why follow his instructions when he cannot be bothered to attend?* Elizabeth stood abruptly to move back to the basin of water. She gritted her teeth and banished the unjust thoughts from her head. He was not able to be here, for whatever reason, and Georgiana was depending upon her. Fitzwilliam was depending upon her. He had already lost so much. To lose his sister would kill him. She plunged the cloth back into the water and wrung it out.

Focus on what must be done, she admonished herself. *Do not think about anything else. This worked for the Wright boys. It will work for Georgie.* She succeeded for a time, but after Georgiana had fallen into a restless sleep and Elizabeth was sitting quietly, alone in the dark, small hours of the night, she could no longer keep her fears at bay. She loved the young woman before her as much as her own sisters, and could not bear to think that she might not recover. Georgie was not as strong as she, but then, not many women were. She laughed silently at herself. *What conceit!* Mrs. Reynolds, in her day, had probably been twice as strong as she, and Mrs. Cronk was still.

You are growing quite conceited, she admonished herself. *Remember who you are, Lizzy.*

She stretched, trying to relieve the soreness in her back, and moved back to the window. The rain was not as heavy as it had been, but the grounds would still be terribly flooded. If only she knew what the weather was like in London. She yearned to speak to her husband and yet she wished him far away. She reached into a small pocket in her skirt and felt for the miniature she had taken from her study. She rubbed her finger along the edge of the tiny frame, drawing strength from it, like a talisman.

Elizabeth tried to move her mind to other concerns. She wished to visit the children in the cottages in the morning and see to their relief as well, but how could she manage it? Georgiana needed her, there were other servants taken ill below stairs, and the two sets of cottages as well as the outlying pensioner cottages out a bit farther from the main house. She would not have time to visit them all each day as she wished, and Mr. Waters was not here to travel between them himself. She puzzled out possible plans for over an hour before she turned to the only one that made any sense. When she had thought it through she stepped out into the hall and asked for Mr. Harrison.

Close to an hour later, the steward stood in the dark hallway, again shifting uneasily from one foot to another as Mrs. Darcy outlined her plan. He shook his head, but she continued to speak to him a calm, steady voice.

"I would ask that you oversee the preparations, Mr. Harrison. We shall need to deploy men in several directions about the estate to gather everyone together in the ballroom. The maids and I will work to clean the room out and set it up for your arrival. John Briggs will help you."

"Briggs? The groomsman? What use will he be?" The man's disdain contorted his features into something almost grotesque. It made Elizabeth think, briefly, of a gargoyle.

More than you shall, I am certain, Elizabeth thought, trying to maintain her composure. "John Briggs has been with Pemberley since Mr. Darcy was a child, Mr. Harrison. He knows where everyone on the estate is located, and in the absence of Mr. Darcy, he is most qualified to help you assign men to each area so that we are sure to check in with everyone. If we are to contain the spread of the contagion and offer assistance to anyone who requires it, it is essential that we are thorough."

"Forgive me, Mrs. Darcy, but I believe this is not a plan that the master would ever approve. How am I to explain to him that I put the household at risk? I should lose my position." He twisted his hat in his two rough hands, his head ducked, but it was an artificial attempt at deference. His head might be lowered, but his eyes remained fixed on hers, daring her to defy him.

Elizabeth scowled and met his gaze. This was not a man concerned with his position, but with self-preservation. He was a bully and a coward. While she understood his fear, she was unimpressed, even angry with the man for giving way to it. It was his job, his responsibility to act honorably and assist her. She had heard wonderful stories about the past two stewards, who had spent a combined thirty years caring for the estate. Would that she had such a steward now!

"Mr. Harrison, in my husband's absence I must act as I see fit for the best care of everyone connected with the estate. In this I know the master would fully agree, and as he is not here to offer his own plans, we shall have to follow mine." She lifted one eyebrow and set down the challenge. "Are you able to complete this assignment, sir?"

Mr. Harrison continued to stare at her for a moment, but when she did not look away, he snarled,

"As you wish, madam, but I will discuss this with Mr. Darcy when he returns. You put all of us at peril with this nonsense."

Elizabeth only smiled as charmingly as she was able. If Mr. Harrison had been a bit more intelligent, he would have understood the danger in that innocent expression.

"See that you do, Mr. Harrison. I am certain he will take your complaints with all the seriousness they warrant. Please meet the men in the stables by seven tomorrow morning. Good evening."

She stood in the same place for some time after Mr. Harrison's departure, attempting to school her features and cool her ire. When she finally felt in control of herself, she turned to the nearest footman and said, quite politely, "Peter, please send for John Briggs. I will be with Miss Darcy until he arrives."

***

Elizabeth took her candle to the small writing table she had asked be placed in Georgiana's room. Sliding one sheet of paper to her, she propped Fitzwilliam's miniature up before her and began to write.

Dearest William,

As I cannot know when I should expect to see you, I will write what I wish you knew, to explain what I intend to do and why I have done it. It is a relief to the press of my thoughts to release them here, where my doubts can cause no mischief. I miss you terribly and only wish I could speak with you and ask your advice.

Georgiana is very ill. Her fever is high, and her sleep is broken. She is attended by Mrs. Reynolds and myself. There is still no word from Mr. Waters, and I fear that he may have been taken ill as well. John has returned from town with no news of him, but can tell us that the illness has not spread to Lambton. Of course, the townspeople now know they should not directly approach Pemberley until we send word, and that is some comfort.

As to Pemberley itself, the ill are spread all about the estate. I know that you would tell me to send food and medicine out to the afflicted, my dear, but the truth is that there are not enough of us well to tend to those who are not.

I have had to make a decision, William, one which I daresay will not please you but that I hope you will come to accept. In the morning, if there is a break in the rain, we will strip the ballroom down, set up cots, and make it our sickroom. We will bring the sick to us so that we may offer proper care to each patient. Georgiana will remain upstairs and the others downstairs, and in this way I may be able to better manage both our resources and their care. I pray that I will soon be joined in this task by Mr. Waters.

I know that this exposes us, William, and I have struggled, knowing you would not have me do such a thing, but it is certain that we have already been exposed. We must have been, or Georgiana would not be ill. John takes your position admirably and tells me with his stoic manner and disapproving looks that this is not something a proper Mistress of Pemberley should undertake. He believes that it should be left to the families to do the nursing and that this is what you would wish. You know your stubborn wife and will not fault him for my actions, indeed, when you return you must thank him for taking your part. He has seen I am determined to do this with or without his help, and has promised to assist me if only to keep me safe, an office it is clear you have asked him to perform.

Dearest, I am convinced that while this may not be the proper course it is yet the correct one. The staff at Pemberley may not be our blood, but they are both our family and my responsibility.

If we can care for those who are now ill, William, I hope that no one else will be stricken. If I am wrong, I can only beg your forgiveness.

Your devoted Elizabeth

Elizabeth closed her eyes for a moment. She had left out her conversation with Mr. Harrison, but she would have to discuss the man with Fitzwilliam upon his return. He was insolent. She had been affronted not by his protest of her plans, but his refusal to accept her authority, his attempts to cow her into abandoning her convictions. This was a test, somehow, one she was determined to pass. She believed herself in the right. If Fitzwilliam did not agree with her decisions, they could have that discussion when he returned, but it was not Mr. Harrison's place. In contrast to Mr. Harrison, John Briggs had thought about the plans silently, his bushy eyebrows pushed together in deep contemplation. He had stated his objections directly, and then simply nodded when she had explained her reasons. Her lips curled in a tiny, satisfied smile as she recalled how he replaced his hat, bowed, and stated that he would have the men assembled at the stables before the appointed hour. He had made his farewell with one word.

"Mistress," he had said as he turned to leave. She listened to his footfalls growing farther away and thought that this was the first time he had called her by that title.

Elizabeth sprinkled sand on the letter and left it to dry on the desk. Standing, she moved over to the bed to check on Georgiana. The fever did not seem to be any higher than it had been an hour ago, but neither had it eased. She thought back to the Wrights and began the process of cooling Georgie down again. When she finished, she sat heavily in the chair next to the bed. She put one hand over Georgie's and then leaned back, closing her eyes. She just needed to rest for a moment.

It felt as though she had just fallen asleep when she felt a tapping on her shoulder. Elizabeth started. Without being aware of how she had managed it, she found herself on her feet. She did not immediately recognize the room. Where was she? She glanced at the bed, where Georgiana seemed to be sleeping deeply now.

"Mrs. Darcy," came a whisper from just behind her, "I can take a turn now. You should retire." It took a moment for Elizabeth to realize that it was Mrs. Reynolds who was speaking. Her racing heart began to resume a more normal rhythm.

"What time is it?" she asked quietly, glancing at Georgiana.

"Five o'clock, ma'am."

Elizabeth rubbed her eyes, trying to clear her mind. There was much to do and little point going back to sleep now. She stepped to the window as Mrs. Reynolds put a hand on Georgiana's forehead. The weather had cleared a little, enough to put her plans into motion.

"I'll send up more water and have the kitchen bring up some tea for you both. Please keep trying to get her to drink, even if she resists. Should her fever remain high we shall have to prepare a cold bath for her." Elizabeth picked up the empty basin on her way to the door.

"Oh, ma'am, no need for that. Agatha can fetch the basin."

Elizabeth paused to place a hand on Mrs. Reynolds' arm.

"I am not yet so fine a lady that I cannot carry a basin," she said with something as close to levity as she could manage. Mrs. Reynolds responded with a small, tight smile and a nod before she sat on the side of the bed.

When Elizabeth had reached the stairs, she recalled her letter. Turning, she strode back down the hall and reentered Georgiana's bedroom. Mrs.

Reynolds was now sitting in the chair she had abandoned. Elizabeth shook her head when the housekeeper moved as if to stand.

"Ma'am?"

"Please do not get up, Mrs. Reynolds," she said, "I am simply here to retrieve my letter."

"Yes, ma'am," the older woman nodded. Her lips curved up very slightly before she sat. Was that a smile? *I have seen her give that smile to William.* Elizabeth blinked, but it was already gone. *I am beginning to see things*, she chastised herself, and hurried down to the kitchen, where she dropped off the basin. She knew Agatha would refill it and carry it back upstairs. She saw the girl who had spoken yesterday.

"Marta," she said, "would you please send word to John Briggs that I shall be outside shortly to speak with him? He should gathering men out at the stables."

"Yes, ma'am," Marta replied, bobbed a quick curtsy, and left the room

Elizabeth thought through her list. She needed to change her clothes, meet with John, and get him to hitch up the wagon. Mr. Harrison would know where everyone was located and could make sure each home was checked. John would select some of the men to accompany him around the estate to collect the ill and bring them to the house. In the meantime, she would work with the housekeeping staff to prepare the ballroom. She would need to speak with Mrs. Cronk about splitting the staff into shifts so there was always someone working in the kitchen and laundry. She squared her shoulders and took a deep breath. There was no point delaying, so she turned and once more headed above-stairs.

Chapter Fourteen

SEYMOUR FILBEE AND Marcus Barrow were standing in Bingley's study conversing in hushed tones when Darcy entered. The sky was still dark and only the kitchen staff were about. This part of the house was quiet.

"Gentlemen," he grunted with a nod as he strode to the chair behind the desk. It was not as imposing as his own, and he thought, briefly, whether he ought to remove to Darcy House. It would suit him better to have his own staff attending him as privacy was an issue, but the sudden removal from his friend's home might cause offense and give rise to rumors.

The men nodded. They looked a little rough, these two, with their threadbare coats and dirty trousers, a proper uniform to gain the intelligence they needed. Darcy knew these men were not only capable and well connected in ways he was not, but that they were also men of great discretion. They had kept the secret knowledge of Georgiana's near elopement in Ramsgate two years before and had demonstrated the same kind of loyalty in many other, smaller concerns.

Barrow stepped up first. "You have something for us, Mr. Darcy?"

Filbee tugged a frayed cuff down to his wrist with a shrug. "Suits me if you do. I be getting as fat 'n lazy as Prinny soon, what wit' a salary and naught a bit 'a work to be done."

Barrow chuckled. "Mr. Darcy offers us the wages of an honest life, Filbee."

Darcy looked at them both, assessing their appearances. One would think that Barrow had worked for the Prince Regent and Filbee in Bow Street, but it was in fact the reverse. Barrow was long and slight, his light hair carefully trimmed and his nails meticulously clean. Filbee was shorter, broader, with a head of long, unruly dark brown hair. He often looked as though he had only moments before been pitched from a tavern, rumpled, soiled, and stinking of whiskey. Yet each could speak in a multitude of dialects, moving from one to another effortlessly. Darcy had been privy to the fluid changes in speech patterns on some occasions and had been nothing short of astonished. Filbee spoke fluent French and Barrow's German was nearly perfect, but the way they spoke now was their preferred method of discourse. He had always considered them an odd pair. The differences were jarring when they stood together like this, but their skills complemented one another. Darcy had complete confidence in them. They were the men for this job. He motioned for the two to sit and lowered himself into a chair as well.

"Gentlemen, I have something of a mystery I need to solve," he began slowly, eventually relating his cousin's story. He left out the more personal parts of the narrative. He related only that Colonel Fitzwilliam was searching for Miss Evelyn Hawke, the sister of a young captain the Colonel knew and who had fallen abroad. He explained the problem, what had been done so far, and watched Filbee pinch his forehead in thought while Barrow's face remained smooth, thoughtful.

"Seven Dials," grumbled Filbee. "I may be able to get a bit more there." Darcy handed him a piece of paper with the direction. Filbee chewed on his lower lip thoughtfully as he read it.

"I may take a stroll around the Mayfair address, then, if that suits, Seymour," Barrow said quietly. "We can meet again around noon to speak in case we need to revisit anything before returning here." Barrow looked at Darcy, "Will that meet with your approval, sir? I presume you would like to be notified of our progress today given the early summons this morning?"

"I would," Darcy said firmly. "Neither the Colonel nor I can predict how long he will be allowed to remain in England. He is eager to satisfy this duty before he must return to his regiment, and I have pledged my assistance."

"Then," Barrow responded with a nod as Filbee also rose, "I should return to my lodgings to change. I will draw too much attention in Mayfair in my current attire."

"The servants at Darcy House have been told you may stop by this morning and to offer any assistance you might require," Darcy said to them both. Barrow nodded and turned to go. Filbee remained a moment longer.

"Mr. Darcy, sir?"

"Yes, Filbee?"

The man shifted his weight from one foot to the other. "This mightn't be as easy as ya think."

"You will be well rewarded for accomplishing your task."

"No, that an't it. T'aint about the money. You pays us well."

"What, then?"

Filbee scratched his head. "It's just that, well, the direction in Seven Dials. It's not unknown t' me."

Darcy felt the hair on the back of his neck rise. He waited, noticing that Barrow had paused, listening, one hand on the doorknob but not turning it. Filbee thought for a moment before he continued, "It mightn't be nothing, sir, but two years ago it was those flats or sums real close by that was used by some 'er Prinny's men. Not sure what fer, but if she be any ways mixed in with them..."

Darcy watched as Barrow's face slipped into a hardened mask, and knew his had done the same. He nodded at Filbee.

"See what you are able to learn, Filbee. Discreetly, as always. We shall reconvene here at five today. Send me a message if that must change."

"Aye, sir." Filbee turned to follow Barrow out, leaving Darcy drained and weary, with a long day still stretching out ahead.

***

A few minutes before the hour, Colonel Fitzwilliam was announced and stepped into the foyer. Bingley welcomed him and then left the two cousins to talk. Darcy nodded at Richard and led him back to the study to await the report. Barrow was exactly on time, but Filbee did not show until nearly ten after the hour. Both Darcy and the Colonel were uneasy, and the interval was excruciating.

"Apologies, Mr. Darcy," said Filbee as he stepped inside and removed his hat. "Unavoidable." His face was unreadable, his accent unusually formal.

"Fine." Darcy quickly made the introductions. "Tell us what you have learned."

Barrow stepped forward. "I have little, so perhaps I shall go first."

Darcy and the Colonel nodded at him.

"I made inquiries in Mayfair. Miss Hawke lives with her uncle, who took her in as his ward after a fire in her family home in Staffordshire many years ago."

Darcy blinked. He had thought perhaps the girl was related, but he had not expected this. "I believed the entire family perished in the fire."

"I would not know, sir, but this is what I heard. Also that there is apparently another sister who survived but that she does not live with them. No one seemed to know her name."

"Is she married?"

"Nobody seems to know, Mr. Darcy. She apparently left them some years ago."

The Colonel rubbed his chin, deep in thought. "So the other sister was the one living in Seven Dials?"

"I thought that as well, Colonel," said Barrow quietly. "However, I have no evidence. There was some curiosity about the uncle and Miss Hawke, indicating that they had not been in residence long."

Darcy briefly thought about what might have happened to Georgiana if George Wickham had been successful in his attempt to elope with her. Knowing the man's habits, it might well have been her in Seven Dials. Until this business of Richard's he had not thought much lately about Lydia Bennet and her unfortunate marriage, as engaged as he had been in the happiness of his own. The reminder was painful. He felt certain that this was a relation to Evelyn Hawke, probably a sister. It would make sense that the reason Evelyn Hawke felt it necessary to steal away to see a sister was the other girl's disgrace, and it would further explain why this additional sister was not mentioned in the letter to the Colonel. It would even explain why the uncle had removed both girls rather than simply retrieving Miss Evelyn. But where had they gone? If it truly had been years since she left, it seemed unlikely that a ruined niece would now be reconciled with the uncle. Had he meant to move her? Whatever the case, it might well be a mistake to intrude. He glanced at Richard, whose forehead was wrinkled in thought.

"Anything else?" Darcy asked.

"I'm afraid not, sir. Precious little, other than. . ." his voice trailed off, and he shuffled uncomfortably from one foot to the other, twisting his hat in his hands. The fidgeting was uncommon for Barrow. But then, this was turning out to be more complicated than any of them had believed.

He nodded in encouragement and prompted Barrow to continue. "Yes?"

Barrow did not answer immediately. He was not a man to rely much on feelings, though he did not exactly ignore them, either. "It is only that while the young woman excited some gossip that there seemed to be more than the general reluctance to talk at all about the uncle even so far as to mention him by name. I am unable to account for it. Truly, I hesitate to mention it without further evidence, but he seems to be genuinely feared."

Filbee cleared his throat and the three men turned to him.

"You've got the right of it, Barrow. The man that's got them girls is their uncle, but he's a powerful man."

"Anything else, Filbee?"

"Yes, Mr. Darcy." Filbee cracked his knuckles before he spoke again. "Dinno the men traveling wit' 'em, but the uncle 'tis Archibald Hawke."

The Colonel's head shot up and he met Filbee's serious gaze.

"Archibald Hawke?" he asked almost breathlessly. "Of the Home Office?"

Filbee bit his lower lip and nodded once, curtly.

Barrow tugged at his coat. "Gentlemen," he said solemnly, "I think we should decide now whether this is a task worth pursuing."

Darcy was thinking the same thing, but his thoughts were interrupted by his cousin's retort.

"Are you crying off, Barrow?" asked the Colonel with just the trace of a sneer.

"Richard," said Darcy reprovingly.

Barrow's eyebrows drew together and his eyes narrowed. "No, Colonel, I am not." He looked at Filbee, who nodded at him. "However, I believe it important to confirm our resolve before we begin. Should we wish to proceed, we shall need to think carefully about how best to accomplish our goal and extract ourselves with some degree of safety." He nodded at Colonel Fitzwilliam. "I mention this both for ourselves and the ladies we seek. And Mr. Darcy," he added, turning to his employer, "Filbee and I will likely need to bring in others to assist. Have you any other resources of which we should be aware before we begin to discuss our own contacts?"

Darcy shared a look with his cousin and raised his eyebrows with a look he knew his cousin could read: *Richard, how far are you willing to take this?* His cousin met his gaze with a stony determination. He could almost hear Richard's voice in his head, *Debts of honor must be paid.*

"We may have some additional connections," Darcy said softly. He nodded at the two investigators and set a time for them all to meet the next morning, after they had taken Bingley into their confidence and discussed who might be of use. After the door clicked shut behind the two men, Richard filled two glasses, with brandy this time, and both men sat nursing their drinks and reflecting on the grim nature of their business. *Well, Bingley,* Darcy thought, *you wanted to help. By the time we are finished we may end in prison, or Elizabeth and Jane may ship us to the Americas, but you will not be left out. God help us all.*

Chapter Fifteen

BY MIDDAY, ELIZABETH was in the ballroom directing the staff as they converted the space into a large sickroom. She had heard her husband and Mr. Waters speak about the British and French field hospitals, and as usual, she had asked many questions about them. At least she had a model for her work, she thought grimly, though her room would be luxurious in comparison.

Nearly twenty years prior, George Darcy had hired several carpenters and their apprentices to build a number of wooden cots that could be easily folded down and moved to accommodate those who had been rendered homeless by a terrible flood. They had been used a few times since when large parties arrived with servants, but no one on the staff could recall deploying so many since that grim event, where scores of tenant homes had been flooded and nearly fifty people forced to evacuate. Those who had been there all those years ago still spoke with something approaching reverence of Lady Anne's gracious attention to their comfort and her husband's particular involvement in the required repairs. There were even some who still remembered a small boy of seven or eight who had ridden with his father to inspect each home and listened with rapt attention as his father explained the work that would be done.

"Each cot should have one set of these," Elizabeth said, handing bedclothes and a blanket to Christine, who nodded and hurried off. She took a set herself and began to make up the beds closest to her. She was on her third bed when she saw Christine stiffen at the other end of the row.

"Oh, ma'am," she said almost involuntarily, "We can do this. You need not make up the beds."

Elizabeth smiled at the young housemaid and glanced around the room. Five women, all recommended by Mrs. Reynolds as being both willing and trustworthy, were scurrying about making beds, dragging tables, rolling up carpets, and moving chairs. "Would you all please give me your attention for a moment?" she said, raising her voice to be heard.

The women stopped. Slowly, from around the room, each straightened or turned or stood up from their work to face the mistress. They had all heard Christine's outburst, and they were embarrassed for her. The girl blanched and stood, her breath coming in tight, frightened bursts.

Elizabeth watched them kindly. She suspected that none of them thought this was a good idea, but that they were doing as they were told in deference to her and, she thought wryly, to her husband. She saw the humor of this, as her husband would likely have sided with them. Still, there was not much time before the children would arrive, and she needed to make something quite clear. Once all eyes were on her, she cleared her throat and began.

"When I told you all that we would be required to do many jobs to which we are not accustomed," she said. "I meant *all* of us. Pemberley is my home and you are all a part of Pemberley. So please, let us just accept from the start that many of the rules of propriety must bend to the needs of our current situation." She saw some of the older women nod. "I mean to be of use wherever I may, and I would not like to have this conversation again." She looked over at Christine, who nodded and cast her eyes down.

"Christine," she said mildly, and the girl looked up.

"Yes, ma'am?" she replied, her cheeks bright red.

"I am not in the least angry. Indeed, I am grateful that you are thinking of my comfort."

"Yes, ma'am," Christine nearly whispered, bobbing a curtsey and beginning her work again.

Making up bed after bed was not difficult work, but Elizabeth had not slept much the night before and her back was stiff from sleeping in a chair. After Mrs. Reynolds had relayed the mistress' orders to set up thirty of the cots in five rows of six, she had sent the staff scurrying to all areas of the estate to locate the stored beds and to gather additional linens so that they would have enough. John entered with the last cot slung over his shoulder and set it down at the end of the final row, moving the legs into place. She dropped the final set of bedclothes on top of it and turned to face him.

"Ma'am," he said gruffly. "The first eight children are on their way with their parents. We have them in the wagon, and the parents are walking up. Once we have them unloaded here, we will continue to the west and collect the others."

"Has Mr. Harrison made a survey of the other homes?"

"He did say he had completed checking the south meadow, ma'am."

Elizabeth frowned. "I wonder that he did not offer a full report to me. Where is he now?" Was this yet another way Mr. Harrison meant to demonstrate his contempt?

"I wanted to talk to you about that, ma'am." His voice was steady, but low, controlled. She nodded and began to walk out of the room so they could speak privately. When they had reached the hallway, he looked around to make sure nobody was walking past. His face was a mask, Elizabeth thought, but it was masking anger. Was it for her?

"Mrs. Darcy, have you sent Mr. Harrison on an errand of any kind?"

This was an odd line of questioning. "No. He was just to make note of the homes we should visit to collect the ill and to check the homes in the south meadow. Then he was to return here." She waited as John's features hardened.

"He is gone, Mrs. Darcy," John said evenly.

This was unexpected. Perhaps she had misheard. "Gone?" she repeated, keeping her voice low, controlled. Her eyes flicked to the hall behind him. Still clear.

"Yes, ma'am. He met me early this morning to say he had checked the southern homes and all was well. I left him, but apparently he took a horse directly after and is not to be found on the estate."

"Are you sure?" Elizabeth asked, bewildered. She tilted her head, thinking. She did not know Mr. Harrison well, but his behavior the day before had certainly led her to distrust him. If he had truly abandoned them, she was surprised, but as she searched her feelings, she was forced to admit to herself that she was not shocked.

"Yes, ma'am." John looked down. He appeared ashamed, but Elizabeth could not fathom why.

She felt a belated rush of anger. Mr. Harrison was the steward! He should have been taking charge of the staff, working as her representative, not abandoning them all in some misguided attempt to save himself. Did he believe himself the only one who was afraid? He had tried to bully her into complying with his own plans to deal with the crisis, but failing that he would flee? Despite his elevated position, he was the only one who had left the property, and against her direct orders. She was silent for a moment before she replied in a pinched voice dripping with derision.

"I see."

She was sure that John would fault her for losing her composure. However, as he looked up to meet her gaze, his face was no longer lined with shame. Instead, it was alight with what she recognized as barely controlled fury. Elizabeth thought with a grim satisfaction that she would not wish to be in Mr. Harrison's place should he ever return to Derbyshire.

"Should we pursue him for the horse, ma'am?" John asked. She shook her head slowly, her eyes bright with indignation.

"Not now. Mr. Harrison undoubtedly realizes that I am obligated to keep everyone who has been exposed confined to the Pemberley grounds. We shall have to hope he does not make anyone else ill and deal with him later."

For perhaps the first time since Mr. Darcy had introduced his new wife to the staff several months ago, John Briggs understood her. Mrs. Darcy was angry. She could not keep the contempt out of her voice, and he had no doubt that this violation of duty would be addressed. He allowed himself a brief grunt of approval. He would request the honor of tracking the coward down himself when Mr. Darcy returned. However, there was also the matter of the horse. As head groomsman, he was responsible for the animal.

"My boys have not been exposed, ma'am. They could at least travel to the nearest posting stations and inquire about Ares."

Elizabeth raised her eyebrows. "The boys have not been exposed?" How had they escaped? "That is excellent news."

John nodded curtly. "They are with their grandparents in Lambton to help with some repairs," he said. "They left Friday last."

The sound of wheels on gravel came from outside. Elizabeth thought quickly. John had enough worries. How could she keep the Briggs boys away? "Until the weather improves, I would not have your boys leave Lambton. However, when the roads are sufficiently dry, perhaps they would able to take a message to Mr. Darcy in London? I have several letters to send, and the boys would be more reliable than the post. You may tell them from me that nobody who is currently away from Pemberley is to return until the illness is gone."

John swallowed hard. He was deeply grateful for the suggestion. It was providential that his boys had been assisting his parents, but he knew they had too much loyalty, both to him and the Darcy family, to remain there long once they heard the news. Sending them to London with important letters for the Master would satisfy both his impulse to keep them safe and the boys' need to be of use.

"Yes, ma'am," he said with a nod. "They would be pleased to be of service." He could walk to the village in the evening, after dark. He was not ill, and if he stopped nowhere else, it should be sufficient. He would slip the letters with his instructions under the door, and the boys knew their way around the stables without requiring assistance. It would answer.

"Excellent. Please tell them that this is my particular wish." Elizabeth knew they might ignore their father, believing him at risk, but they would not ignore a direct request from the mistress. "I will leave the letters with Mrs. Reynolds," she said, beginning to walk away. She stopped, turned back. "Thank you, John," she said pointedly, meeting his gaze, and he nodded gruffly.

*Thank **you**, Mrs. Darcy,* he thought, before following her outside.

Chapter Sixteen

IT WAS EVENING. Twenty-five of the beds were occupied, the ill propped up on pillows and covered with blankets, being cared for under Elizabeth's direction. She had wandered the rows, humbled by the magnitude of the venture and hopeful that her makeshift hospital would not allow the outbreak to spread through the house.

She had strictly limited access in and out of the sickroom and asked the kitchen staff to simply leave things in the hallway where she or one of the others could collect them. They would leave the dirty dishes and bedclothes in the hall in the same way. Of course, Elizabeth was leaving the sickroom each evening to repair upstairs and see to Georgiana's care, so it was not a perfect system. It would simply have to do. Mrs.

Cronk had created a schedule to keep the kitchen staffed both day and night. The two women had spent several hours in conference to inventory the supplies and create a plan for feeding everyone now residing under the roof. Because they would not be able to bring in more food for some time, it was essential that nothing be wasted. In particular, Elizabeth insisted that those who would be required to work longer hours or at more difficult tasks than normal be well fed.

There was a fire in the hearth on the east side of the ballroom, the wood crackling as the flames grew higher, and Elizabeth thought of the last time she had been in this room after dark. Fitzwilliam had insisted on a ball a month after their arrival as a way to introduce her to the neighborhood. Many of the local gentry who had been invited had been more curious than polite. Elizabeth closed her eyes, remembering, briefly, the hastily covered surprise and icy formality of the women that indicated they found both her beauty and manners lacking. The men had been infinitely worse, and she had found herself subject to several barely contained leers when Fitzwilliam's attention had been drawn elsewhere. She had said nothing to him, knowing full well how he would respond.

Despite her distaste for most of the company, there had been several women who seemed more sincerely interested in making her acquaintance. She thought of young Mrs. Rebecca Tilden, not much older than Elizabeth, who had asked what Mrs. Darcy thought about the neighborhood and had laughed enthusiastically when she had answered simply that she loved Pemberley.

Elizabeth sighed and opened her eyes to the present. As she gazed around the room, she could almost hear the strains of music, the swish of skirts, the tapping of feet all stepping in unison. Most of all, she imagined her husband standing next to her in the receiving line, intentionally brushing his fingers against hers. No, this would not do. She brought herself back, forcefully, to the present.

Few of the men had been taken ill, none of them younger than sixty, and Elizabeth thanked God for that. She needed their strength to accomplish many of the tasks she could not. Each patient had been bathed as well as possible. She had spent several hours visiting one at a time, instructing caregivers and tending to those who had none. She pulled a small journal from a pocket in her apron and stepped out to her study. There, she sharpened her pen and began to copy over the new, complete list of the afflicted. Then she began a separate page for each charge, noting everything she had just learned about each case. When she finished, she closed the book and took a sheet of paper. After a moment of consideration, she began to write.

My dearest husband,

It is done. We have our hospital within the Pemberley walls, cleaner and warmer than any hospital in London and surely a healthier setting than the field hospitals you once discussed with Mr. Waters.

Here is what we have accomplished today. Fifteen children, ten boys and five girls, all under the age of twelve and six of our more elderly servants and pensioners have been afflicted and are in residence, along with their families. The illness does seem to be worse for the young and the old, and as of yet most of the men seem well, for which I am profoundly grateful. We are prepared for up to five more, though I do hope we shall have no need to fill those beds.

There is one rather disappointing matter that I hesitate to relate, but must. Mr. Harrison has vanished, William. John confirms that the man took a horse this morning but is no longer on the estate. I am afraid he has abandoned us, my dear.

Elizabeth paused, pen in the air. Fitzwilliam would be as furious as John had been, and there was no profit in stoking that fire when he was so far away and unable to act. Dipping the pen and tapping it against the glass, she continued:

However, John has taken on Mr. Harrison's duties so completely that we are perhaps better off that he has gone. Mr. Wilkins, of course, still runs the house, but everything that I might have expected Mr. Harrison to do, John has done, and well. You never told me how a man who knows so much about the estate remains the head groomsman and a preferred coachman for your wife, my dear. Perhaps this is something we should discuss when you return.

There. Better to end with a jest, though she was serious, too. In the less than two days since this whole debacle had begun, she had learned to trust John's stoic good sense over all the other servants except Mrs. Reynolds, even over Mr. Wilkins. The butler, whose impeccable manners had not allowed a single muscle in his face to move when he had been told what she had planned, had merely nodded and replied, "Very good, ma'am." She far preferred the dubious expression and suppressed storm she had seen in John's face to the butler's stony countenance.

She was discovering, little by little, that John had been following Mr. Harrison's work with a keen, critical eye and knew a surprising amount about the management of the rents, the tenants, and the work that should have been done but was languishing. Mr. Harrison had been relatively new, and John seemed to have decided that he was not yet to be trusted, a judgment that had proved correct.

Dearest, I must end for now. I am expected upstairs. I will not allow Mrs. Reynolds to assist downstairs, but it has been impossible to keep her away from Georgiana, and indeed I have neither the heart nor the resources to insist upon it. She has been with our sister all day and must be relieved of her watch.

I pray for your health and safety, my love.
Elizabeth

When Elizabeth reached Georgiana's bedroom, Mrs. Reynolds was waiting for her. She stood and took Elizabeth's arm, steering her outside.

"Ma'am, a bath has been drawn for you. Once you have bathed, Sarah will relieve me. It is important that you rest."

Elizabeth relented without argument, merely smiled and thanked Mrs. Reynolds. She would take the bath and then return to Georgiana's room later.

"A bath sounds wonderful, Mrs. Reynolds, I thank you. How is Georgiana?"

"Still feverish, ma'am, but she has been speaking with me a bit." This was good news, Elizabeth thought with pleasure.

"Has she been taking the draughts?"

"Yes, ma'am. She has been a right lamb, doing everything you asked without complaint. She has even been drinking her tea though I can see she would rather not."

"Excellent. Thank you, Mrs. Reynolds. Have you eaten?"

"Oh yes, ma'am. Mrs. Cronk has been very attentive."

"Indeed she has. You should head to your rest, then. We shall have need of you in the morning."

"Good night, ma'am." The housekeeper bobbed her head.

"Good night, Mrs. Reynolds." Elizabeth waited for her to turn and leave, but while the housekeeper nodded she did not move, and it was her mistress who finally turned. Mrs. Reynolds continued to watch until Elizabeth entered her own rooms and shut the door behind her.

Elizabeth glanced at her bed, momentarily tempted to lie down, but instead called for Sarah to help her undress. She slid into her bath gratefully, scrubbing her back, her legs, her arms and hands, leaning back in the hot water as her muscles unknotted and relaxed. This was one luxury she would be loath to lose, even now. Mrs. Reynolds was so kind to think of it with everything else that was happening.

She took half an hour to soak, washing her hair and then drying it by the fire, letting it hang down her back while she dug through her belongings for a dress more suited to the work she had yet to do tonight. She had already ruined two gowns when her apron had not been sufficient, and while she did not necessarily mind buying new gowns when Georgiana was with her, she thought with a smile, having to stand for fittings was a maddening waste of time. She reached into the trunk she had brought with her from Longbourn and found a short-sleeved blue muslin with small yellow roses embroidered around the hem. The skirt was creased a bit, but no worse than after an outdoor ramble. She was easily able to dress herself by buttoning up the back, leaving only the final four buttons undone, and pulling it over her head. She shook her hair out, toweled it again, combed through it, then plaited it and put it up in a simple twist. Finally, she reached behind her to fasten the remaining buttons. She was out of practice, and it took her several tries. She pulled on her stockings and shoved her feet into sensible boots. Warm and comfortable, she looked in the mirror to be sure she was presentable. There was a familiar woman in the reflection.

"There you are, Lizzy Bennet," she said with a smile.

Chapter Seventeen

ELIZABETH PEEKED OUT into the hall. It was dark, lit only by candles, and entirely empty. She stepped carefully down to Georgiana's chamber, and slipped inside.

Sarah stood when Elizabeth entered.

"Ma'am," she said, disapprovingly. It had become their charade over the past few nights. "I thought you was asleep."

"No," Elizabeth answered. "I could not sleep. Please go to bed, Sarah. I will sit with Miss Georgiana."

The set of her mouth showed Sarah ready to protest, but she could not dispute the mistress.

"Sarah," Elizabeth called as the girl moved to the door.

"Yes, Mrs. Darcy?"

"Remember that should Mrs. Reynolds wakes you in the morning, you will tell her only that I replaced you early." A small lie, to be sure, but it was true she would never be able to sleep in her own bed with Georgiana so ill.

She heard a small sigh in the dark and then, "Yes, Mrs. Darcy."

When Sarah was gone, Elizabeth sat on the side of the bed and evaluated Georgiana. She was flushed and uneasy, and Elizabeth's heart sank. She helped her sister struggle to sit up and lifted a teacup to her lips, slipping one arm behind Georgie's back for support. Elizabeth could feel the heat of her skin through her thin summer nightclothes. Georgiana did try to drink, but was only partially successful before she began to shake as though she was freezing. Elizabeth moved to the hearth with a towel to pick up two warming bricks, replacing the cold ones in the bed.

The hours ticked by, and Georgiana did not improve. Rather, she grew steadily worse. Just after one, she began to whisper, addressing people who were not in the room, calling plaintively and repeatedly for her brother. Elizabeth spoke soothingly, stroking Georgie's flushed cheek, pushing wisps of honey blonde hair from her eyes, wishing desperately that Fitzwilliam could answer her himself. After a time, the frenzy subsided and Georgie gazed vacantly at the foot of her bed, breathing heavily, but not sleeping, caught in a kind of fevered stupor. When she finally closed her eyes, looking for all the world like a small, defenseless child, Elizabeth paced the floor, tortured by being trapped inside for so many days and suffering a terrible need to act, to do something, *anything.* If only Mr. Waters was here. He would know better what to do than she.

That was it. She could at least send John for Mr. Waters. He would be at the stables tonight. She stood, painfully, stretching her aching muscles, but she sat on the edge of the bed as Georgie began to cry softly. It had been days. Mr. Waters had to be at home by now, and well. He had to be. Elizabeth stroked Georgiana's hair until the girl fell into a restive, troubled sleep.

***

Once Sarah had resumed her post next to Georgiana's bed, Elizabeth nearly ran to the stable to look for John. He had taken to sleeping there to protect the horses from anyone bold enough to try to sneak onto the estate. She thought it highly unlikely that thieves would dare the fever to steal a horse, but

John pointed out that one horse had already been taken.

She had scolded herself when she realized that was not thieves from outside that worried him, but that there would be a defection from within. It was sobering to realize that John did not trust the staff. She could not believe that any of the upper servants would flee. They had all been with the family far too long to repay the Darcys in such a way. The underservants were younger, had been a part of the household for a comparatively short time, and many, she had to admit, were afraid. Her unconventional response, bringing the illness into the house, certainly had not helped. John had said none of this aloud, but neither had he denied the understanding he saw settling on her.

She found the stables empty, other than the sleeping horses. Aggravating man! He had been so stern about remaining on watch. Where was he? She huffed, frustrated. She had to find Mr. Waters and it could not wait. There was no time to search for John now.

She looked around her. There was nothing else to be done, she decided. She would have to ride, and ride with speed. She could not do that side-saddle. She would have to break yet another sacred law of propriety, and this one she would have to hide, both for Pemberley's protection and her own. She moved back to the kitchen and entered the laundry where she found one maid sleeping in a corner.

Within a few minutes, she reemerged in trousers, a shirt, and coat. She held a boy's brimmed hat in one hand and a pair of boots in the other. Quickly, she tucked her hair up into the hat, jamming it down tightly on her head, and slid into the boots. Everything was a bit too large, but she could not worry about that now. She returned with great haste to the stable.

It was easy to get Plato up, but she staggered under the weight of the men's saddle, and it took three tries to toss it successfully across the horse's back. She tightened the girth and adjusted the bit as she stroked Plato's head and spoke quietly to him. *I hope this is correct*, she thought. Until she had come to Pemberley, there had been little riding for pleasure, and John had always prepared Plato for her rides, though she had, as always, watched carefully and learned. She swallowed hard. This was no time to be a coward. Georgie's cries for her brother, her vulnerability, the fever, all the children ill in the ballroom, the servants looking to her for reassurance, it all washed over her at once, and Elizabeth shuddered. She could not reveal it to anyone, but she was terrified. *What else can I do? This is for Georgiana. She needs help. I must go.*

Hurriedly, she stuck a foot in the stirrup and pushed up, swinging her free leg over Plato's back. She pulled her hat just a bit farther over her brow and wheeled Plato around. The horse, desperate for exercise, burst out of the stable at a speed quite unsafe for the dark. *At least there is a little moonlight tonight*, she told herself, declaring it to be as she wished it was, and did not attempt to slow Plato. She did not have much time. She had to find Mr. Waters. Even if she could not find him, she would have to make her way back before anyone realized she was gone. There were always servants awake at Pemberley now, but they kept mostly to the house at this hour.

At least she was finally *doing* something. She prayed it would be enough.

***

It was silent on the road back from Lambton as John returned to Pemberley. He had delivered his message and Mrs. Darcy's letters to his parents' home. The boys would find their instructions in the morning.

The roads were still soft and muddy, so he had chosen to leave the horses at the stables and come on foot. It was unlikely anyone would try to take a horse at this hour, with the roads in this condition and the night as dark as his mood. He would never forgive Harrison for abandoning Mrs. Darcy and Miss Georgiana. The coward had even stolen a horse, and for that, John promised himself, he would see the man hang. He blew on his gloveless hands and pulled the collar of his weathered greatcoat up to protect his neck. Although it was summer, the night hours and the rain meant that it was still damp and rather cold.

Halfway back up the road to the Pemberley turnoff, he heard a horse. It was running, far too fast for the road and the dark, so fast that he could barely jump into its path to try to stop the rider. Even in the dark, he knew the horse—it was Plato. He cursed out loud. Could he not step away for a moment, even in the middle of the night? Above all, to take Mrs. Darcy's mount? The fury he kept burning for Harrison burst into hot flames as he waved his hands and tried to slow the horse. The rider banked, hard, sending a shower of mud flying. As John tried to see around the mud and grab for the reins, the rider cut to his left in one fluid motion, then moved back to the road and was gone.

John's curses were loud and increasingly foul. There had been a boy on the horse. Where in blazes was he headed? He considered following the thief, but he was on foot, and a sudden thought struck him—Mrs. Darcy may have sent the boy—something might be wrong at the house. *Worse* at the house, he corrected himself, though it was difficult to see how. He would need to check in on the women, make sure they were safe. His anger flared into panic, and he began to run.

Elizabeth reached the apothecary's home more quickly than she would have thought possible. Even before Plato had come to a full stop, she was sliding off his back and knocking at the door. She had not quite worked out how she would remain in disguise, as she would have to speak, but there was no time now. The house was dark. She waited a moment, then pounded on the door in desperation. She knew he lived alone, preferring to have his housekeeper come only during the day so as not to disturb him more than necessary. That would be a blessing, if only he would answer the door!

He did answer, suddenly throwing open the door while holding a candle in one hand and rubbing his face with the other. Her relief was overpowering.

"Yes?" he asked thickly, trying to shake the sleep from his voice.

Elizabeth tried to pitch her voice to match that of a young boy. "There's fever at Pemberley, sir. Miss Darcy is very ill. Will you come?"

Waters leaned against the doorframe, staring blearily at the boy standing before him, or rather, at the top of the boy's hat. The rider was slight. He was so very nearly swallowed by his clothes and the hat with an unusually wide brim that it might be comical in a less solemn situation. Still groggy, he scratched his chin and hesitated. *How can he even see to ride a horse in the dark let alone with that hat blocking his view?* The meaning of the boy's words was slow to penetrate, but when it did, it forced him awake instantly. *Miss Darcy. The Wright boys.* He leaned forward to grab the boy's arm.

"Influenza?"

The boy nodded, but did not speak.

Waters released the boy and stepped back inside. He was already thinking about what he had on hand. "I will gather what I need and follow you back."

"Bring everything you have," said the boy, and turned to his horse.

It took two attempts for the small messenger to mount the horse again. *Not an experienced rider,* Waters thought, distracted momentarily before he ran both hands through his hair in an effort to clear the remaining fog. He closed the door and moved quickly to his store of medicines, packing what he would need. *Bring everything you have. Why?* Behind him, he heard the horse galloping down the road and thought, *that boy had better take care or he will be my patient before I ever reach Pemberley.* Within ten minutes, he had packed his cases and was on his own horse, making his way with haste, but more caution, to the great house.

Elizabeth finally slowed Plato's pace as she approached the stables. She was fairly sure the figure who had tried to stop her on her way to town was John. What had he been doing on the road? She briefly considered dismounting and sneaking into the house, leaving Plato to wander the final quarter mile home on his own. Her dress and boots, however, were rolled and hidden in Plato's stall. She needed them to enter the house, and even were that not the case, John would find her clothes if indeed he had not already. Better to face his disapproval now, when she could explain her errand in private. She dismounted but kept hold of the reins, stroking the horse's head and offering him the carrot she had grabbed from the larder on her way out. The ride had been terrifying and exhilarating. She had nearly lost her seat more than once, and while she was sorry to have been forced to it, she could not regret it. She could not have remained indoors a moment longer, and now she would have help. Resigned, she walked Plato into the stable.

As she suspected, John was there, arms crossed.

"Boy," he hissed, seizing the reins from her and beginning to evaluate the horse. "What in blazes are you doing with Mrs. Darcy's mount? You could have destroyed him in the dark and all this mud. Mrs. Reynolds tells me the mistress is asleep upstairs and could not have given you permission to take him." He ran his hands down Plato's legs carefully, checking for injuries.

Elizabeth's mind raced. Could she still talk her way out of this? It took only an instant to realize that such an attempt would be folly. Mr. Waters was not long behind her; she had no time for subterfuge. She would have to place her trust in John. *Better to do this quickly and have it over.* She braced herself and removed the hat.

She had never seen anyone more astonished. He blinked several times and nearly fell over from his squatted position in front of the horse. It would have been amusing had she not been in such a hurry.

"Mrs. Darcy!" he exclaimed. "What... how...?"

Elizabeth said sternly, "I needed to find Mr. Waters and you were not here. Fortunately, he was finally returned home."

She couldn't wait until the morning? The urgency in her voice caused John to feel sick himself. What had happened to push her so far?

"No, ma'am, I went to deliver the letters you gave me. I wished to pass unseen, so I waited until the neighborhood would be at rest."

Elizabeth closed her eyes. *Of course that was where he was. At my request.* She opened them. *No matter.*

"Miss Darcy has taken a turn for the worse, John. I could not find you and there was no one else awake. I had no time to waste. Mr. Waters was finally home. He was not fully awake and I do not believe he recognized me, but he is on his way. I need to change to meet him upstairs. Please allow me to pass." She slid into Plato's stall to gather the bundle she had left there. She was relieved to see that John would not require more of an explanation before she realized, three steps later, that he had no choice. She was the mistress, no matter how shockingly wanton he found her behavior. Unlike Mr. Harrison, John respected at least the position of mistress enough not to protest, even if he did not think well of her in particular. Well, there was no time. She would have to find a way to speak to him later, to be sure he kept this to himself. She turned to look at him, and saw, even in the dim light, something in his face that had not been there before. Elizabeth knew, without being told, that he would not reveal her secret.

With a relieved sigh, she nodded at him once and said, "Good night, John."

"Good night, Mrs. Darcy." Was his voice more stoic than usual? He sounded almost hoarse, and she found herself worrying that he too might be ill, but she could not linger to decide. Quietly but with haste, she made her way back to the laundry.

When Mr. Waters arrived downstairs, scarcely a quarter of an hour after her own entry to the house, she had just entered Georgiana's room and was dismissing Sarah. She sat in the chair and stroked Georgie's arm. The girl was sleeping, but moaning, writhing in pain, and Elizabeth could not be anything but glad she had risked the ride.

There was a soft knock on the door and Elizabeth sighed. It had been a very near thing. She touched her hair to be sure there were no telltale signs and stood. Mr. Waters nodded to her from the doorway and she gestured for him to enter. He strode directly to the bed and sat next to his patient. He checked her fever, her pulse, and began asking a steady stream of whispered questions she recognized from his treatment of the Wrights: Was the fever higher or lower than earlier in the evening, how long had she been in this state, had there been delirium? Was she drinking? Elizabeth answered each with clear, direct responses. Mr. Waters nodded at each and then began to prepare some laudanum.

"I will only give her a small dose, Mrs. Darcy. She is rather slight and I do not believe it will require much. I only wish for her to sleep soundly. Rest is what she needs. Otherwise, you should continue your treatments. I have another medicine you can try in the morning." Elizabeth nodded, her heart in her throat.

"Will she recover, Mr. Waters?"

The young man sighed and ran a hand through his hair. "I cannot say, Mrs. Darcy. We must be patient." She felt her heart grow cold, but simply nodded.

He bade her sit in the chair next to Miss Darcy's bed. He could not remain in the room alone but wanted to stay at least until the morning, when he would examine his patient again. He guessed that it would not be long off, perhaps another two hours. He rubbed his face and grimaced at the stubble rubbing against his fingers. Normally he would not have appeared in the Darcy household so disheveled.

"I must apologize," he said quietly, "that I was not available to assist you before this evening. Mr. Proctor had an accident a few days ago, breaking his leg in a rather nasty way, and I have been tending to him since."

Elizabeth nodded. Life at Pemberley had come to a halt, but she was reminded that the rest of the world had not.

"You have care of a great many people," she replied. "I was simply concerned that you might have been taken ill yourself, or that others had been."

He shook his head. "I had not even heard," he said regretfully. "If I had. . ."

"You would still have had your duty to Mr. Proctor."

He shook his head again. "I could have left him in his wife's care. Knowing of no other obligations, I chose to remain."

"You are a man of honor, Mr. Waters," she said firmly. He recognized that this was her way of ending the conversation. Clearly she must already be agonizing over her sister, and indeed, her shoulders were slumped and her face drawn. She did not need to take on the job of reassuring him. He looked her over critically. This was not the same woman who eagerly asked questions and teasingly demanded that he recount his treatments in every detail when they met on the paths of the estate. This was less a girl growing into her marriage to a wealthy man and more a woman who had taken on her new position as a sister and mistress of an estate. How had he missed the transition? While he had always thought well of her, he found that this demonstration of her fortitude raised her in his estimation.

They sat in silence, Elizabeth finally nodding off for a few hours, head propped against the side of the chair, until the sun began to rise. There was a knock at the door and Mrs. Reynolds slipped in.

"Oh, Mrs. Darcy," she said, surprised, as Elizabeth woke and rose. "Forgive me ma'am. I had thought to find Sarah here."

"She was, Mrs. Reynolds, but Miss Darcy took a turn for the worse last night and we sent for Mr. Waters. Fortunately, he had returned home."

Mr. Waters nodded to the housekeeper, whose kind face was lined with concern.

"Mr. Waters has given Miss Georgiana some laudanum to help her sleep, Mrs. Reynolds. Would you mind taking my place here while I accompany Mr. Waters downstairs?"

"Of course, ma'am," Mrs. Reynolds replied.

"Mr. Waters, if you would follow me," Elizabeth murmured.

He nodded as he stepped out into the hall after Mrs. Darcy.

"Mr. Waters," she said with a small, tight smile that was not reflected in her eyes, "I meant to speak to you after you examined Miss Darcy, but fell asleep instead."

"Clearly you required the rest, Mrs. Darcy."

"You should have awakened me. In any case, Miss Darcy is not to be your only patient."

"I'm sorry to hear that," he said sympathetically. "Is Mr. Darcy well?"

"Mr. Darcy is from home," she replied, the ache in her voice impossible to conceal. "Come with me, if you please. It will be easier to show than to tell you."

She led him downstairs, to the ballroom. He looked at her quizzically. What were they doing here, of all places? She opened the door and stepped inside. He stepped into the room behind her. The sun was beginning to stream through the windows weakly, rendering the candles unnecessary, and a servant was in the process of extinguishing a number of them. He looked tiredly from the servant to the ballroom floor and suddenly stopped, eyes widening, heart twisting in dread. Worried faces, mothers, he guessed, looked up at the new arrivals, but Mr. Waters quickly returned his attention to the rows of small beds filled with patients, mostly children. Some slept, some moaned or spoke aloud, others stared vacantly at the ceiling. All were flush with fever. Like Miss Darcy. He struggled to maintain his equanimity, but failed. He turned to Mrs. Darcy, who had lifted an apron from a table near the door and was slipping it on over her head.

"Mrs. Darcy," he whispered. "How long have you. . ."

"We begin our fifth day, Mr. Waters."

"Good God," he said feelingly. He had toured the hospitals of London, but this was the last place he would have expected to see such a sight.

"Language, Mr. Waters," Mrs. Darcy prompted, nodding at the children.

"My apologies, ma'am," he said immediately, and rubbed his palms nervously against his trousers. He took a breath and let it out slowly.

Now that the initial shock was over, his exacting eye noted that the small wooden cots were evenly spaced, with room for a small table and chair next to each. While the beds were the same, the tables and chairs were a variety of shapes and sizes, taken, he expected, from many different rooms. Some of the chairs were filled, other patients were alone. The bedding looked clean. Clean bedding on the fifth day meant they were laundering the bedclothes. Saline draughts and tea infusions filled a long table to the left of the fire, and several kettles of water hung above the flames. Mrs. Darcy was certainly listening when he explained his treatments, he thought. She had done so much.

"Shall I speak to you of each patient, sir?" He looked over at her sharply, but her face betrayed nothing other than a fatigued resolve. She had assembled a hospital inside her own home for the servants and their children to be treated, had done this not knowing when or if any help would arrive. Was she nursing them all in addition? Clearly she had help, but there had to be close to thirty patients here and then her young sister so ill upstairs. How was it possible?

He knew. He had done it himself. She simply had not taken the time to eat much and likely had slept less. If her brief sleep upstairs was an example. . . he frowned.

"Yes, ma'am, but then you must eat something and take more rest. You will be of no use to any of us if you do not." She nodded once, but he narrowed his eyes at her and said in a low, commanding voice, "I am quite serious, Mrs. Darcy. In this situation, you must take your orders from me. Your health cannot be allowed to falter. If it does, who will take care of the rest?"

"You, Mr. Waters," she said with a trace of her old humor. He refused to be teased. He met her gaze directly.

"Not I, ma'am. I could never treat so many all at once without your assistance."

She smiled at the criticism couched as a compliment.

"Very well, Mr. Waters," she replied, lifting a book that resembled a ledger from the table behind her. "Let us begin."

Chapter Eighteen

OVER THE NEXT FEW DAYS, the Colonel, Darcy, Barrow, and Filbee worked on their plans. They had determined those amongst their acquaintance who could be employed to inquire after the carriage and its occupants, had sent word to men along each road out of London to keep watch, and through the intelligence that resulted, had determined that the carriage was at last moving north.

This being the case, Bingley's contacts from London to Scarborough might be of use, and Darcy sat him down to explain why the Colonel had called. Bingley was surprised and uncharacteristically stoic as he clapped Darcy on the back and murmured that he was pleased to offer his help. He had immediately gone to his desk to write the necessary letters, and Darcy could not help but notice that the blots and illegible handwriting that had once marked most of his friend's correspondence were absent. His writing was still not consistently legible, but his hand was far more assured and careful than it once had been. Darcy smiled to himself. Jane's influence, no doubt.

When Bingley had finished his letters and walked out to the stable to select mounts for their journey, Darcy wrote to Thomas Tilden, discreetly requesting information on the Hawkes of Darlington in Staffordshire. Tilden's estate, Bidewell Manor, was situated almost precisely between Pemberley and Darlington. Darcy believed that Tilden, who was some years older than he, had been living at Bidewell at the time of the fire. He hoped to gain any information he could about the family, and he trusted Tilden to be discreet. The note was quickly written and sent off with Barrow, who had secured a few boys to ride as private messengers.

While waiting for news from Filbee and Barrow, Darcy wrote Elizabeth and took care of his original business as quickly as possible. Based on the incredulous looks his solicitor gave him, the man likely believed him mad for insisting on such speed in what were otherwise a rather mundane reconciling and clarifications of quarterly accounts, marriage articles, and the confirmation of a purchase of a small piece of land adjacent to Pemberley. Jane herself had remarked mildly that she had hoped to spend more time with her new brother, but understood that he was anxious to return home. Her smile softened even this mildest of reproaches, but he did feel a bit guilty that he had not visited much with her. He was, quite simply, desperate to have his own work out of the way by the time he received any word that might take him out of London and was attempting to complete a fortnight's worth of week in less than half that time. He hoped, rather than believed, that Richard's business could be concluded quickly and delicately with all the help they had marshalled and that he could then return home directly. After all, Richard only wanted to speak briefly with the girl and offer her his assistance should she require it. How had such a straightforward commission become so complicated?

Darcy finished reviewing the contract laid out before him and signed it, standing to stretch his back and flex his writing hand. He walked across the room to glance out the window to the street below. In the eight days he had been away from Pemberley the weather had alternated between steady rain and a pale, sickly sunlight with little warmth. He had heard nothing from his wife since their arrival, and the separation had already begun to wear on him, his mood reflected in the gray sky. Closing his eyes, he imagined what she might be doing now. Was she walking along the lake? Laughing with Georgiana? Was she perhaps thinking of him? He wondered if Wright had made it back to Pemberley yet, given the deplorable state of the roads. He almost wished he had held Wright back to help him with Richard's request, but Elizabeth had made him promise to send the man home, and he had no wish to keep the man's older boys without a parent any longer than necessary.

Until Richard had mentioned something about it, he had all but forgotten that most servants did not have children. That was true, more or less, for his staff in London, but it had always seemed right to have children at Pemberley. For a very long time, he had thought that while he was master, they might be the only children to play in the woods or the meadow. Now he had a young, beautiful, intelligent wife at Pemberley and where was he? London, and then points unknown, to interfere in the personal affairs of a man from the Home Office. He sighed impatiently. Only for Richard would he do such a foolish thing. He thought about that and heard Elizabeth's voice telling him that he would do such a thing for anyone he really loved.

Darcy checked the signed contract to see whether the ink had dried. It had, and he folded it up and sealed it to send to the solicitor with his man. One more contract lay on his desk, and then he would be free to leave whenever there was word. He hoped it would be soon.

***

At last, that afternoon, there was news. The Colonel reported that before heading north, one of his soldiers had spotted the carriage near the Inns at Court, and that it had held two young women and an older man. He was able to provide a few more details on the carriage that might prove useful, and had learned that the solicitor had been asked to change some kind of legal agreement either about guardianship or inheritance, or both, but that the solicitor had not agreed to any alterations. Darcy had mulled that piece of information over for some time. He asked for the name of the solicitor, but shook his head when Richard gave it. He had no connections there.

Darcy was increasingly frustrated with the bits and pieces of information that were sent to him. How old were the girls? Were they related? Was the man an uncle to them both? Were both young enough to be under his guardianship or only one? Why was there dissatisfaction with the guardianship? Why in the world were they headed north? There was nothing left at the estate in Staffordshire. He badly wanted to see the whole picture, a picture that was stubbornly refusing to be drawn. He did not want to make plans without knowing everything, but that was looking increasingly unlikely.

By the end of the day, Barrow had sent an express saying that the carriage had stopped at an inn near Kempston the night before and had set out early, still heading north. A knock on the door pulled him from his thoughts, and he saw Richard slip into the study, Bingley not far behind him.

"What news?" Richard asked immediately, seeing the letter in his hand.

"Still headed north, Richard. I think the time has come to follow."

Bingley dropped into a chair, his face thoughtful. "I think we should all go. It may be necessary at some point to split up, and in such a case, an extra man would be helpful." He looked up at the Colonel.

"I understand that this is your mission, Colonel, and that you are in command." He held out his hands, palms up. "I merely offer my services as a foot soldier."

Richard looked at Darcy, skeptical. This man was soft, young, and worse, undisciplined. Darcy saw what he was thinking and shook his head slowly.

"Bingley is quite a good rider, and what is more, he is a good shot."

"Forgive me, cousin," Richard said to Darcy and then bowed to Bingley politely, "but this is not to be a country hunt."

"Actually, I think it is exactly a country hunt." Darcy looked over at Bingley, who tugged once at his waistcoat.

"I will not hold you back, Colonel," he said. "What Darcy tells you is true. I am not a military man, but I am not entirely without useful skills." His voice was serious though his blue eyes still twinkled just a bit. "I am not as good with a sword as your cousin, but I believe I am a better shot, and can nearly match him as a horseman. Can you not use such a man, if for nothing else than to run messages?"

"Better shot, Bingley?" asked Darcy, amused, "truly?"

"Any time you wish to match me, Darcy, I stand ready," said Bingley, almost chuckling.

Richard held up his hand. "Enough," he said with a sigh. "I will be glad of your help, Bingley. We must determine what is to be done. They are more than a day ahead of us, and we will need to proceed carefully. We cannot afford to let Archibald Hawke know that he is being followed unless we are ready to intervene."

Darcy stood. "Agreed. At the moment, they are taking the same route we would take to Pemberley. I believe that for some reason they are headed for Staffordshire. Shall we simply announce I am headed home? There is no reason to explain your reasons for traveling with me, Richard, but we will need an excuse for Charles. What could induce you to leave your lovely bride so soon?" He smiled at Bingley, who was only just realizing that his insistence on joining his friends would indeed separate him from Jane. Bingley thought about it for a moment before recalling the purpose of their sudden removal to London in the stink of summer.

"I might be seeking to remove to Derbyshire with my lovely bride in the near future and wishing to examine eligible properties."

Darcy raised his eyebrows. "Why, Charles," he asked innocently, "have you outgrown Hertfordshire so soon?" Richard snorted.

Six months before, Charles Bingley might have blushed at the merest hint of this incivility. Now he only grinned knowingly. "I would not say outgrown,

Darcy, only that we seek the solitude and *privacy* of a more rustic location."

The other men nodded, smiles still playing about their lips as they turned to the task ahead.

"We shall ride, William, yes?" Richard said anxiously. "The carriage can follow with the trunks and go straight on to Pemberley."

Darcy nodded. "I will write ahead and make sure we have mounts waiting. As we have no idea if or when they will leave the main roads, it would be best to ride rather than try to deal with the carriage." His mind was filled, suddenly, with all that needed to be done before they could be on their way.

"Charles, we will be traveling light. Anything that cannot fit on the horse we shall send ahead to Pemberley. You should go tell your wife." Bingley nodded, and without so much as a flicker of regret, stood, straightened, and walked out of the room.

"Not quite so much a puppy as when I saw him last," was Richard's only concession.

Darcy nodded. "So it would seem." He sat again and began to write his letters, stealing a glance at Richard from time to time. His cousin had his head tilted back and was staring upwards. Finally, Darcy looked up, too. "Richard, is there something amiss with the ceiling?" he asked archly.

"Not with the ceiling, cousin." He paused. "I am simply considering whether I wish to remain in active service."

Darcy put his pen down. This was the first time he had ever heard Richard suggest that he might resign his commission. As much as his heart leapt at the news, he was cautious in his response. "Is there a particular reason?"

Richard nodded. "I find I no longer have the heart for it. That being so, would it not be wrong to ask my men to follow me?"

Darcy sighed softly. *There are plenty of men who have never had a heart for the fight, Richard, and yet they suffered no pangs of conscience for leading their men to slaughter.* "Is it your injury?"

"No, I have been injured before. I still have all my limbs, they all still work well enough." Richard's voice yet held a trace of merriment. "I never thought I would want anything more than a soldier's life, William. Now I find that such a life is not enough. That is not a comforting thought." He smiled ruefully. "I am not prepared to be anything different."

Darcy swallowed his hope. *Be careful what you say.* "Richard, whatever you might wish to pursue, I would be honored to assist you." He motioned to the letters on the desk and said wryly, "As you have ample proof."

Richard laughed. "Your assistance and Bingley's port? How can I not end a success?" Darcy laughed in response, but when Richard did not continue, he knew enough to let the conversation die.

Richard stood and stretched. "We leave in the morning, cousin?"

"At first light, Richard."

"Excellent. I will meet you both here." He strode to the door, his limp almost entirely gone, before turning and addressing Darcy. "Please know I shall not allow any harm to befall you or Bingley." He winked before adding, "I have no desire to tangle with your wives."

Darcy responded only with a grimace, his mind already on the details of their travel. Richard shook his head and closed the door on his way out.

Charles Bingley rose early the following morning. He gently kissed the forehead of his sleeping wife, and pulled the covers over her shoulders. Jane had not been pleased to hear that he was leaving with Darcy and the Colonel. He had explained that he was helping the Colonel track down the family of a man who had died on the battlefield, but she clearly understood that there was much he was not saying. He frowned. Though the second Bennett sister was generally considered the wit among her family, the eldest sister possessed no mean intellect. She had seen through him easily as if he had been made of glass. Her temper burned all the hotter for its fire being rarely lit, and he had been a little surprised at its intensity.

"My love," he had said soothingly, "the girl may be in trouble, but she may not. This is truly all I know."

"And if she is in trouble, Charles? What will you do?"

"I will support the Colonel and Darcy." He paused before adding "We shall not take unnecessary chances, Jane."

"What precisely does that mean, husband?" she asked, her voice calm, but her displeasure keenly felt regardless.

"I do not know, Jane. I shall not know unless we are successful in locating her."

"I see."

"Do you?"

"I see enough. Good night, Mr. Bingley." He was left somewhat befuddled by the suddenly cold address. It was difficult to determine her mood as they had never truly argued before. Was this an argument? He was not certain he could tell. She was unhappy with him, that much was clear, but was it because he was leaving or rather that he could not tell her more about why? He did not know what lay ahead, and therefore could not tell her more. It took another hour and two glasses of port before he realized, with a start, that she was frightened. He was heading into something possibly dangerous, somewhere she could not follow. He tried to consider how he would respond were she to insist on doing something that might put her at risk, but had to break from those thoughts rather quickly. It was too much to bear. *Idiot,* he thought.

"Oh, Janie," he thought regretfully. He put down his glass and went upstairs to hold his wife.

As he tucked the blankets around her in the early dawn and prepared to depart, he felt her eyes on him.

"I am sorry to wake you, my dear," he said gently.

She motioned to a letter on the table.

"For Lizzy." He nodded, placing it in his jacket pocket.

She then held her hand out to him and he took it, running his thumb gently up and down her palm. "Please, Charles, just promise me you will be careful." He looked into her clear blue eyes that were darkening with worry and was lost.

"I promise, my dear. I shall be very careful. And when we are through, you shall join us at Pemberley."

He bent to kiss her hand, lingering just a little longer than necessary before turning to leave the room.

As he reached the bottom of the stairs, he heard Darcy's voice in the foyer. His friend had already eaten and was headed outside to check on the horses. He had apparently dispatched several servants to fetch things they would need, and was seeing to the loading of their trunks on the carriage as well. Charles smiled. Darcy could not help but be the master, even when he was no longer in his own home. He would have to speak with his friend about that, but not now. Instead, he turned to the breakfast room. He intended to eat enough so that he would not feel the need to stop until evening, but he would have to hurry. The Colonel would not be in the mood to brook any delay, and he still needed to check that his weapons were properly loaded and stowed. He would carry both his rifle and a pistol. He was nearly worthless with a sword, but kept a hunting knife with him as well. He thought it unlikely that they would be needed, but there was no sense in being unprepared.

Well-fed and more at ease and focused than he had thought possible, Bingley stepped outside to see his horse saddled, rifle in its place, and Hanson holding the box with his pistol. He opened the box, checked his firearm, stored it with its ammunition, then pulled the rifle out to check that it was loaded and that there was ample ammunition stored in the saddle bag. He looked up to see the Colonel and Darcy doing the same. He entirely missed the approving glance of the Colonel and the smug look Darcy tossed his cousin's way. With a nod to the Colonel, Bingley swung up into his saddle to await his orders. When the others were ready, Colonel Fitzwilliam simply nodded, and then they were off.

It was not until quite late in the afternoon that two very muddy, very tired young men leapt from their horses and knocked urgently on the door of the Bingley townhouse. When Mr. Hanson opened the door he was taken aback at the sight of the bedraggled messengers from Pemberley. The young men insisted that they had important letters for Mr. Darcy, and were quite discouraged to learn that he was not within.

Chapter Nineteen

IT HAD TAKEN Mr. Waters several hours to relate the particulars of each sufferer, but Mrs. Darcy's notes were detailed and exact. He had examined each and found them more or less at the same stage of the illness. Clearly, they had fallen ill nearly all at once. Only a few of the women seemed to be in the earlier stages, one young housemaid and a few mothers who had taken ill while tending their children. Whether it was due to Mrs. Darcy's insistence on separating them from everyone else here in this room or not, he could not say, but there did not seem to be many others falling ill. It was a blessing, he thought, considering how many were already abed.

Of all the children, it was the Wright boys who most concerned him. They were much the same as

Miss Darcy. He felt great sympathy for them, so ill and all alone, their mother and younger brothers on their way to Cardiff and their father still in London. The weather had continued so wet that the roads were in terrible condition, but perhaps their father was already on his way.

He had a great fondness for the boys, being as they were always up trees, pretending to be pirates, and battling dragons, causing endless but harmless mischief. He knew they would settle down soon enough under their father's calm hand and become fine young men, given the chance. He was used to the sickroom, but even for him it was difficult to see these boys in such distress. Mrs. Darcy seemed to feel the same way, remaining near them a little longer, wiping their heated little faces and quietly coaxing them to drink.

As they finished, he held out his hand.

"May I have the book, Mrs. Darcy? I wish to add some notes."

She nodded and passed it over.

"Now, if you please, food and sleep for you."

"Very well, Mr. Waters," she said, casting a look back at the Wright boys. He raised his eyebrows at her and she smiled.

"I will be in the breakfast room." She paused. "When I am finished, I beg you would also take something to eat. Shall I have a tray sent in?" He nodded his acquiescence, eyes on the book.

"There is a writing desk in the far corner near the windows. I believe you will find everything there that you require."

"Thank you, ma'am."

"You are welcome, Mr. Waters." She moved to the door and, as she placed one hand on the knob, turned back to see him sit at the desk.

"Mr. Waters?" she asked.

He stood.

"Yes, Mrs. Darcy?" His voice was clipped, clinical.

Her voice betrayed a deep sense of relief. "Thank you for coming."

***

Elizabeth sat alone in the breakfast room. She nibbled on a thick piece of dark bread studded with walnuts and raisins and sipped a cup of steaming coffee, thinking the current meal among the best she had ever tasted. She had not realized how hungry she was until the food was placed before her, and it took more than a little willpower to behave as though she were not ravenous. She managed it, however, by going over the numbers in her head again as she ate. She counted everyone on the estate, subtracted young Jacob and Harry Briggs, Mr. Wright, and Mr. Harrison. *Harrison*, she thought, wrinkling her nose. The coffee was helping her to think more clearly despite her lack of sleep, and though she had run these sums before, she realized, with a start, that they were not adding up. *No, I must be wrong,* she thought, pouring another cup of coffee and resolving to begin again.

The third time through, she had eaten her full, swallowed two cups of coffee, and concluded that not everyone had been accounted for. It was possible that nothing was amiss, but she would not be able to rest until she had confirmed it. She thought briefly of Mr. Water's instructions. It would indeed be a pleasure to follow them, but until she dealt with this she would not be able to sleep.

When she discussed her concern with John, his face was grave. He admitted that he did not know whether or not those who lived on the southern part of the estate had been visited. Elizabeth noted without comment that John's thoughts immediately moved to the area Mr. Harrison was supposed to visit.

"We were so busy with the children," he said slowly, shaking his head, "and Harrison said he had gone. I assumed then that he had sent Jonas and

Peter, but," he continued, "I cannot honestly say whether that is the case."

He strode away, and in a few minutes returned, his face stormy.

"I will leave Jonas here to tend the horses," he said, "and see to this myself, ma'am."

"I believe that there are several women there, John. I should like to accompany you."

"Ma'am," he said carefully, "might you not need to rest?" He met her gaze unflinchingly. "After last night you must have need of it."

"I am surprised to hear you speak of it, John," she said with a slight smile. "Do you mean to frighten me into compliance?"

John stiffened. He was genuinely bothered by her lack of rest. More to the point, he meant to spare her what he feared might be awaiting them, but the headstrong woman would not admit his meaning.

"I would not dream of it, Mrs. Darcy," he said, barely suppressing his frustration, "for what good would it do?"

"None," she replied lightly, but then looked up into his face. "I thank you for your solicitude, John, but a woman must go and I do not wish to make a scene. Everyone is frightened enough. With any luck, they will all be fine and we can simply return to the house without alarming anyone."

"Shall I prepare the wagon, Mrs. Darcy?" was his only reply.

"I thank you, yes."

"You will ride in the seat this time?"

Elizabeth started, but there was nobody else around. She tilted her head and glared at the man. To bring her nighttime ride once was quite enough, but twice? She was completely shocked when her glare produced only a twinkle in his eye and a softening of his expression, not unlike the one William often bestowed upon Georgiana. She was shocked by the thought that came to her unbidden, *Good Lord, is that a look of approval?* Then the moment was gone as he turned towards the stables and she went to find her pelisse.

***

John drove the wagon to the final two homes on the edge of the southern meadow. He had been heartily relieved when, at the first several stops, all had been well. Perhaps they would have the luck Mrs. Darcy had hoped for and this afternoon's journey might end in nothing more than a way to remove her from the sickroom and get her out of doors for a time. That would not be an unwelcome outcome.

He counted only two more stops before they could return to the great house. The next visit would be to Mrs. Amelia Blunt, a young woman whose older husband had left her a widow not four months ago, just before the master and mistress had returned from their wedding journey and only a month before the birth of the Blunts' first child. Amelia Blunt was nearly a child herself, he thought, too young both in years and experience to be married, let alone with child, but her parents had seven children and had been pleased to accept Mr. Blunt's offer for their eldest. Upon John's recommendation, Mrs. Reynolds had situated her here, near old Mr. and Mrs. Gibbons, after the birth of the child. As he suspected, the pensioners had been only too pleased to help with the infant, their own children being grown and gone. Their home was just a short distance away and would be the day's final stop.

He pulled the wagon to a halt but Mrs. Darcy stepped down before he could assist her. He shook his head, not for the first time on this sojourn, and rubbed the back of his neck in irritation. In her diligence to do her own duty, she would not allow him to do his own. There was no answer to her knock, but perhaps Amelia had taken the child for a walk or was visiting with the Gibbonses. He frowned as Mrs. Darcy slipped inside and called the girl's name. He tied up the horses and moved to follow her, proper or not. If she could set propriety aside for the better care of the staff, then he would not be forced to stand on ceremony and remain outside.

He stepped inside to find the home cold, not surprising after the chill and rain of the past days, and moved to the fireplace. The fire had gone out long ago, he judged, holding his hand over the coals.

Elizabeth slipped into the dark bedroom. "Amelia? Are you here?" she called softly. When her eyes adjusted to the dim lighting, she saw a figure in bed, her head propped up on several pillows, an infant resting against her shoulder. They were sleeping. Elizabeth moved to the bedside and put her hands on the child to make sure the babe did not fall. When she lifted the tiny body to place him upon her own shoulder, his skin was cold. Very cold. Her own breath began to come only in short huffs as she reached down to feel Amelia's arm. It was the same. Amelia's blonde hair was neatly braided and laid across her pillow. Her eyes were closed, her face pasty, her arms limp. Elizabeth placed her free hand on the girl's chest. She knew, but she had to be sure. There was no reassuring beat to tell her she was in error. She choked back a sob and gently returned the child to his mother's embrace before stumbling back towards the door.

She felt ill. Wretched mistake. Awful, terrible mistake. Harrison had told John he had checked the southern homes. She *knew* he was not to be trusted. When John told her Harrison was gone, she should have sent Jonas directly to be certain. She was responsible for them all. How could she not have thought to check Harrison's word, knowing the man that he was? Poor Amelia. She was so young. The child, without even a chance to live. She put a trembling hand on the doorknob.

"Mrs. Darcy?" John called from the front room. He stepped towards the single bedroom in the back.

The mistress reentered the hall from the bedroom. She held up a shaking hand to arrest his progress. He was alarmed at her appearance. She was deathly pale and unsteady, but as he reached to assist her, she shook her head.

"No," she said weakly and put her hand to the wall. "I am well."

Her words were belied by her appearance, and he took her arm.

"Come outside, Mrs. Darcy," he insisted. "Please, ma'am." This was all he needed, for her to fall ill. Thankfully, this time she accepted his help and soon they stood outside in the chilly sunshine. The mistress leaned against the stone wall of the small home, breathing heavily, blinking back tears as her color slowly returned.

John Briggs did not understand the young wife of the master. She was independent to a fault, teasing, and frustratingly stubborn. Yet in the past days he had also begun to admire her strength, particularly in the way she had taken leadership of the staff in the master's absence. Her tenacity in the face of Harrison's abandonment had impressed him, as had her anger. John had been reassured to see that anger. It meant she would bear up well under the stress of the news. Her fearlessness in seeking help for Miss Darcy had even won her his gratitude. He shifted from one foot to another. All he could do now was wait for her to recover. He hoped it would be quick. He needed to get her back to the house to rest. He did not wait long.

"Too late," she said quietly, closing her eyes, a pained expression on her face. John waited for her to continue, but he knew. He had known as soon as she stepped out of the back room. This was precisely what he had feared all along, why he would have left her behind. No, it was worse than he had feared. To have the first victims be a young girl and her infant child? He knew Mrs. Darcy to be very fond of children, and that she had a sister at home not much older than Amelia Blunt. This was a particularly cruel blow.

An irrational flash of fury burned through him. Why could she not have just remained at the great house? Why must she see to everything personally? Did she not trust the staff to do their job? Did she not trust him?

Just as quickly, the ire subsided. John certainly did not relish the conversation this trip would occasion with the master upon his return, but as much as he was loath to admit it, a woman had to make the trip and she had been right not to make a scene. The staff was grateful to her, for they all witnessed how hard she drove herself to take care of them all, but they were still very frightened. Those who might best have accompanied him in her stead were needed in the sickroom or were asleep. Word would get around, it always did, but at least it would be known that most everyone out on this part of the estate had not taken ill. He ran a hand through his thinning hair.

She was looking at him now, her brown eyes truly sorrowful.

"I see you are angry with me, John," came a small voice weak with grief. "I am sorry. I know you would have preferred that I not come for just this reason."

How did she do that? He grimaced. "You have done so much already, Mrs. Darcy. I wish you had trusted this to me." He waited for her to argue, to protest that it was her duty to be here, which he knew she felt to be true. *Damn it all, trust Fitzwilliam Darcy to select a wife as duty bound as he.*

"I do trust you, John," she said seriously. "My husband trusts you, and that means everything, as you well know. I am only sorry that you do not trust me." She looked away but continued, "However, I never thought Mr. Harrison honest. When he proved that to us, I should have sent someone to confirm that these homes had been checked. I did not, and Mrs. Blunt and her child have paid a heavy price for it. So perhaps you should not trust me after all. I have not earned it."

John pursed his lips to keep from swearing in frustration. How could it even occur to this aggravating woman that *anyone* on the estate would not trust her, especially now? Mr. Darcy's approbation had been enough for most, but the way she had acted in the past se'nnight had amply demonstrated her superior character. Who else would have done so much? Not even Mr. Darcy, of that he was certain. The master's actions would have been compassionate and prudent, but he was not a nurse, and it would not have entered his mind to do more than what was expected. It would not have entered *anyone's* mind to do more, except Mrs. Darcy's. What other woman of her station would have put herself at such risk to summon help even for Miss Georgiana, let alone what she had done for the staff?

No, this young woman was possessed of uncommon courage and compassion and he believed his master had chosen his wife exceptionally well. At the same time, he knew that even her strength must have a limit, and he meant to do what he could to prevent her from reaching it. Why must she make that task so damned difficult? He glanced at her face. She was still staring into the distance.

Distract her, he thought suddenly.

"There is nothing more we can do here, ma'am," he said, his voice rough, "but we have not yet stopped at the Gibbonses'."

Mrs. Darcy's eyes snapped back to his. "I had forgotten," she said quietly, and moved quickly to the wagon. She allowed John to hand her up, and the wagon carried them away from the cold little house and down the lane.

Chapter Twenty

THEY WERE OUTSIDE of London before the city woke, and Darcy was relieved to be out in the country again, even on such an errand as theirs. Richard seemed more relaxed than he had in days, whereas Bingley seemed mostly to appreciate that their speed had slowed. They had a good deal of road to cover, though with the horses it would be easier than in the carriage which would follow behind. Barrow and Filbee had decamped a few days earlier and would be riding back to them with news as they had it.

As they rode, Darcy pulled his horse astride and tried to speak with Richard, but the Colonel was very far away. Darcy was hoping to begin planning an approach should they be fortunate enough to track down the girl and her uncle, but knew that it would be of no use to try to intrude upon Richard's thoughts. The Colonel rarely fell silent, but when he did there was generally nothing else to do but wait.

Richard rode through the countryside without noticing much about the land around him other than the fact that his cousin Darcy and Charles Bingley were riding nearby. He thought briefly that they were making good time, but to what end? He had felt so sure of his course in London, but now he had doubts. It might be nothing. It probably was nothing. Still, he could not quite persuade himself that this would be a simple case of finding Miss Evelyn Hawke and relaying his tale. That being the case, what the blazes was he doing involving Darcy and his friend so deeply in something like this? They were newlyweds, for heaven's sake. He should have asked for the use of Darcy's investigators and just come alone.

He considered what the boy had done for him and shook his head. He had saved men himself. He had been saved before by others. It was the life of a soldier during war. What was it then that made Oliver Hawke different? Perhaps because this time the death had been so personal, as he came from Kent and had spoken well of his cousin Anne. Perhaps it was because the captain had been so young. Perhaps it was that the sister seemed to be in difficulty.

Perhaps it was because this was the last such debt of honor he ever intended to owe and he felt a tremendous need to see it satisfied.

He was trying to recall the feeling of staring into the barrel of a French pistol, but there was nothing. He still felt numb, and it was a strange sensation not to feel something, anything about his near death. In the middle of this deliberation, he vaguely understood that Darcy had ridden over to speak to him, but it did not pull him from his reverie. He laughed to himself as he saw the frustration on his cousin's face as he moved away. Darcy had always been one to plan everything to the last detail. He needed to learn that not everything could be planned. There were times one just had to be ready to act as events unfolded.

When they reached the inn in Kempston, it was nearly dusk, and they were weary and dusty from travel. They were all tired from the many hours in the saddle, but Bingley seemed to have the worst of it. They agreed to head to their rooms to change and bathe before meeting in Darcy's rooms for dinner. As they all sat down to their food, there was a soft knock on the door.

"Enter," called Darcy, and Filbee slipped into the room.

"Sir," he said quietly. "'Tis an answer from Mr. Tilden." He held out the sealed letter.

"That was quick, Filbee, I thank you," Darcy replied. Richard saw the slight tension in his cousin's face indicating surprise.

"We had men stationed on the way. Each took a leg." Filbee shrugged. "'Tis no hard thing when there be money enough. Mr. Tilden responded while the boy waited." He stood patiently awaiting orders as Darcy broke the seal and turned the page over, noting that both sides of the sheet were filled with close, neat script. He had not expected so much.

"Read it out, Darcy," said Richard stiffly.

"Shall I wait outside, sir?" asked Filbee.

"No, Filbee. I would just have to repeat the information a second time. Will you be so good as to relay anything we learn to Barrow?"

Filbee nodded and clasped his hands behind his back while Darcy cleared his throat and began to read.

Dear Mr. Darcy,

I admit to being puzzled by your inquiry into the fire at Darlington twelve years ago. I should have thought that your own good father had relayed the details of a tragedy so close to Pemberley. However, your letter indicates you seek to assist Miss Evelyn

Hawke, and for her sake I shall gladly offer what little I know.

I was seven and twenty at the time of the fire, and working with my father on our estate. The Hawke and Tilden families were friendly, and as such I had made the acquaintance of both Mr. Hawke and his wife. They had three children, and while I understood that Mrs. Hawke had experienced several disappointments, she was again with child.

As you know, Bidewell is twenty miles distant from Darlington. Our groom spotted smoke after dinner and we set out with men immediately, suspecting that Mr. Hawke would require assistance. We did not know then that it was the great house that was afire.

The housekeeper later told my father that Evelyn, the youngest, was led outside by her sister Sophia. The older girl then returned to the house to rouse the upper servants, who were able to escape. Her brother had gone to wake their parents, but all three were trapped in the house and perished. The butler tried to reach the lower servants' quarters, but their rooms were cut off as well. Including the girls, only seven members of the household in residence that night survived the flames.

My father and I took the girls home with us. Sophia took care of her younger sister, who was inconsolable. They remained under my mother's care for a fortnight when their uncle arrived to claim them.

I do not know much about the uncle as he dealt more directly with my father, but I will say that he seemed a calculating sort of man and that my parents did not like him. My father asked that I attend a formal meeting where he offered to keep the girls with us as wards. My mother had grown quite fond of the Hawkes, and she was concerned that their uncle had no wife. Mr. Hawke pretended, I believe, to consider my father's offer, but in the end he took the girls with him to London. My father wrote a number of letters to inquire after them, but all communication was at an end.

When her parents and brother passed, Sophia became the heiress of Darlington and both girls came into quite a fortune. We all suspected that the uncle's interests had more to do with securing control of his nieces' funds than it did an interest in the girls themselves, and my father did exert himself on their behalf by engaging solicitors and barristers to protect their inheritance. I believe that Miss Sophia Hawke should have had full control of the estate at the age of her majority, and my father thought she might return at that time to rebuild. That would have been three years ago, however, and as far as I know, she has not come, nor does anyone seem apprised of her whereabouts. Miss Evelyn should herself be nearing her own majority now.

As far as I know, the steward from the time of the fire remains in place. The tenant farms are still leased and seem tidy and profitable. Someone is managing the estate in the absence of the family, but to whom the steward answers and where the funds are sent I know not. I will ride over to inquire should you wish it, though Mr. Hobson is a rather close fellow and may be unwilling to reveal such information.

Mr. Darcy, I have tried to relate the facts of the matter without becoming mawkish, but I shall never forget the sight of two small girls standing together in the dark, wearing nothing but their nightclothes, watching their entire lives being consumed by flame. If there is any way I can assist the Hawkes, I stand prepared, as does my wife. We do so not only for the girls, but for the memory of my parents who cared deeply for them.

I wish you success in your endeavors, Mr. Darcy.

Your servant,
Thomas Tilden, Esq.

The men sat in silence as Darcy finished reading. He folded the letter and tapped it lightly against the table.

Richard shook his head. "Oliver Hawke died in the fire."

Darcy pursed his lips. "Are you sure the captain's name was really Oliver Hawke?"

Richard grunted. He turned to Darcy to reply, "I only know how he introduced himself. He was using that name with his own colonel. It is how he introduced himself to me."

"Is it possible the boy survived the fire? Could Tilden be mistaken?" Bingley asked.

Richard grimaced. "Doubtful. If Tilden was there, he would know whether the boy had survived." He looked up at the ceiling before asking, "So who was the boy who *claimed* to be Oliver Hawke?" His jaw tightened with frustration.

Darcy saw Richard's response and silently agreed. This was growing more complicated by the hour. "It is not an uncommon surname. I would think he might have been another Hawke entirely were it not for the letter specifying Miss Evelyn Hawke's direction in Mayfair."

"And that Evelyn was his sister. Not his cousin nor a distant relation." Richard pressed his lips together in anger.

"Is it possible he was an imposter and wanted some claim upon the inheritance?" Bingley asked.

"But why ask me to help his *sister* in a letter to be delivered only after his death?" Richard rubbed his hands roughly over his head. This was giving him a terrible headache.

Darcy stood and stretched himself to his full height.

"Richard, if the captain was not Oliver Hawke, he was not the girl's brother. You are released from any debt on the basis of that fact alone."

Richard shook his head. "I am not. There was still a debt incurred, though it was not Oliver Hawke who created it. I must still speak with her."

Darcy held Richard's gaze but shook his head, a few dark curly strands of hair falling over his forehead. "You are basing this chase on the word of a liar, Richard. This is not your responsibility."

Richard stared at his cousin. He was the son of an Earl and if Darcy thought he could match his haughty stare, he was utterly mistaken. Darcy might have had more practice, but Richard used it less often, giving it more power. Finally, he spoke.

"You are a fine one to make such a claim. You take on the responsibilities of everyone around you, whether they ask you to do so or not. It matters not who the boy was. He has made a request of me and I must see it fulfilled." He shrugged. "You need not accompany me." The staring continued unabated for a few moments more.

Bingley rolled his eyes at the display and interrupted it. "Putting aside the identity of our mystery rifleman for a moment, it seems likely the uncle wanted the girls' fortunes. Any idea how he might manage that, Darcy?"

Darcy turned away from his cousin. Grudgingly, he replied, "He might attempt to take legal guardianship and control the funds that way. Had he been successful at separating the girls from their inheritance, though, he might then have returned them to the Tildens."

"Depends on the amount," Richard grunted. "If he was unable to gain what he wished directly, he might keep the girls, wait until the elder reached her majority, and then attempt to extort her with some threat to the younger. Did Tilden mention how much was at stake?"

"No," Darcy replied quietly, unsurprised that Richard would see the seamy possibilities so quickly. "I would imagine Darlington was worth about six or seven thousand a year when Mr. Hawke was actively running it." Darcy knew it was nearly two-thirds the size of Pemberley, rich with timber and fertile soil, and that his own father had believed Hawke a shrewd but fair man. Bidewell was a good deal smaller, but Tilden had worked to make the land more efficient and seemed to make a good profit with what he had. "It would likely make less now, but without a household to maintain, the profit might not differ substantially. I have no idea whether the estate was his only source of income or whether there were other funds or investments." He shrugged. "The late Mrs. Hawke might have come to the marriage with a large dowry, or there might have been additional money in the accounts." He glanced over at Filbee, who nodded.

"I will make inquiries, Mr. Darcy." Something flickered in his eyes. "I know just the man."

"How long can we keep this quiet, Filbee?" asked the Colonel.

Filbee considered that carefully. "Depends on the source himself. I'll not tarry."

Darcy rubbed his forehead. "Filbee, beyond the estate numbers, if you would. Find out as much as you can about the legal situation. I should very much like to know whether the uncle has any actual rights to the girls or their funds." If Richard was so determined to see this through, he would of course remain. If these young women were indeed in trouble, he could not turn away regardless of the reasons that brought him into their lives. He was already thinking about offering the Hawkes escort to wherever they might wish to travel. Certainly they could not desire to remain with their uncle.

Richard grinned as Darcy's eyes focused on a far corner of the room. He knew exactly what his cousin was thinking. This was why he had asked Darcy to come along. Even when they disagreed, he knew Darcy would support him. He would work through the solicitor's papers to identify weaknesses. Perhaps they would be on the side of the law here and would not have to fight to remove the Hawkes from their uncle. Archibald Hawke was a powerful man, but he was not powerful enough to break laws with impunity. *He is not*, Richard thought ruefully, *a peer*. Now in an improved humor, he stood and moved to the door, where a tray of food was being brought in by the innkeeper.

Filbee nodded at Darcy.

"Do we know where they are tonight?" Darcy asked. Filbee shook his head.

"Barrow be back shortly wit' news."

"Well, gentlemen," Bingley broke in brightly, standing with the intention to join Richard. "Shall we eat while we wait? I dare say we will have another long ride tomorrow."

Darcy rubbed his chin thoughtfully and stood. As difficult as this problem was, he put it aside to stride to a window. Hands clasped behind his back, he gazed out at the dark and wondered, again, what his wife was doing. Had she had received his letter? Was she worried? Now that he was off his horse and had time to think, he felt again how much he missed Elizabeth, missed talking with her, seeking her advice. He missed the curve of her waist and the taste of her lips on his. He missed being in their bed.

His hand went absently to the pocket in his waistcoat, where he kept her miniature. He was grateful that she had posed before leaving for the wedding tour. It had been ready when they returned and he normally kept it in his study, but he had been unable to leave Pemberley without it. He pulled it out to gaze at her face, but kept it close to his chest, blocking the view of the other men. Silently, he slid it back into its place. *I will return home soon, love.*

He glanced over at Richard and pondered idly whether this time his cousin might really be considering a livelihood in England rather than in the battlefields abroad. The Colonel had seen action from Copenhagen to Vitoria, had returned home wounded several times, and Darcy was nearly desperate to keep Richard in England. He wanted not to feel ill every time he picked up the paper and saw the war news. He had already lost both his parents. He did not think he could bear to lose Richard.

He watched the other men through the reflection in the glass and tried not to let his hopes overwhelm his good sense. With his marriage, he finally felt grounded, happy. He just wanted Richard to feel the same way.

Barrow did not arrive until quite late, after the men had eaten their fill, had a few drinks, and retired to their chambers. Darcy was still dressed, though his coat had been tossed over the back of a chair and his cravat had been removed. He was beginning to unbutton his waistcoat when there was a knock at the door. Darcy opened it to see Barrow, mud splattered on his boots, his angular face streaked with dust. He inclined his head to indicate Barrow should enter, and Barrow took off his hat and slipped inside.

"Forgive my appearance, sir, but I wished to report before you were asleep. They did not make ground today." Barrow's eyes danced with mirth. "The running gear appeared damaged."

Darcy rubbed his eyes. "The running gear? The axels?"

"I believe so." Barrow was fighting a smile.

"What is it, man?" Darcy demanded. Barrow rarely smiled.

"We may have help," Barrow replied with a shrug. "It rather looked as though someone had taken an axe to it. Not a subtle maneuver."

There was another knock on the door and Richard entered without waiting for Darcy to open it.

"Come right in, Richard," he said dourly.

"What news?" Richard asked, ignoring his cousin.

Barrow glanced at Darcy. Richard nearly growled. He was having difficulty accepting the command structure with Filbee and Barrow, but he knew the men were paid by his cousin.

Darcy nodded at Barrow. Before Barrow could speak, Bingley strode in and closed the door. Richard nearly rolled his eyes, but he trained them steadily on Barrow instead.

Barrow shuffled his feet a bit and began "The coach was damaged. Intentionally. Someone is impeding the journey. I do not know who, but it means we might be able to have you gentlemen at the same inn tomorrow if you wish."

"I am not sure," Darcy said thoughtfully. "I would much rather have answers about the legal situation before we intercede, as we would know what we might legally offer in way of assistance. Of course," he said quietly, turning to Richard, "you might be able to discharge your primary duty by simply speaking to Miss Evelyn."

From a corner of the room Bingley muttered, "It is beyond that now."

All three men turned to look at him.

"Is it not?" asked Bingley, as he leaned against the wall. "Should we make contact prematurely, we may not be in a position to assist the girl, but we will most certainly have alerted the uncle to our presence and made her situation more difficult. Before we approach, we should ascertain her legal situation at the very least. Truly, we do not even know her relationship to Colonel Fitzwilliam's phantom captain."

Richard sighed. He was wrung out. His leg throbbed after the full day of riding, the pounding in his leg matching the drumbeat in his head. He hated to wait when they were so close, but he liked the notion of approaching the girl without knowing her situation even less.

"How long?" he asked Barrow. The man shrugged. "Mr. Darcy sent out inquiries before we left London, and we had word that there are some documents for Mr. Darcy. Filbee set off as I arrived."

"Back to London?" Darcy asked. Barrow nodded. "He will make the next leg and send another man on from there. He will sleep where he is while he waits for the return rider and catch up with us by the afternoon, he hopes. Perhaps there will be more news than merely the solicitor's name." His scowl indicated he had been unimpressed with the earlier efforts.

"Then we wait," Darcy said. Richard nodded reluctantly.

"Should we try to close the distance a bit more?" Bingley asked.

Richard nodded again. "We should wait to approach, but I do not want to be too far behind. Clearly, someone is anticipating our arrival."

Chapter Twenty-One

IT WAS LATE in the afternoon when Mr. Waters looked up from his medicines to see the door open and several footmen bearing two stretchers enter the room. His heart constricted as he motioned towards the last few empty cots. Was the contagion spreading? He waited until the new patients, an elderly man and woman, were made comfortable, and then began an examination. He quickly saw that they had been ill for some time without the benefit of the care the others had received. Mrs. Darcy entered behind them, removing her bonnet, and his expression must have shown his disapproval. Why was she not abed? She rubbed her forehead as she moved to him.

"Mr. and Mrs. Gibbons," she said softly. "They were still in their home in the southern meadow. A miscommunication led us to believe that we had checked every home, but we missed a handful of them."

"Am I to expect more patients, then?" he asked, mentally gauging how long it would be before he would have to leave to replenish his stores.

Mrs. Darcy shook her head. "No."

He thought she would say more, but she was silent.

"Mrs. Darcy," he said, scolding.

"Yes, Mr. Waters. I am headed upstairs now. How is everyone?"

He nodded, relieved that he would not have to ask someone to escort her to her chambers.

"Much the same, Mrs. Darcy, but at least no worse. I have been to see Miss Darcy. She was able to take some broth, and I have given her another dose of laudanum." He paused. "I hesitate to give you false hope, Mrs. Darcy," he said, "but she does seem a bit improved."

"I will not foster an unreasonable expectation, Mr. Waters," Elizabeth said tiredly, "but I will allow that it does me good to hear it." With that, she nodded, turned, and headed upstairs.

She stopped by Georgiana's room to see for herself the truth of Mr. Waters' words. Georgie was in a deep sleep, as was to be expected, but her face did seem a little less flushed, her fever a little lower. Mrs. Reynolds fussed with the tea that Mrs. Cronk had sent up when she heard the mistress had returned, and Elizabeth was happy to sit and have some.

"Now, Mrs. Darcy," Mrs. Reynolds said, "you must repair to your bath."

"What?" Elizabeth nearly laughed. "Another bath?"

"You have been out riding to the southern meadow, ma'am," said Mrs. Reynolds with a firm, calm gaze. "You must have a bath to remove the dirt and dust."

Elizabeth nodded, feeling rather sheepish. The speed with which news spread through the great house put the best gossips of the *ton* to shame, but she felt that the confidence of the staff was at least no worse than it had been earlier. Finding only two additional people ill had felt like a blessing of a sort, the more so because they seemed to have fallen ill about the same time as the children. It was not a sign that the fever was spreading. She would not think of the other two who had not lived long enough for assistance to arrive.

Elizabeth drew a deep breath as she entered her chambers. It felt oddly jarring to be planning something as mundane as a bath after what she had seen today, and despite her attempts to push away the memories, she saw them again in her mind's eye. The girl had been so young. *Lydia's age*, she told herself, but stopped. It was becoming a habit, to halt her melancholy before it could grow, to set it aside for later. She thought briefly how these burdens were accumulating, wondering how she would ever be able to face them all. If she waited much longer, there would be so much. Too much. *William will return. He will help me sort it through.* Elizabeth's heart beat a bit faster as she wished for her husband to return. *How long until he receives my letter? Today? Tomorrow? Then three days to travel home?* She knew it might be longer, with the roads in such poor condition, but she was certain he would be on his horse within an hour of reading her messages. She would not wish for him to come home while there was still the chance of him becoming ill, but the danger of infection seemed to be passing, and she longed for his comfort, his kiss, his arms wrapped around her. She closed her eyes. It felt an age since she had been comforted by her husband.

Her weariness notwithstanding, she doubted very much that she would sleep tonight. The bath, however, would be most welcome.

Elizabeth lowered herself into the hot water with a relaxed sigh and closed her eyes. Despite her stubborn belief that the events of the day would keep her awake, she was asleep before Agatha had finished washing her hair. An hour and two pails of steaming water later, she sat up suddenly, sweating, heart pounding, a scream strangled in her throat.

Elizabeth scrubbed herself with the soap, trying to wash the dream away. She rinsed herself, stood, toweled herself off and dressed, moving soundlessly to Georgiana's room to relieve Sarah. She would not risk having that dream again tonight.

Later, at the desk in Georgie's room, she rubbed her eyes and set the candle a little closer before beginning another letter.

My dear husband,

The fifth day of the illness is at last over. It has been the most trying day thus far, but Mr. Waters arrived early this morning and remains here with us. He believes Georgiana is improving slightly, and indeed, her fever seems a bit lower. Further, his presence in the sickroom below stairs has freed me for other tasks that must be completed, and I am deeply grateful. You will be pleased to learn that both he and John have used their authority to order me to eat and rest, and I do what I can to comply.

Mrs. Cronk has been a blessing, running the kitchen and supervising the laundry with a military efficiency that Colonel Fitzwilliam would heartily approve. Mrs. Reynolds remains by Georgiana's side all day while I am with the others, and John guards the horses and keeps the estate running. We have heard nothing of Mr. Harrison, and I doubt very much that we ever will.

The weather has improved, and I believe the Briggs boys should arrive in London soon. They will check at the changing posts for Ares, but I asked them not to delay. The roads are still muddy, and their travel will be difficult enough. I hope they will be safe and find you well, my love.

There is something that weighs heavily on me, William, and I dare not speak it to anyone else. In all the confusion of Mr. Harrison's departure, we did not send to the homes on the southern meadow to confirm he had checked them. When John and I travelled out there this afternoon, Mr. and Mrs. Gibbons were very ill. Mr. Gibbons had been nursing his wife, we believe, before he was himself brought low. It is possible they were exposed by Amelia Blunt and her infant, who. . .

Elizabeth halted, pen in the air. Writing the words was difficult. Thinking of the orders she had given when they arrived back at the house for the burial had been harder still. She exhaled painfully. Then, determined, she set the pen to paper again.

. . . were both beyond the reach of our care. I will not attempt to deny that it is a difficult loss, William. To think, nay, to know that they might have been saved had we reached them in time is very hard. She was so young, my dear, younger than Kitty, and all alone with her babe. I have been able to keep a stout heart throughout all, William, until today.

I would not have you think me remiss in my attentions to my duty, however, and I am resolute. I shall conquer this despair, my dear, and I will be well.

May God watch over you and bring you home safely to us.

Your loving Elizabeth

She put down her pen, moved to the chair by the bed, and rubbed her eyes again. Tears threatened, but did not fall. *I promise, I will be well.*

Georgiana's fever continued, but a little lower, and she slept with more peace than the night before.

Elizabeth, despite her assurances to Mr. Waters, began to feel her hopes rising. She extinguished the candle, rested her head on her arms on the side of the bed, and soon was sleeping lightly. She woke several times though the night, but Georgiana slept on.

Mrs. Reynolds entered Miss Georgiana's chamber to find Mrs. Darcy asleep, head tilted to the side against the back of her chair. She clucked impatiently. It had been more than a week since influenza had come to Pemberley, and even Mr. Waters insisted that the mistress needed to rest. Sarah should be here, but she knew that the maid could not dispute an order from Mrs. Darcy, and so she could not be angry, though she had been growing increasingly worried. She thought to wake her young mistress and send her to bed, but thought better of it. At least Mrs. Darcy was sleeping. There was no way to predict what she would be off to do next if awakened.

The older woman tiptoed to the other side of the bed to check on Miss Darcy. She gazed at the girl's face, reminded suddenly of Miss Georgiana, the child she had been, peeking out from behind her mother's skirts, large blue eyes in a tiny smiling face. She placed her hand on the girl's forehead and was relieved to find it cool to the touch.

"About three o'clock," said a low voice from the chair. Mrs. Reynolds looked over to see Mrs. Darcy, awake and looking at her, but otherwise unmoving. "The fever broke around three."

"Thank the Lord," said Mrs. Reynolds fervently, reaching out to stroke the sleeping girl's cheek.

Mrs. Darcy just smiled and closed her eyes. Soon the mistress was asleep again, and Mrs. Reynolds sat on the bed and thanked the Lord for that, too.

***

Mr. Waters opened his eyes. He was exhausted, and did not immediately move to rise. As his eyes grew accustomed to the late afternoon light, he made out the figure of Mrs. Darcy tending the Wright boys, having each roll first to one side, then the other as she carefully removed the old bedding and replaced it with clean. Both boys were responding to her gentle ministrations, answering her quiet questions about how they felt. They were not well yet, but he felt it would only be a matter of time. Mrs. Darcy stood, carrying the old bedding to a large basket by the door before returning to the boys.

He was still very concerned about Mr. and Mrs. Gibbons. Mrs. Gibbons was very ill, and though her husband had not been quite as ill and should have been improving, he was not. *Sometimes,* he thought sluggishly, rubbing his face with his hand, *it is not only a matter of medicine, but of will.*

He blinked a few times trying to clear his weary mind and considered tossing back his blanket, but before he could, he heard something. It was Mrs. Darcy's voice, low, melodic, sorrowful yet comforting, coming from where she perched on the edge of Matthew's cot. *The boys must have asked her for a song.* The notes seemed to float above the room, suspended somewhere between waking and sleep, a song he seemed to recall from his boyhood, about a soldier returning from war. Her voice was deep and resonant, sweet, painful, and impossibly hopeful. This was not drawing room music, he thought with a weary chuckle, but a folk song. Her voice was expressive rather than polished, but it was hauntingly lovely. It was the soul of the music she conveyed, and her audience could not have been more appreciative. Mrs. Darcy, he thought, was endlessly surprising. The boys settled back and closed their eyes. Mr. Waters listened until she had finished, watching as she tucked the boys in and kissed their foreheads.

Mr. Gibbons had insisted that his cot be positioned directly next to his wife's, and Mrs. Darcy had placed their cots together to create one larger bed and placed them a bit apart from the others, in a position where they could look out the French doors that opened to the grounds yet be sheltered from any drafts. When she had finished with the boys, she wandered over to check on them. Mr. Waters tossed his blanket aside and sat up. He saw that Mrs. Darcy had turned to him, motioning silently to the desk, where there was coffee waiting. He thanked her with a nod and stood to pour himself a cup. They had all been drinking so much tea that the change was most welcome.

He was still worried about Mrs. Darcy. Despite the fact that she repaired upstairs each night, she did not look rested. There were dark circles under her eyes and she moved as though her muscles ached. While he was severe about her taking dinner each evening, he had overheard the servants complaining that once he was asleep in the morning, she was not eating much the rest of the day.

Mr. Waters sipped his coffee and watched Mrs. Darcy sitting with the Gibbonses, gently coaxing Mrs. Gibbons to drink. Mr. Gibbons was pressing his wife's small hand in his large, leathery one, and muttering something to her. It sounded like encouragement from where he stood, but he could not be sure. Mrs. Darcy seemed to have some success. She set the cup back in its saucer, eased the woman back down onto her pillow, patted her fragile hand

and gently brushed the elderly woman's unkempt white hair from her forehead before standing to meet his gaze. She smiled a little and nodded. He returned the greeting and motioned her to the French doors. Her eyebrows raised a bit, but she stepped outside and he followed her.

The air was fresh and not as warm or damp as it had been. The day had been sunny and fine. Mrs. Darcy took a deep breath and let it out slowly.

"Lovely," she murmured.

"How long has it been since you walked out of doors?" Mr. Waters asked.

"Too long," she said with the ghost of a smile on her face.

"Perhaps you could stroll a bit in the garden before coming inside to relieve me in the morning. I can certainly wait a bit longer for you to begin."

"Perhaps," she replied, "when Georgiana is able to come downstairs." *A clear dismissal*, he thought.

They walked through the tall hedges past a stone bench in a clearing, and he motioned for her to sit. They were still visible from the house, but far enough away to converse privately. She took a seat, but he remained standing. She regarded him patiently, her hands in her lap.

"If you would allow me, ma'am. . ." he began haltingly and glanced at her. She nodded for him to continue. "I know we have not had time to spare before, but the worst seems past. I wanted to say to you how extraordinary your preparations and nursing have been."

Elizabeth smiled tightly. She would not allow him to continue. "We are not finished yet, Mr. Waters. Let us not borrow trouble."

He had been hoping to get her to quit the sickroom now that things were well in hand. "Most of the children are mending, and nearly all of the others."

"Not the Gibbonses," she replied, her gaze directed over his shoulder into the distance.

"No ma'am. Not the Gibbonses. They were on their own so long. . ." he nearly bit his tongue. Damn. Why had he said that? He searched her face, wary of her response. Her expression did not change.

"Yes," she agreed, and closed her eyes for a moment.

Fool, he berated himself. He could hear the sorrow in her voice. It was not difficult to see that she blamed herself for not catching the error soon enough, but why? Did she not realize how few patients she should have expected to survive such an outbreak? Did she truly believe that she was the only one who should have realized? Should not the blackguard who had lied and abandoned them not bear the brunt of her recrimination? He scowled and shoved his hands into his coat pockets, a bad habit of his when angered. When he looked up, she met his gaze with scrutiny.

He plowed ahead. "Mrs. Darcy, this simply will not do. The staff looks to you. If you push yourself too hard, they will, too. If you fall ill or are injured because you lack enough rest to make sound decisions, I cannot guarantee that all the sick will be cared for properly. The immediate crisis is past. You must agree to sleep more and take more food." He looked up at her slyly. "Mr. Darcy will have my head if he sees those circles under your eyes, ma'am. Please consider my well-being, if you would."

Elizabeth pondered this silently. She knew she had been foolish. Had she injured Plato, she would never have forgiven herself. Had she injured herself, William would have been as devastated as she would be were he hurt. John had said as much, though in fewer words than Mr. Waters. She had to quiet this desperation that was driving her. It was time. She could not clearly articulate this shift in her thinking, though, not yet. She would have to consider it more fully. In her heart, she promised to take better care of herself.

"Mr. Waters, my husband understands that I am stubborn," she said quietly, and then, wishing to change the subject, "There *is* something I wish to know."

Mr. Waters frowned. "Yes, ma'am?"

"Why do you practice as an apothecary?"

He was surprised at the sudden change in topic. What was she asking him? What had she heard? "I am not certain I understand the question, ma'am."

She smiled, a real smile this time. "It is a simple question, sir."

"Because I *am* an apothecary."

Mrs. Darcy shook her head, her dark brown curls dancing. He would miss that when this was over and her hair was no longer casually pulled back but instead pinned neatly, properly restrained, and tucked beneath a cap or bonnet. "Yes, but you are far more, is that not true? There is no hiding that you are skilled with medicines. However, you are equally skilled in the sickroom. You are well read. You refuse to bleed fever patients. . ."

Mr. Waters began to explain, "That is because. . ."

"Stop." She said, holding up a hand. "That was not a complaint, Mr. Waters. Allow me to finish." She thought for a moment and then continued. "You have clearly studied modern medical techniques quite thoroughly, have completely discarded some traditional methods, and you have contained the illness almost entirely to those first affected."

He demurred. "I am afraid, madam, that I can take no credit for halting the spread of the disease. You did that yourself by gathering the ill in one place, keeping it clean, and limiting access."

She shook her head, "I followed the course of treatment you offered the Wright boys. We discussed it."

Mr. Waters shook his head. So ready to take the blame for everything but not willing to accept praise. Frustrating woman.

Mrs. Darcy waited only a moment before continuing. "You have a most active intellect and are always adding to your knowledge. Forgive me for saying, but in my experience, that is not often true of apothecaries. Most are more interested in selling their wares than curing their patients. Are you in fact a physician, sir?"

He laughed. "No, ma'am, I am not. A physician would not actually tend the sick, as you know." *Just like most fine ladies, physicians give orders and leave others to carry them out. We are neither of us physicians.*

She pursed her lips and shook her head at him. "A surgeon, at least..."

"No." He was firm.

Her eyes narrowed. She did not believe him, and was keen to win her point. He would play this game with her if it helped her forget his earlier remark. He was unprepared, however, for her next attack.

"What do you think of Dr. Croft?" she asked pointedly. "He is well regarded in London. Shall Mr. Darcy employ him for the family when we are next in town?" She knew her husband did not intend to change physicians, but she was interested in Mr. Water's response. She was not disappointed.

"Absolutely not, Mrs. Darcy," he said sternly. Croft? Blast. This was no game. What was she about?

"Why is that, Mr. Waters?" She tilted her head at him and arched a single eyebrow, challenging him to ignore her.

"Croft is a fool!" he spluttered, offended by the question.

"Explain," she said, her tone almost imperious.

He muttered something too low to hear.

"What was that, Mr. Waters?"

"I said, ma'am, that with all the bleeding he relies upon, he will one day kill someone he is meant to cure. That is, if he has not done so already."

"Truly? Yet Mr. Croft is quite well-known and sought out, even, I believe, by the royal family."

"He is old-fashioned and dangerous, Mrs. Darcy. I beg of you not to employ him."

"Indeed?" Mrs. Darcy raised her eyebrows. "Is that the opinion of an apothecary?"

He stopped. How had she wound him up so quickly? He tugged his waistcoat and met her gaze. "It is the opinion of *this* apothecary, ma'am."

She nodded, both eyebrows now arched in a look he could only describe as triumphant. "Shall we simply agree that I believe you to be as knowledgeable as a physician but far more useful?"

He grinned and rubbed the back of his neck, glancing up at her with a look that could only be described as boyish. "If you wish, Mrs. Darcy."

"Well," she said, standing, brushing out her skirts, "Now that we have that settled, shall we return to the house?"

She was slipping through the door to head upstairs before he recalled that he had asked *her* outside, and that he had never been able to gain her promise to leave the remaining sick to him. She had neatly turned the conversation around on him to avoid discussing her own health. He shook his head as he watched the door close behind her.

"Tomorrow," he said softly to her retreating form. "You will not distract me tomorrow."

Chapter Twenty-Two

THE DAY DAWNED bright and warm at last, and Colonel Fitzwilliam was out early checking the horses. After speaking to the groom he returned to the inn for coffee. He sauntered outside, mug in hand, and thought briefly about his commission. If he meant to sell it, he should think about sending a letter to the major-general and then the army agent. His parents would be happy, he thought dispassionately. They had begged and bullied him to sell out for years and as careful as Darcy was not to broach the subject, he knew his cousin would like to have him home as well. He had fought on after Ciudad Roderigo, but if he was honest, even before he had been wounded at Vitoria, the brutal behavior of the troops after taking the fort had, more than anything, forced him to question whether he could remain. He was exhausted, as tired as he had ever been. His body was no longer young and he could no longer maintain the pretense that war was an honorable profession, regardless of the need for it.

However, the very thought of leaving the army to face Napoleon without him made him restless. He wanted to be there when that Corsican dog was finally brought to heel. The thought of the marriage mart his mother intended to subject him to was another reason to reconsider. The world of his mother and the women she would select was so very foreign to his own, his experiences so beyond that of an innocent, sheltered peer's daughter or even that of a wealthy widow, that he knew there was little about which he could truly speak with them. It was not possible to converse about what he had seen to anyone unless they had been there, and sometimes not even then. So he teased, flirted, joked, and hid his troubled dreams by retiring late and riding out early. His mother hoped he would marry a woman with a title, but he believed her hopes fantastical, what with his positon as a second son and his lack of fortune. No, he was in little danger there. His father only insisted upon a healthy dowry, but despite using the need for money as an excuse in the past, he did not believe he could bring himself to it in the end. What need had he for the luxuries of the Earl's life? All the things he had once believed important, fine clothing, the ability to keep a stable, a house in town in a fashionable neighborhood, none of it mattered. Well, he must admit that a few excellent horses would not go amiss with him. Still, after living so long as a soldier he was mostly content simply with good food, dry boots, a soft place to sleep, and a sound roof over his head.

As a Colonel, Richard would bring little wealth with him into a marriage. All he could offer was himself. That being the case, he was determined that he should at least love the woman, respect her, desire to make her happy, and spend his days working to achieve that end. If he was entirely honest, he was nearly desperate to find a woman that could love him, too, despite his lack of significant fortune, despite his own myriad of shortcomings. *William's marriage has ruined me for more mercenary considerations.*

Therein lay the problem. What woman could bear to be with a man so broken? Love a man whose soul was in such disrepair? He snorted at the thought and then grinned a little. Perhaps he should try his hand at penning Gothic novels. He was behaving like an overwrought girl about to face her first season. He gulped down the watery coffee and scowled. At least it was hot.

There was no sign of Barrow, and Filbee was not expected to reach them until the early afternoon. He knew that Darcy would likely be up already, plotting twenty different scenarios for rescuing the damsel or damsels in distress and making mental lists of approaches and the contacts he could use for each one of them. He loved to tease Darcy about his need to plan and organize. It was a compulsion. He grinned wider as he acknowledged that his fastidious cousin's services were actually invaluable, particularly now. His own mental faculties were at a low ebb and he was grateful for the help.

Since Vitoria, Richard had to be careful. Every time he tried to concentrate on anything important, it took only a few minutes before his eyes began to water and his head began to pound. The headaches were both less frequent and less severe than they had been a month ago, but he could not have done this on his own, as much as he might have preferred it. The unseasonably cold, rainy weather the past week had not helped alleviate his pain. He hated having to rely on Darcy yet again, but there was little to be done. He would have to adjust to it until the headaches finally stopped. Even after he was entirely well, if he sold his commission, he would be a dependent again. Thanks to Darcy's good advice, he had managed to invest and save, but his fortune was still smaller than the dowries of many women in the *ton* his mother loved so well. Richard knew his brother would continue his allowance should his father die and that Darcy would try to offer him a place to settle, but it grated. A man wanted to provide for himself. If he meant to marry, he must be able to provide for a family as well. *Should have gone into the Navy. Lots of money to be made in the Navy.* He snorted. *Too bad I get seasick.*

Outside, in the quiet of a new day, he turned his mind to Captain Oliver Hawke, whoever he was. What could have possessed the boy to lie? Fighting under a false name could be a hanging offense, at the discretion of his colonel. He worked at a hole in the dirt with the toe of his boot. Yet, whoever the boy had been, the captain had saved his life. That could not be dismissed. Nor could the letter asking for his help. Clearly the boy had known Evelyn Hawke was in trouble. But how?

He felt a dull ache begin behind his eyes, and fished a packet of powder out of his pocket. He dared not use anything too strong before riding, but the headache remedy took the edge off the pain. He poured it into his coffee, watching it dissolve, and finished the brew in three large gulps. As he turned to enter the inn, he spied Darcy exiting to find him.

Darcy opened the door to the inn just in time to see Richard pouring some sort of medicine into his coffee and swallowing it down. He knew his cousin was still in pain. It had been clear enough to him when Richard could not focus on their map, and last night his limp was more pronounced after a long day on horseback. His own back and legs were sore, but a hot bath had eased the ache and allowed him to sleep. He put his head down and continued through the doorway so that Richard would not see him looking. He glanced up a few moments later, as Richard turned and gestured with the hand that held the empty mug. Holding the door, he allowed Richard to return inside. Darcy followed him, determined to keep a closer watch.

Bingley rose late, but they were soon off, reaching their destination close to noon. They were only a few miles from the inn where the Hawkes had supposedly been detained the day before, a good time to change out the horses and eat something. As the men swung out of their saddles, there was a commotion on the road behind them. Filbee was riding up at full speed, what remained of the mud on the road flying up behind his mount. The men turned to watch as he catapulted out of his saddle to present Darcy with a sheaf of documents.

"It took some days, sir, but these like to be helpful to ya."

"Where did you get these, Filbee?" Bingley asked. He was astonished that the men had found anything, let alone the stack of papers in the man's hand.

"I canna' say, Mr. Bingley."

"You cannot or you will not?" Bingley asked, smiling.

"Is all ta' same ta' me, sir," Filbee replied with a shrug and a grimace. His brown hat was battered, his dark hair sticking out from beneath the brim at odd angles. His horse was hired. He wore brown boots that were scuffed and worn thin, his trousers were threadbare at the knees, but Bingley noted that there was a very fine pistol tucked away discreetly beneath a faded blue coat. Highwaymen were scarce now, but any robbers hiding in along the road to waylay a wealthy rider would certainly have allowed this poor messenger to pass them by.

Darcy was already looking at the writing on the first document as he spoke. "Charles, I pay them to get the information, I pay them to make certain it is sound. I am careful not to pry into the affairs of others if there are no lives at risk, and no one is to be harmed to procure it. However, I do not ask otherwise how that information was obtained. Generally that is something I neither need nor desire to know." Without looking up, Darcy said firmly, rather than asked, "Of course, Filbee, you have broken no laws."

Filbee wore an expression of perfect innocence. "No, sir. Not I."

Richard grunted his approval. Ramsgate had changed Darcy more than he had realized. *No*, he thought, *not just Ramsgate. He now has two women to protect. He finally understands that there are times propriety must be set aside.* "Shall we ask for tea?"

Darcy nodded. "We will need a private room while I try to make sense of these. Filbee, get yourself something to eat and ask about a room. I will speak with the innkeeper."

Filbee nodded, grateful. "Mr. Darcy." He tossed the reins of his horse to a startled groom and walked inside. The other men did the same. As he passed, Bingley pressed a coin into the man's palm.

"Thanks to you, sir!" said the groom with delight, and began to walk the horses back to the mews.

Thirty minutes later, Darcy was studying the nearly twenty pages of contracts and notes spread wide across a table, pointing out particular passages to Bingley as they muttered together softly. Richard was ready to hang them both from the rafters. What the devil was taking so long? He had tried to read the small, even script, but his headache threatened to return after only ten minutes, so he had taken to pacing instead. Finally, Darcy nodded and sat down. Bingley poured a glass of wine and offered it first to the Colonel, then to Darcy, but each declined, and Bingley sat with it himself. The tea arrived and Darcy looked up as the servant bowed and closed the door behind him with a soft click. Richard grabbed a plate and began to eat, barely tasting the food but knowing he could not go much longer without something more than coffee in his stomach. His anxiety did not ease. Finally, his cousin spoke.

"Another piece of the puzzle, Richard," he said calmly.

"Good God, Darcy," Richard exploded, sliding his plate forcefully to the side. "Tell me what you know or I shall throttle the both of you!"

Bingley looked amused, but Darcy remained nonplussed. He rarely responded to Richard's outbursts, as not reacting was a sure way to drive Richard to Bedlam. After a moment, he remembered the medicine in his cousin's coffee and took pity on him, steepling his fingers and leaning back in his chair, speaking hesitantly as he worked it all out for himself as well as the others.

"According to these documents, when Miss Sophia Hawke came of age three years ago, she became legal guardian to Miss Evelyn. What I do not understand is that she apparently became mistress of Darlington with access to all of the funds," he paused, still wondering, "the moment her parents and brother passed. Her solicitor in London was the executor and he was required to approve any removal of funds until her majority. She seems not to have drawn on anything beyond a modest quarterly allotment." He shook his head, unsatisfied. He sat forward to flip one document over and read the back, then another, "Currently, the estate profits are being reinvested in the property and the rest is sent to several accounts in London, both in the funds and other investments. The personal accounts have not been touched beyond about three hundred pounds total over the past three years." He paused, glancing at one of the documents. "The funds seem to have been sent to Dover." He considered whether the elder Miss Hawke might reside there or perhaps on the continent. It was not much to live on for an heiress. "We know Miss Evelyn has been living in Mayfair with her uncle, but there are no guardianship papers here for him. Filbee's source says there are no such documents, so the uncle does not appear to have the right to keep Miss Evelyn with him if her sister does not wish it." *Why had her sister not arrived to collect Miss Evelyn when she had the legal standing?*

Richard heaved a great sigh. This was knowledge worth waiting for. "What do we know of her sister? Is she the woman from Seven Dials?"

Darcy cocked his head at Richard. "I do not know, Richard, but if I was forced to guess. . ."

Richard completed the sentence "You would say yes."

Darcy nodded. There was silence for a moment before Bingley cleared his throat and indicated that Darcy should continue. "If these contracts are accurate, Miss Hawke made several changes when she was about sixteen. She increased her steward's salary substantially, moved all of her accounts to a new solicitor," he glanced at the name and then mumbled something in surprise before continuing, "and finally, she transferred her dowry of £20,000 to Miss Evelyn with the stipulation that the additional money remain in her sister's control even after marriage. The principal is invested in the funds and may not be withdrawn. She may take the interest quarterly as an allowance." He looked at Richard, a dark and serious expression on his face. He held up one of the documents. "The way these have been written. . . Miss Hawke has been very clever. Nobody can access the original dowry without the guardian's approval until Miss Evelyn is five and twenty. Even once married, the additional monies cannot be touched by her husband. If the uncle is trying to get at the funds, he will find it difficult. He may be hoping to coerce Miss Hawke into altering the contracts."

Richard rubbed his chin. "He could force a marriage and threaten Miss Hawke with her sister's safety."

"You are reading too many novels, Richard," Darcy replied half-heartedly. The Colonel shrugged, and they let the matter drop.

Bingley set his glass down. "You believe she had help drawing up the documents. More than just the solicitor."

Richard grunted. "Most solicitors would not deign to do business with a woman, let alone a sixteen-year-old girl without any man to speak for her."

Darcy tilted his head to gaze at the ceiling. This solicitor he knew. He considered how to broach it with his cousin.

Richard was already moving towards the door with purpose, picking up his coat along the way and stuffing his arms into the sleeves.

"We must go. There is no telling how long they will remain at the inn."

Darcy put up a hand. "Richard, we cannot rush out at this moment. We need fresh horses. Sit. Finish your tea. They cannot be far."

Richard slumped into a chair. He badly wanted to be moving, to be doing something, and sitting again was almost painful. His foot tapped the ground impatiently. He knew Darcy was right. The horses were blown, they needed new mounts. He squeezed his eyes shut and leaned his head back against the chair. He understood these practicalities and bowed to their necessity, but he badly needed this chase to be at an end. As he sat, his foot stilled but his mind began to race. Without entirely realizing he was speaking out loud, he asked, "Why would the sister be in Seven Dials if she was an heiress? Even had she truly been ruined it would not preclude her from taking up her inheritance and living quietly on her estate. Wealth covers a multitude of sins. Perhaps it is not her sister at all."

Darcy and Bingley glanced at one another and then Richard, who shook his head and continued without opening his eyes. "I feel it is the sister, though I cannot account for it."

Bingley shrugged, but Darcy nodded in silent agreement. Richard continued. "She was not ruined."

His eyes opened and he stood, saying what he had been considering ever since Filbee had mentioned Archibald Hawke. "She was hiding. From her uncle." He opened his eyes, stood, and began to pace. Just as suddenly he stopped, his back to the other men, and said, very quietly, "If we are able to recover the Hawkes, I think I should take them to my father, and you two should go to Pemberley."

Darcy asked, softly, "Do you think the Earl is involved?"

The Earl of Matlock was famous for his stands in Parliament in support of workers and the poor, who loved their champion unreservedly. His fierce defense of those who he felt had little voice in the House of Lords had consequences, of course. Along with his many allies and friends, he had collected, along the way, a number of very powerful enemies. One of them was Archibald Hawke.

"I know he has no love for Archibald Hawke. I never made the connection with Captain Hawke. It is a common enough name and we were so far from home." He pursed his lips, thinking about the reference the boy had made to Anne de Bourgh and said, quite suddenly, "The boy's name. It is just the sort of thing my father would do. He has a great love for symbol."

"You think it was the Earl's intention to set this entire situation in your path?" Bingley was skeptical.

Richard halted in mid-stride, sighed, and rubbed his forehead, staring out the window. He was remembering his father's reaction to the boy's name.

"I do not think even he could manage that. However, I would not be surprised to learn he was involved."

"Richard," said Darcy quietly, touching the tip of his finger to a page on the table. "Is not Silverman and Jones your father's firm?"

There was a soft knock at the door, and a servant's voice informed the men that their horses were ready. Darcy gathered the papers with a sweep of his long arm. Bingley gulped the remainder of his tea and stood to follow Fitzwilliam and Darcy, who were already walking outside.

Chapter Twenty-Three

THE FINAL DAYS of the epidemic passed quietly in as much comfort as Elizabeth's new routine could offer. The days began to blend one into another until she was not sure what day it was or how long her life had consisted of changing sheets, bathing fevered children, feeding those who could not drink or eat by themselves, and sleeping in her sister's room during the night hours. Although Georgie was no longer burning with fever, Elizabeth felt an unrelenting fear that it might all be an illusion, that if she let down her guard for one moment, everything might go horribly wrong.

This morning she had been confronted directly by Mr. Waters, who insisted she sleep in her own bed, and they had finally agreed to compromise on having a long chaise moved to Georgiana's room. She was to allow Sarah to sit up while she slept, and to this she had willingly consented. Her primary fear now was simply being too far away should Georgiana want her. So tonight, she fell asleep quickly, tucked up carefully in a light blanket, head on a marvelously soft pillow.

Unfortunately, the dreams had not stopped. Tonight, she dreamt that Fitzwilliam had come home. He could find nobody in the house and was calling her name. She called out to him, but he could not hear her, and his voice grew increasingly frantic as he searched each room in turn. Finally he was yelling Georgiana's name, and Elizabeth could bear it no longer, waking with a gasp and a pounding heart. She could not allow the dream to become real, he could not leave home with his sister in health only to return and find her gone. The younger Wright boys had seemed to best their fevers, and had begun to roam the house again only to return to their beds less than a day later. She would not allow Georgiana to make the same error.

She stood, the blanket pooling on the ground, and stepped to the bed. She pulled Georgiana's bedclothes straight and tucked them around the girl very gently, but she was restless. Sarah brought a cup of tea to Georgiana's lips and gently persuaded her to sip. Elizabeth almost reached out to take the cup, but held herself back. *It makes me feel better to help,* she scolded herself. *It must make Sarah feel better, too.* She thought briefly about adding a drop of laudanum to the tea, but she disliked it when she herself was ill and could not countenance giving it to Georgie unless truly necessary. Her sister did seem to be on the mend, but Elizabeth could not be easy. It was yet too soon. Reluctantly, she retrieved her blanket and returned to the chaise. She took a deep breath and closed her eyes, determined to make good on her promise to Mr. Waters.

As the dawn began to light the room, Elizabeth blinked herself awake and rose. Sarah was nodding off in her chair, and Elizabeth began to snuff out the candles. Mrs. Reynolds had scolded her for that, but there was no need to ask a servant to leave her duties when every hand was needed elsewhere. Because she had insisted on setting propriety aside, she was beginning to realize just how much work the servants truly did around the house and how grateful she was to be the mistress. She had always been appreciative of their service, but she had to admit to herself that even she had no idea the vast number of tasks that they managed as a matter of course. She was exhausted just contemplating it.

Elizabeth had been kept quite busy running the larger sickroom during the day, tending to those who had no caretakers and then tending to Georgiana in the evening, but she had found the strength to tease Mrs. Reynolds about the bath that awaited her each twilight between her tasks. The normally affectionate housekeeper had actually grumbled at her last night, something about not allowing the staff to do much of anything else for her. She was only partly mollified when Elizabeth took her by the hand and promised to allow them to help more. She had been making a real effort to delegate some of her workload to the staff, to their surprise and relief, but every time she tried to step to her room or she passed one task to someone else, yet another need would arise. She knew that in setting herself up as the one who had done everything from the start, she had trained the servants to come to her with all problems, even if they wished to solve them on their own. She was now facing the consequences of her stubbornness. She had made herself indispensable. *My fault for not listening to John and Mrs. Reynolds from the beginning*, she scolded herself. *My fault for allowing Mr. Harrison to rattle me.*

In the end, keeping steadily busy was helpful. She found that moments of relaxation simply resulted in more time to think about all the fears and self-recriminations she had locked away. She knew that they were not far along enough for her to stop and examine them. Any brief moment of rest was interrupted by at least one nightmare. She would rather work. It was just that now, she understood the importance of allowing others to work, too. It was good for her, but it was also good for them. She reached for Fitzwilliam's miniature and kept it in her palm for a moment, gazing down at his likeness. *You would have known this already, my love. I am learning. I will do better. I promise.*

"Lizzy?" Georgiana asked, blinking in the early light.

Elizabeth slipped the miniature into her pocket and moved to the side of the bed to pat Georgie's hand. "Yes, my dear?"

"I cannot sleep. Would you mind telling me a story?"

Sarah's sleepy head lifted.

"Of course," Elizabeth replied. "What would you like to hear?" She stood to consider the books on the table, but turned when Georgiana said that she did not want "a book story."

"I would rather hear about growing up with four sisters," Georgiana said with a shy smile. "Or one about you when you were young. Fitzwilliam says you were quite fearless."

Elizabeth laughed. It felt wonderful. "Yes, fearless is likely an apt description."

Georgie smiled. "I wish I were as brave as you, Elizabeth."

Elizabeth returned the smile. Georgiana's face was very pale and she was still quite weak, but she did seem to be improving. She took a breath and endeavored to portray a lightness she did not feel. "Even when I should have feared, I am afraid I did not. Perhaps it was foolhardiness rather than courage."

"Surely not, Lizzy," replied Georgiana, squeezing her hand.

Elizabeth thought for a moment. "I suppose that part of being fearless is simply not thinking about what one should fear, so I am not certain it is something for which I am due such praise." She thought for a moment about their current trial. "My approach to being brave, Georgie, is to pretend that I am even when I do not feel it, and soon I find that I can manage quite well." She smiled, recalling an old conversation with her husband. "And as William can attest, my courage always rises when someone, or something, tries to intimidate me. Perhaps it is just plain stubbornness."

Georgiana nodded and closed her eyes. "I am ready for a story about courageous Lizzy," she said with a teasing demand in her voice.

Elizabeth turned to Sarah, who was doing her best to melt into the furniture, and smiled. "Now Sarah, this is all strictly in confidence," she said with a smile. Sarah smiled a little in return and nodded.

"Of course, ma'am."

Then Elizabeth turned back towards the bed and began to tell Georgiana a story about her father teaching her to tie sailing knots. They had been reading a book together and Lizzy had wanted to try herself. Once she thought she had the knot mastered, she had climbed high into a tree to tie a stout rope to the branch that hung across a large, deep pond on the grounds at Longbourn. She explained in detail and with wry jests how she had nearly fallen several times as she shimmied out along the branch, tearing the hem of her new blue dress, though she had at last managed to secure the knot.

"Then, before I even had an opportunity to benefit from all of my own hard work, John Lucas grabbed the rope and swung out. I thought I had the right to go first, of course." Lizzy's lips quirked up in a small smile, remembering. "I am afraid I was quite cross with him."

Elizabeth watched Georgiana's lips tug upward as though she was imagining the precise way in which the young Lizzy had expressed herself. The girl's eyes opened to meet hers. "What did you *do*, Lizzy?" Georgiana asked.

"Why, whatever do you mean, Georgiana?" she asked coyly. It felt marvelous to be teasing Georgie again.

"I just *know* you punished John Lucas somehow. What did you do?"

"Oh dear," laughed Elizabeth, "I am teaching you to think very ill of me."

"Not at all," Georgie said softly. "I am sure you only taught him a well-deserved lesson, but Lizzy, it can be so very funny when you lose your temper!"

"I dare say that your brother would not agree."

"I dare say he would so long as you do not lose it with him," Georgie said slyly. Elizabeth smiled as she thought of Fitzwilliam. Her hand went again to her pocket and she touched the frame of the miniature with the tip of her finger.

"Well, as it happens, there was no need to teach Mr. Lucas anything other than not to trust the knots I tied." Elizabeth laughed at the memory. John Lucas had been a little more than five years her senior and was just back to visit from his first year at university. She had not approved of the new haughtiness and sense of superiority that had returned with him. "Some sins carry their own penance." She smiled, recognizing that this applied to herself as well. Fortunately, her only penance thus far seemed to be fatigue. She met Georgie's shining eyes, noiselessly begging her to continue.

"He never made it to the water at all," Elizabeth explained, "and great large boy that he was, he could not sit down for many days. Although I had not done it on purpose, I did laugh. I could not help it. Then it was his turn to be quite cross with me."

"Was he very angry, then?" Georgie asked, clasping her hands on her lap in delight.

"Well, perhaps I did remain in the tree rather longer than I had planned. In fact, it was my father who finally came to retrieve me. He was not amused to see me perched on the limb like a colorful but recalcitrant bird. The entire day was a bit of a disaster and I was confined to the house for a week. I believe I had the worse punishment after all."

Georgie's hand covered her mouth and suddenly she began to giggle in peals of musical laughter, thin, reedy, but very, very welcome. Elizabeth sighed contentedly. Hope was a risk, she thought, but she began to think of the day when Georgie and all the others would really, truly, be well.

Chapter Twenty-Four

THE ROAD WAS STILL a bit damp, though the sun had dried it enough that it was comparatively easy to ride, and Richard set a bruising pace. He was sure that that the carriage would soon be repaired or replaced and he would lose his chance if he did not run his horse nearly to death. His cousin and Bingley rode behind, not trying to keep up, but not so far back that he was out of their sight. The way Richard was riding, Darcy was concerned that they had not waited for reinforcements to arrive, though he had left word of their destination.

It was a little more than an hour before they began to descend into a small valley and Richard knew that they were nearing the inn. He looked back, waved once at Darcy, and plunged down the road.

Swearing under his breath, Darcy stood in the stirrups to watch his cousin bolt down a gentle incline. The inn was close, and he had hoped Richard would wait. He would prefer not to rush into a confrontation, but it appeared Richard had finally reached the end of his patience. Darcy urged his horse into a gallop and headed after him. In perfect health, Richard was a formidable fighter fully capable of taking on several men at once, but he was not himself. From the corner of his eye he noted that Bingley had kept pace with him as they closed the distance between Richard's horse and their own. As they rounded a turn at the bottom of the small hill, the inn came into view.

A carriage was standing at the entrance, the driver perched atop the box holding the reins but nobody else in view. He saw Richard dismount and peer into the carriage. Apparently there was nobody inside, as he then turned to the driver. Only then had Darcy and Bingley managed to reach the front of the inn and dismount. They tied up their horses and moved to join the Colonel, who was now involved in an increasingly hostile and apparently fruitless interrogation. The driver gazed at the three men, bewildered, and offered little of value. Either the man was an idiot, or he was pretending to be one. The

Colonel seemed to believe the latter, and his voice, though controlled, was growing icy and dangerous.

"I will ask again. Who owns this carriage?" he growled.

The man shrugged.

"Where are the Hawkes?"

The man shook his head.

"Enough," Bingley interjected softly, placing his hand briefly on Richard's shoulder. "Stay here in case they arrive and allow us to check inside. We do not even know that this is their carriage."

Richard looked at Darcy, and lightly tapped the door. A coat of arms had been painted over. It was unreadable, but he was almost entirely certain the carriage was Hawke's. Darcy nodded, and Richard grunted his assent, leaning back against the front wheel with his arms crossed over his chest, glaring at the driver who shrugged and resumed his seat. Darcy and Bingley stepped towards the door of the inn when it flew open just in front of them. They stepped away, Darcy to one side, Bingley to the other.

A short, stout man with a few wisps of dark hair on a mostly bald head stomped out first, hat in hand. He was followed by a young woman with perfectly coiffed, light brown hair tied up in ringlets that grazed her shoulders. She was wearing a dark jonquil traveling dress and carrying a bonnet by its ribbons, but made no move to place it atop her head even once she had walked through the door. Darcy judged her to be about Elizabeth's height, perhaps a little shorter, and of a similar build. She carried herself with none of the confidence of his wife, however. Her shoulders were slumped and her back slightly bent. Her face was pale, and the way she rubbed her hands together betrayed her anxiety. Both men noticed that her blue eyes were rimmed with red and she was staring straight ahead. She seemed almost dazed, unaware of anything happening around her. She was followed by a footman. Darcy glanced quickly back at Richard, who was now pushing away from the carriage to gain his feet, his eyes locked on the young woman. A few feet behind this group was another young woman, a bit older than the first, who was followed by two footmen, one of them rather larger than the others.

Darcy eyed the second woman with interest. She was perhaps three or four and twenty, though she might possibly be younger, and she was the opposite of the first in nearly every way. She was tall and slender, almost thin, whereas the first had been petite and rather buxom. Her hair was fair and fell just below her shoulders in soft, untouched curls. The only similarity between the two women was the shape and unusually intense blue of their eyes. They were identical. Sisters, Darcy thought. He felt a sudden rush of certainty. Sisters. This had to be the Hawkes.

He stepped up to the second woman and bowed, halting her progress while using her body to block him from the sight of her escorts. Silently, he mouthed his name. Her eyes were quick to catch it.

"Good day, Miss Hawke," he said in a voice loud enough to be heard by the footmen who stopped behind her, "it is a pleasure to meet you here."

The woman seemed to have been waiting for just such an opportunity, as without any hesitation, she responded to his greeting.

"Good day, Mr. Darcy," she replied, her voice catching just a bit on the "a" and drawing it out just a moment too long. "Whatever are you doing so far from town?"

"Believe it or not, madam, we have been traveling with a message for your sister, Miss Evelyn." A brief expression of confusion crossed her face before she could control her response. She quickly smiled and nodded at the men behind her. The footmen made no move to intercept him, but he was clearly being inspected. He stood to meet their gaze.

"Mr. Darcy and his friends have a message for Miss Evelyn. We will delay until they have delivered it." Her voice was commanding. She stepped away from the footmen to lead Darcy back to the carriage. The men followed her but did not intercede. Miss Hawke's step was quick, and she reached Miss Evelyn just as Richard moved to block her entrance to the carriage. Miss Hawke took Miss Evelyn's arm and smoothly steered her sister away, back towards the inn. Richard followed. Darcy noted that the first man to exit the inn was already inside the carriage and was turning to sit down. He had not yet noticed that his charges were no longer with him.

"Evelyn, dear," Miss Hawke said soothingly, "Mr. Darcy and his friends have brought a message for you." Bingley wordlessly moved to take the Colonel's place near the carriage as Richard stepped around and in front of the women to greet them. The footmen still hovered behind the women as Darcy listened to his cousin introduce himself at last.

"Ladies," he said calmly. "I am Colonel Richard Fitzwilliam. I have a message to deliver, but also a few questions, if I may." He turned to Miss Evelyn. "Would it be too much to ask to have you and Miss Hawke return inside for a few moments?" He turned to look at the three footmen and raised his eyebrows in challenge. There was a muffled roar from inside the carriage, and the stout little man flew out, nearly giving way to his rage before tugging uselessly at his waistcoat and placing his hat firmly on his head. Bingley blocked his way.

"You will not importune my nieces, sir," the man growled, waving one arm to try to knock Bingley aside. "Step aside." Bingley matched his movements without raising his hands, making it clear that he would not yield. Only when the man had controlled himself did Bingley allow him to pass. However, he remained inches from the man's shoulder. Richard stepped over to them.

"Mr. Archibald Hawke?" Colonel Fitzwilliam asked, his voice low and dangerous.

Hawke narrowed his eyes and spat, "I have not been introduced to you, sir, and if your father believes he can take what is mine he is sadly mistaken. Step off."

Richard observed the man before him. Overweight, florid complexion, not carrying a weapon. No walking stick. Even if he had a knife stashed in his boot he could hardly have bent to reach it. His eyes flashed in annoyance at the interruption. "Clearly you know who I am, Mr. Hawke. Need we stand on ceremony?"

Darcy saw Bingley tense slightly and followed his friend's gaze. Each footman's coat revealed the bulge of a pistol. Richard's mad dash meant that they had ridden ahead of their support, and while armed, they had the ladies to protect.

"Richard," he warned in a low voice, inclining his head very slightly to indicate the pistols. Richard's face hardened and his right hand dropped to his own weapon.

As the men stared at one another, daring one another to make the first move, there was a distracting flutter of silk and a strong, clear voice. As Miss Sophia Hawke moved to her uncle, stepping directly between the two men, Richard noticed that the blue at the bottom of her skirt was much darker than the rest of the gown. The hem had evidently been let down several inches.

"We do not belong to you, uncle," Miss Hawke said firmly, with a small, tight smile. She turned slightly to respond to Richard. "He is not our guardian. I am of age and my sister is my responsibility."

Darcy stepped up hurriedly. "That being the case, Miss Hawke, I find we simply need the answer to one question. Do you prefer to continue in Mr. Hawke's company?"

Miss Hawke's eyes glinted with pleasure. "We do not." She took a step away from her uncle. "We will hear what you have to say, Colonel, so long as my uncle and his friends are not granted admittance."

"The devil you will," sputtered Hawke, grabbing her arm and yanking her back roughly. Miss Evelyn gasped as two of the footmen stepped towards the pair to hem Miss Hawke in. "Get in this carriage now, girl." He pulled at his niece, trying to shove her to the steps. She staggered into her uncle, her shawl falling over her arm. Quickly, though she found her feet, dug in, and refused to move farther.

The Colonel, Darcy, and Bingley all stepped forward to separate the two, but Miss Hawke stilled them by raising her free hand. "Uncle," she said again in an eerily calm voice, "you will unhand me." Then she bowed her head and whispered something to him. He glowered, but threw her arm away as though it burned him. She stumbled but regained her balance without falling. Though barely perceptible, Richard thought her back stiffened a little at the movement.

"You have always been an ungrateful. . ." he began angrily but she cut him off.

"Let us not have any lies between us, uncle," she said evenly, quietly but loud enough to be heard by those who surrounded her. "Let us dispense with your melodrama. You were never going to win. Whatever you may have told your friends here, you merely want what is ours, and I believe you must finally accept that you will never have it." Two of the footmen appeared confused, though they did not change their positions.

Darcy watched the scene unfold before him as though watching a theater performance at Drury Lane. There was a decided sense of unreality about the confrontation. He had teased Richard earlier about reading novels, but the convoluted plots of the stories Georgiana sometimes read were nothing to what his cousin had stumbled into, and shockingly, it had all begun at Darlington, only forty miles from home.

Still slightly behind the Colonel, who carefully shielded her from her uncle's approach, Miss Evelyn peered at first her uncle's face and then her sister's, her face even paler than before, were that possible. In her hands she twisted a snowy white handkerchief into knots. Archibald Hawke's round face was flushed with anger.

Sophia Hawke was neither flushed with anger nor pale with fright. Her voice was steady and a tiny, quite unladylike grin was actually tugging at one corner of her mouth. Her shawl was still draped over her right hand, and she made no move to replace it on her shoulders.

Nobody present was fooled into believing that her uncle would give way, but for some unfathomable reason, she was acting as though he already had. The only two who were not shocked at her response were Sophia and Archibald Hawke, who stared intensely at one another before the little squat man broke the gaze and looked away.

Miss Sophia Hawke took up her sister's arm, and led her gently back to the inn. Darcy and the Colonel followed them in, and Bingley followed carefully, never turning his back to the four men they left behind. He thought at least one of the footmen, the large, burly one who had followed the elder sister, looked a bit relieved, but the others were stone-faced as they waited for orders. Hawke glared after the retreating party, but finally jerked his head at the men and climbed up the stairs. Bingley waited until he was inside the coach, and then, bowing slightly, moved inside the inn.

Darcy was already with the innkeeper requesting a private room. Bingley continued to watch the front door and the Colonel scanned the room for a rear door or other entrances. The dining room had a few travelers who had not yet departed, but was largely deserted. The front door was the only way in or out unless they circled through the kitchen. As he took a few steps into the dining room to evaluate it as a point of entrance, he saw a small, dark young man sitting at a table in the back corner with an untouched mug of ale in his hand. The man rose, stretched lazily, jammed a hat on his head and strode through the front door.

He looks familiar, the Colonel thought. Darcy had turned in time to see it, too, and Richard raised an eyebrow at his cousin. *I think,* he struggled to dredge up the memory, *do I know him from Matlock House?* The innkeeper joined Darcy and the entire party was shown into a small but comfortable private room.

Miss Hawke guided Miss Evelyn to a seat at the table before placing her shawl on the table. She smiled to herself, a mysterious little smile that irritated the Colonel. He reached over and removed the shawl from her arm to reveal that she had been holding a pistol.

"My uncle always allows his anger to get the better of him," she said as she set the weapon down and moved to place her hand on her sister's back. "It does get him into trouble sometimes."

"I presume that was his weapon?" Richard asked.

"Indeed, though what he thought to do with it, I have no idea," Miss Hawke said scornfully. "He would more likely have shot someone inside the inn who had no congress with any of us. I have been waiting for days to get close enough to take it."

The Colonel picked up the pistol and placed it on the sideboard. It was a nice weapon, an expensive one. Perhaps she would allow him to keep it.

She turned her face to the window, observing the activity out front, and pursed her lips. "He is heading south," she said thoughtfully, nearly to herself. "That is not what I would have expected from him."

"Oh, Sophia," cried Evelyn, distraught, "why is he acting this way? I know you two have quarreled, but ever since he met you again he seems another man entirely." She crossed her arms on the table and buried her face in them. Sophia moved to her side and placed a gentle hand on her sister's back.

"This is the man he has always been, Evie. You are only seeing him clearly for the first time. I am sorry to grieve you in this way, but it was inevitable."

Evelyn gazed up at her sister, cheeks wet with tears. "Me?" she shook her head, bewildered, wispy brown locks falling from her hair pins. "Sophia, I am grieved for *you*. I have been terrible to you. You were right all along and I should have listened. I brought him to us!"

Sophia shushed her sister gently and said "I always understood you loved me. It was safer to let you think he and I were simply at odds in an ordinary way." She turned to the Colonel. "Perhaps we should hear this message that Colonel Fitzwilliam has for you."

Evelyn took a deep breath. "I will, but you must promise to rest afterward."

The men were surprised both by the statement and the sudden strength in the voice of the small woman. Until this moment, she had been quiet, timid. Apparently that was not her typical behavior.

"This is best discussed privately, Evie," Miss Hawke mumbled, suddenly self-conscious.

"No, it is not," Miss Evelyn said, pushing her chair back roughly to stand and glare at her sister with her chin tilted up and hands on her hips. "You will rest, you will allow me to tend you, and you will not push me away when I am trying to help. You are not the only stubborn Hawke sister." It made an odd picture, Sophia Hawke being taken to task by the younger, much shorter Evelyn.

Sophia Hawke sat next to her sister and took her hand, bending her head slightly to speak more privately.

"May we please not spend additional time on this now? Let us hear your message and see what the Colonel and Mr. Darcy have in mind, as I do not believe they mean to leave us to find our own way home."

"Where is home now, Sophia?" Miss Evelyn asked quietly, only loud enough for her sister to hear.

She glanced over at Bingley, who smiled and introduced himself. Miss Evelyn was not deterred. After the introduction had been made, she turned back to her sister and spoke in a quiet, firm voice.

"We will speak about this before we leave this room."

"That will do, sister," was the ambiguous reply. "Colonel?"

Suddenly Richard found himself caught in the intense gaze of Sophia Hawke's blue eyes. He was shocked by the similarity of her eyes to those of the man who had claimed to be Oliver Hawke. The eyes must be a family trait. The sisters both had them. The boy had to be related to the women somehow.

"Have you any other male relatives, Miss Hawke?" Richard asked abruptly.

She paused before saying, carefully, "I do not believe so, Colonel."

"But it is possible?"

She considered a moment before relenting. "I have learned that nearly anything is possible, Colonel." She tucked a golden curl behind her ear.

Richard moved his attention away from Miss Hawke to focus on Miss Evelyn. Her hands were trembling, and she clasped them before her to keep them still.

"I have a story to tell you, ladies," Richard said, specifically addressing Miss Evelyn, "and I am hoping you can fill in some of the holes for me."

"We will try, Colonel," Miss Evelyn replied uncertainly.

Richard gestured for both women to take a seat, and they complied.

"Then let us begin."

After he finished explaining almost all they knew, Miss Hawke looked thoughtful and Evelyn looked stricken.

"Have you the letter?" Sophia Hawke asked. Richard thought this a reasonable request. Perhaps she could identify the handwriting. He held it out to her with an encouraging smile.

"Who would use Oliver's name in such a way?" Miss Evelyn whispered, appalled. She looked at the Colonel. "He was our brother, but he died years ago, in the fire at Darlington. And why would he leave a letter asking you to find me? I was in no distress until. . ." her voice trailed off and she looked at Sophia, confused.

"I am pleased you did not feel distressed, Evie," Sophia said in a low voice, as she read the letter, "but you *were* in danger. As soon as you come of age and are no longer under my legal guardianship, uncle would have made a move to access your funds." She paused her reading to meet her sister's gaze. "I made it very difficult for you to sign anything over, but he might have married you off to one of his men and offered him a percentage of your dowry as a reward. Even had he succeeded in stealing your dowry, I had made arrangements so that you would have something to live on." Evelyn's eyes opened wide. Evidently she had not known about this provision.

Darcy and Bingley both nodded. It was much as they had suspected. The Colonel simply looked pensive.

"Forgive me, Colonel," Miss Evelyn said quietly, breathing a little more rapidly than she had before. She turned her full attention to her sister and nearly pleaded, "You have hinted at uncle's behavior before, Sophia, but how could you possibly know?"

Sophia Hawke took a breath before responding. "Evie, be honest with me." She glanced around the room. "Be honest with us all. The day of your majority is fast approaching. Had uncle not already begun to invite men to call on you in order to orchestrate a marriage?"

Miss Evelyn looked at her lap. "Three," she whispered.

"Three different men?"

"He said it was my choice." Sophia's voice was high and pinched.

"But your choice was limited to those three? He never offered you a coming out when you were eighteen, or a season in town to meet other potential suitors?" Sophia Hawke's voice was flat in a way with which Richard was quite familiar. Darcy's voice hit the same kind of note at times of great stress.

She is struggling to control her anger, Richard thought. *She is not as collected as she appears.*

Miss Evelyn whispered, "No, he said I was an heiress and he wanted me to meet only men he could trust."

Darcy huffed a little, startling the younger woman. "Forgive me," he said. "Please continue." He felt his fist clenching involuntarily as he considered how vulnerable Evelyn Hawke had been. This was unconscionable. Archibald Hawke appeared to be a worse scoundrel even than George Wickham. *George told lies rooted in truth, but Archibald Hawke uses the truth to mislead with no need to lie. Masterful and inexcusable.*

She shook her head and a lock of brown hair escaped her dainty bonnet. "I asked him for time to think it over. They were all so much older and they frightened me, Sophia." She traced an imaginary line on the table with a long, elegant finger. "And then I had word that you had come and I fled the house to see you. Had you not come, he would have had me married on my birthday." She met her sister's eyes and saw nothing but love there. "I thought he loved me and that he was protecting me. I believed him over you." She ducked her head, and whispered, miserable, "I am such a fool." Her sister kissed the top of her head.

"He is our uncle, my dear. We should have been able to trust him. That he is the man he is cannot possibly be your fault. We have neither of us had the girlhood we should." Miss Hawke turned her eyes to Richard.

"Colonel, you have told us your part of the story," Sophia Hawke said quietly. "Now let me repay you with a bit of my own."

Chapter Twenty-Five

MISS SOPHIA HAWKE stood before the men, smoothing her skirt nervously while considering how to begin. Finally, she clasped her hands together and spoke.

"You have heard the story of the fire from Mr. Tilden. I was nearly thirteen when my uncle took us to London, rather tall for my age, and he thought I could be of use to him in his work."

Here she paused, worrying her bottom lip while pondering how to continue, and the Colonel asked "What work is that, exactly, Miss Hawke?"

She glanced at him inquiringly, and tilted her head, surprised. "I would have thought you knew, Colonel."

"Why would you think that, Miss Hawke?" Richard was flummoxed. Had he missed some important clue? Was there information Darcy's men had missed?

She examined him curiously for a moment, then shook her head. "My error, Colonel." She stood and began to pace. "My uncle is not a fan of your father. In fact, he loathes him, and the feeling is mutual. Everything my uncle taught me had to do with traversing society in London in order to gather information that he might then use to harm or embarrass your father or other political enemies."

"Why would he use a young girl for such an office?" Bingley asked. The Colonel had nearly forgotten that his cousin's friend was in the room.

Miss Hawke smiled sardonically. "Do you have any idea, sir, how much the women know? The things they discuss when separated from the men? The things they learn from their husbands when they are married," she glanced at her sister apprehensively, "and also when they are. . . not married? These kinds of confessions then become commodities to be bought and sold, traded for other secrets. This was a world my uncle could not enter and he trained me to penetrate it for him." She frowned. "I was a very determined student."

"So you enjoyed the work he set you to, Miss Hawke?" the Colonel asked, a little harshly, Darcy thought.

Sophia Hawke stared at the Colonel and he was chastened by the intense anger he saw burning in her eyes. "I assure you, Colonel, even at that tender age, I despised my uncle. Had he truly cared for us he would have left us with the Tildens." She took a deep breath. "Mr. Tilden called me into his study after Uncle Archibald sent word he would arrive. He explained my father's will, and expressed his concerns. My father had been wary of his brother, and in the end, Uncle Archibald was able to use only the funds set aside for our care and our quarterly allowances, which were fortune enough. It was not long before he had run through the principal." She turned away to the window again.

"Once I had spoken with Mr. Tilden, I knew my responsibilities. I had an eight-year-old sister in my charge, and quite unexpectedly, an estate to protect. As Mr. Tilden recommended, I did what uncle required of me and waited for enough birthdays to pass that I might oppose him openly. I knew that the more training I received from him, the more successfully I might challenge him when that time came."

"Is uncle why you were so often at Holland House?" came Evelyn's gentle voice.

"Yes, my dear." She turned to the men. "I was already my full height by the time I turned fourteen, and uncle kept me quite busy. I never looked the same nor used the same name twice unless I was at Holland House."

Richard's head was beginning to pound. Too many pieces to put together. Holland House was notorious in certain circles for clandestine political activity. What might she have learned there? Was his father. . .

"No, Colonel," Sophia Hawke said firmly, breaking his concentration.

"No?" He was certain he had not spoken aloud.

"I never found anything implicating your father. The Earl of Matlock is not an easy man, but he is an honorable one. He has a way of annoying anyone looking for a weakness to exploit." After a moment, she said, almost mischievously, "I will admit fabricating stories about the Earl to send my uncle on one false adventure after another."

"Sophia," Evelyn gasped, while tears were again forming in her eyes, "do not make light of what you did. He was so angry. . ."

Miss Hawke smiled ruefully and arched an eyebrow. Miss Evelyn fell silent. Then Miss Hawke cleared her throat and continued. "We had an unspoken pact, my uncle and I. If I did as he asked, he would treat my sister with kindness. We both knew that I was just waiting for my majority and that he would then lose all access to us and any money. Unfortunately, there was a very long time to wait, plenty of time for him to make plans."

She stood and moved to the window, looking outside for a moment before turning to face the room and continuing.

"Things changed when I turned sixteen. Uncle decided that I was now a woman and might be able to," her eyes shifted to a spot above Richard's shoulder on the far wall, "offer additional inducements to some important Frenchmen to gather information about the war."

Sophia Hawke moved slowly back to her sister and knelt, finally pained by something she was relating.

"That is why I had to disappear, Evie. I am so sorry, but it was too much. He had already destroyed my integrity and my sense of honor. I could bear those things to keep you safe, but I could not let him take my virtue as well. I left you with him and went into hiding. Can you forgive me?"

Miss Evelyn was too shocked to speak and the men were no less horrified. Miss Hawke squeezed her eyes shut briefly when she realized that she had spoken with three men in the room. She had been so wrapped up in her story, apparently she had forgotten.

"I am clearly out of practice with proper topics of conversation. We should speak about this later, when we are alone. My apologies, gentlemen." Before anyone could formulate a question, she stood and began to pace.

"I left the house the night uncle told me what he planned for me, but I had no place to go, nobody who would take me in. From my work at Holland House, I knew that Lord Matlock was aware of my uncle's attempts to ruin him, and therefore believed him to be likewise advised of my own activities. Therefore, I went to visit him." Her cheeks turned pink.

She was embarrassed, Darcy thought with some surprise. Sophia Hawke had hinted at her uncle's base intentions for her without faltering, but she was ashamed of having approached Lord Matlock for help. He wished Elizabeth were here. She was more likely to display righteous anger than shock and always knew what to say to offer comfort. At the same time, he could not help but be glad she was far away, safe at Pemberley.

A short, soft laugh broke through his thoughts. Sophia Hawke was recalling the meeting.

"I accosted the Earl quite suddenly as he left a parliamentary session some seven years ago now. He seemed amused, as though he knew I was coming, and I understand now that he likely did. He invited me to walk with him and I told him everything." She met Richard's stare with her own, and this time he recognized a deep sense of gratitude there.

"He knew what my uncle was, what he is, and was willing to assist me where he could. He sent men to watch over my sister, to privately warn my uncle not to harm her or try to use her as he had me." She paused. "While my uncle has a good deal of antipathy for me, he does seem to care for Evelyn, in his own selfish way." She glanced down at her sister's stricken face. "The Earl helped me to contact Mr. Hobson at Darlington to ascertain what was being done there. I wrote to our housekeeper Mrs. Jamison and found that my father had settled some money on her in his will. She resided nearby and was still in touch with many of the tenant families, helping Mr. Hobson to take care of them."

She paused to clear her throat. "Mr. Hobson had remained to run what was left of the estate and had been dutifully taking his salary and depositing the profits to my father's accounts in London." Darcy noticed she did not mention increasing his pay when she gained control of her fortune. "Even Lord

Matlock agreed that his accounting was meticulous. After nearly four years of neglect, he had not misspent one farthing. I was finally able to make sure the other servants were well." She shook her head. "It is astonishing, the loyalty my parents inspired."

Richard recalled the story of the fire, how the only survivors had been those alerted by twelve-year-old Sophia Hawke, and thought that it was not the parents alone who must have inspired such devotion.

She paused, her face taking on a faraway look before she began again. "Lord Matlock knew the right questions to ask about maintaining the tenant farms, improving the yields, checking the account books, everything I needed to discuss with Mr. Hobson. He found a solicitor who would help me, not my uncle, and the moment I reached my majority he had all the assets transferred to new accounts. He brought Mr. Hobson to London to tutor me on the procedures he had put into place."

Richard nodded. It was becoming much clearer. Only Lord Matlock would have been able to wrest control of her funds from Archibald Hawke, even once she reached her majority. Despite the action being illegal, he knew of no solicitor in all of London who would stand on principle against a man like Hawke to help a young woman take control of her inheritance. Only if promised the support of the Earl would someone have the courage to do what was right. *That* was why the Hawkes used the same solicitor as the Earl.

Miss Evelyn was following this story with disbelief, shaking her head from time to time and weeping silently, tears falling while she dabbed at them with her handkerchief. The men looked at Miss Hawke questioningly. She squared her shoulders and raised her chin. "I actually should not have had to wait. Legally, I ought to have had full control of the estate, with the executor my father had selected, as soon as my parents and Oliver were legally declared dead." Miss Evelyn winced at the word, but it had little effect on her sister. "Unfortunately, neither the Tildens nor I found the executor willing to help me."

Richard grunted. *I knew it. A boy might have stood a chance with Tilden's help, but not a girl.* Sophia grinned at his grunt and he could not help but grin back. She had been through so much, yet her resilience was intact.

"I was a child, and to make matters worse, a girl. I had no regent, as it were," she said with some bitterness. "Mr. Tilden did try. My uncle's friends in town might well have used the courts to hand everything over to him, but Mr. Tilden had already engaged several barristers to keep them from doing so. Because my uncle is a powerful man, there was little else Mr. Tilden could accomplish on my behalf. Checking his progress was the best for which we could hope. Lord Matlock, though," she said with a grim smile, "had the political power Mr. Tilden did not. He was more than a match for the great Archibald Hawke."

Darcy listened without comment. He knew, better than anyone, the difficulties Sophia Hawke would have faced even without the additional obstacles. He also realized that by going directly to the Earl of Matlock, her uncle would see her as a traitor. Who knew what he might be capable of doing now that his final designs were at last being thwarted?

Miss Sophia Hawke paused, paced a little, and turned back to face them. "My father thought he had covered every contingency, however, nobody could have foreseen that my parents and Oliver would die so suddenly and all at the same time, let alone that this could happen before I was grown. There were no provisions for a child to inherit. I was therefore immediately my sister's guardian, too, but my uncle argued that I could not be her guardian until I reached my majority, and he quickly found a judge who signed papers establishing himself as temporary guardian for us both. He arrived at Bidewell with those papers in hand. Once in London, he began to badger me to sign over the estate as well, so he could, as he said, look after it properly. I refused. This went on for over a year. When he finally accepted that I would not be swayed, he began training me. At the time, I thought it was his way of making amends, at least pretending we were working together. Now I suspect he hoped I would be killed doing such work, though I did not realize at first what he was about."

Bingley had been listening to this recital with a great deal of pain. He was of a naturally pleasant and cheerful disposition, but it did not follow that he was unaware that there were men like Archibald Hawke in the world. The story was a jarring reminder of how fragile the situation of a young woman could become upon the death of a father or brother. *My sisters do not have any idea how fortunate they are to have had my protection after father's death. What would my Jane have suffered had her father died before she was wed?* He gazed at the two young women before him, appalled at what they had endured, and he began to wonder what Archibald Hawke had planned for them at the end of their carriage ride to the north. He did not notice the scowl that had etched itself into his face as the story went on, a scowl far more suited to one of the other gentlemen in the room than to him. He could not stop thinking about

Archibald Hawke's intentions. The possibilities were relentlessly grim.

Twelve, Darcy thought, remembering his own father's death. *I lost Mother when I was twelve, but I was through Cambridge by the time I had to assume responsibility for the estate. I was grown, and a man, and still, the avarice of those around me was almost too much to bear.* He began to feel strangely protective of these two young women despite barely knowing them.

Richard's face was stony. He had not known quite what to expect, but it was not this. His own father was intimately involved, but had not mentioned this in their conversation a week ago. Why not? He had a terrible feeling that he had become yet another of his father's chess pieces and that he had just been played to perfection. His father could not take a public position on the guardianship or fortune of Archibald Hawke's nieces. While the man was deplorable, he was not without powerful friends in the Home Office and could not be directly confronted. Who better to send after the Hawkes than his second son, a capable soldier but not a peer, a man largely beneath notice? He would draw little attention yet be trained for just such a mission. He sighed. *You are never completely away from it, Richard. Your family is your destiny, no matter how hard you try to avoid it. Perhaps I have more in common with Darcy than I thought.* He grimaced at Miss Hawke, who had placed a comforting hand on her younger sister's arm while Miss Evelyn was mumbling something that sounded like an apology. *This is already far worse than I believed, and I am not confident that we have yet heard it all.*

"Gentlemen," Miss Hawke said, breaking the heavy silence that followed her story. "I am afraid we must now make plans. It is too late to reach safety today. We may need to remain here at the inn for the night. My uncle has been denied his satisfaction from me, but he will not see this as a permanent defeat. He will not give up until he has my sister's fortune. Her birthday is only three days away, and I believe he means to have her wed." She turned to her sister. "We should share a room, dear, so the men have only one to guard."

Evelyn Hawke shuddered and began to rise, but she was stopped when Mr. Bingley stepped away from the window to voice what they were all thinking. "Miss Hawke, from what you say, it appears clear that he means to have it all. He will come for you first and then your sister. You must also take precautions."

Even Darcy rolled his eyes. Miss Hawke glowered darkly at Bingley at the same time Miss Evelyn gasped and grabbed her sister's arm.

"Sophia, surely not! He cannot be as bad as this. He cannot."

Bingley winced at his error. Of course she already knew the peril. She had known it for some time. The uncle had some perverse fondness for his younger niece, believing that she would still marry as he wished, and she would inherit the entire estate if Sophia Hawke were to die. He undoubtedly believed he could coerce her to sign over the management of the estate to him were her sister out of the way. However, if he felt in danger of losing everything, as he clearly did now, he would simply forge the proper documents and then arrange some sort of accident for them both. *Chuckle-head. She was trying to keep Miss Evelyn calm.* He met Miss Hawke's angry glare with a wordless apology.

"Miss Evelyn," the Colonel said in a deep, solemn voice, "regardless of the identity of the man with whom I served, I am honor bound to see to your safety. That now includes the safety of your sister. Please allow us to assist." Miss Evelyn looked up at him. She was diminutive in comparison to him, and he could see in her face that she thought that he would make an excellent protector.

She smiled wistfully. "I thank you for phrasing this as a request, but I do not think we are in any position to refuse. Colonel, we would be grateful to accept your help."

Chapter Twenty-Six

GEORGIANA WAS IMPROVING each day, but she was not yet well. Each morning, her fever abated, but by the evening she was uncomfortably warm. She did everything she was asked, drank cups of tea, took her draughts, and even began to swallow more than the broth Elizabeth brought up from the kitchen. She only complained a few times about being required to remain in bed, sighing impatiently and settling for being regaled with stories of the Bennet sisters. On occasion, she shared memories of her brother, but she held him in such esteem, her vignettes were unwaveringly admiring rather than humorous, but truth be told, Elizabeth enjoyed every tale.

When Mrs. Darcy finally made a request for solid food to be sent to her sister, it was through the firmly secured kitchen door. She was determined to enforce the separation of the household until she was absolutely sure any danger of infection had passed. Therefore, she had to content herself with hearing what she could only describe as a muffled squeal of delight. Mrs. Cronk was clearly very pleased to hear that *their* Miss Darcy was feeling well enough for something other than broth and barley tea. Elizabeth allowed herself a little smile of pleasure at how much everyone cared for Georgie. She was such a dear girl, she deserved all of their loyalty and love.

Slowly, slowly, Georgiana mended. It was much the same in the sickroom. There was less coughing, fevers were lower or disappearing, and the children in particular showed signs of restlessness at being confined to bed. Elizabeth began to take short naps in her study after she finished the afternoon notations in the journal she and Mr. Waters shared, but despite the press of her duties and her continuing fatigue, she felt as though there was finally a hope that this horrible fortnight might end more happily than they had any reason to expect. The physical shock of touching an infant's icy skin threatened to break through her relief, but she shrugged it back.

It was on the day Georgiana was finally able to come downstairs that Mr. Wright arrived, weather-delayed, dirty, worn from travel, and anxious to see his boys. He had been to the cottages to find the homes all but abandoned, and had come racing to the great house. By the time Mrs. Reynolds mentioned Cardiff and led him to the ballroom, he was panicked. He cut off her explanations as he stepped inside.

The little wooden cots were still occupied, here and there, but most were empty. At the other end of the ballroom near a second fireplace, a thick wool rug had been rolled out, pillows and blankets strewn across it. At one end Miss Darcy was perched upon an overstuffed chair from the library, a heavy blanket tucked around her legs and a shawl across her shoulders, reading softly about Ali Baba and the forty thieves. A gaggle of children sat or laid flat on the pillows, bundled up and preternaturally quiet, enjoying the story. Sitting at Miss Darcy's feet and staring up at her with unabashed admiration were Matthew and Peter.

Judging by their pale faces and unnerving willingness to sit still while listening to a story, Mr. Wright could see that they had been quite ill. He could see, too, that they were now well, or nearly so. He walked towards them, confused but incredibly relieved. He had thought it was the younger boys who were in danger, but Mr. Darcy had told him that they were on their way to Cardiff. Instead he had returned to find that his older boys had been seriously ill. Why were the old cots set up in the ballroom? Who had nursed the boys with their mother gone? As he reached the carpet, the boys looked up and saw him.

"Papa!" Matthew shouted hoarsely and leaped into his arms. Peter said nothing, just grabbed his father's leg and held on for dear life.

Mr. Wright reached down to pick Peter up and hugged both boys tightly to his chest, walking away from the others so that they might have a moment alone. Georgiana smiled, but continued reading to the others in her gentle voice, giving Mr. Wright the time he needed to embrace his boys and compose himself.

The two boys recovered more quickly, talking in loud whispers, interrupting one another in their bid to be the first to tell their father all that had happened since their mother and brothers departed for Cardiff. Peter finally laid his small head on his father's broad shoulder, worn out, and after a moment, Matthew did the same.

Mr. Wright could barely make it all out, but what he heard astonished him. He took another look at the rows of cots, the table of medicines, and a prone Mr. Waters sleeping on a cot in the far corner, one arm folded over his eyes. When Wright entered, he had completely missed Mrs. Darcy, an apron tied over an old gown, hair pulled back simply from her face, tending to some of those still abed. When he finally kissed each boy on the head and set them back down on the carpet, he saw the mistress walking across the floor in his direction. She had not been untouched, he thought, noting the drawn face, the fatigue in her gait, and the slightly looser fit of her gown. He bowed deeply at her approach. She seemed almost embarrassed by the courtesy.

"Mrs. Darcy," he said as he rose, his voice husky with emotion, "I thank you for my sons."

Her cheeks reddened slightly, but she nodded. "We are very glad to have you back, Mr. Wright. How was your journey?"

"Long, Mrs. Darcy. I cannot recall another trip to Pemberley requiring as much time on the road, particularly this time of year." He reached into his coat and pulled out a letter. She took it, a quiet smile on her face.

"From Mr. Darcy, ma'am."

"Would you care for some tea, Mr. Wright? I believe Mrs. Cronk has some ready in the kitchen."

"Yes, ma'am, I thank you." He bowed again and with a glance at the boys, left the room. Elizabeth moved to the doors and stepped outside to the garden. Closing the doors gently behind her, she walked to the stone bench and sat. She took a deep breath and opened the letter.

My Dearest Elizabeth,

We are safely in London, and I am sending Mr. Wright home, as you requested. I have let him know about his boys and wife heading to Cardiff for recuperation. I fear it may be some days before he arrives, as the weather has been miserably wet. It took all of four days to reach London from home, and it may take even longer for him to reach you if it has been raining in the north as well.

Richard has asked for a private meeting with me on a matter of some urgency, though he will not explain until I see him. If I am needed in town longer than I originally planned, I will send word.

We have only just arrived, so I will conclude. Please send my love to my sister, and know that I am counting the days until I see you again.

Be well, and God bless you.
Fitzwilliam

Elizabeth sighed, a little disappointed that the longed for missive was so brief, but she reproached herself for the thought. *What did you expect? Mr. Wright had not heard about our troubles, and the letter is an old one. William should know now what has happened.* She sighed. *I miss him so.* She studied the letter for a moment. He had signed as Fitzwilliam, rather than his typical F.D. She was still learning his quirks, but she thought the signature indicated he was anxious. Perhaps the business with his cousin was something unsettling? *No,* she told herself. It was becoming quite easy to set these worries aside unconsidered, when they assaulted her from all sides. *You still have things to attend to today, and you will not be able to puzzle this out. You have enough to think on for now. Wait for another letter or his return. Whatever it is, I have to trust that William will be able to resolve it. Perhaps he has already.* She thought for a moment what they would have done had Fitzwilliam been at Pemberley the past few weeks. She would not have had her way, of course. He would never have allowed it. As much as she ached to see him, it was good that he had been from home. It allowed her to do what needed to be done and it had kept him safe. With a small sigh, she tucked her letter into an apron pocket and returned to the Gibbonses. She would see them through this to the very end. She would lose no one else.

Chapter Twenty-Seven

MISS SOPHIA HAWKE was already breaking her fast when Darcy and the Colonel came downstairs. Bingley and Evelyn Hawke were down a few minutes later, both of them stifling yawns.

"There seem to be some men arriving in the yard near the stables," Miss Hawke said to the Colonel as she coolly tapped the shell of her egg with a spoon. "Are they your father's, do you think?"

Richard left the room and walked quickly to the back door of the inn, Darcy and Bingley close behind. Indeed, there were about eight men congregating at the rear of the building, changing out horses and checking their weapons. The saddlebags being removed from the mounts had the Matlock crest pressed into the leather. His father's men, though he did not recognize any of them. *I have been abroad too long*, he thought.

The man he recognized as the leader waved him down.

"Colonel!" he called, striding over to offer his hand. "We are sent by your father and are here to relieve you. Miss Evelyn Hawke shall ride back with us to Matlock. Do you wish to join us?"

"What about Miss Hawke?" Darcy interrupted. "There are two ladies here who require assistance."

The man lifted a battered hat to scratch his head. "I was only told to fetch Miss Evelyn, but I've no difficulty bringing another along. Sister?"

"Yes," Richard confirmed. "I will ride with you, but Darcy, you and Bingley should ride on to Pemberley."

Darcy's eyebrows pinched together. "I would feel better seeing this through with you, Richard. Matlock is only a half day's ride from Pemberley, and we can head on from there directly." He nodded when Richard grinned knowingly at him. Only the day before, he had attempted to dissuade his cousin from pursuing the Hawkes. Now. . .

"Shut it," Darcy said good-naturedly. "I own the error. Charles?"

As Bingley agreed that they should help escort the Hawkes to Matlock, the back door flew open.

Sophia Hawke stood in the doorway flanked by two boys, her face tense and anxious.

"Mr. Darcy," she said urgently, "these boys have letters for you from home. They say they have been following you from London."

Darcy recognized the Briggs boys. Reflexively, he thought, *They look tired.* Then he remembered where he was. *What is so serious that they followed me here?* His mind was awhirl with possibilities. *An accident. An illness.* His heart in his throat, he managed to take the letters they offered and send them off to eat, trying not to take their solemn faces as a sign of bad news, but failing dismally. His hand trembled as he read the direction on the first letter. Elizabeth's hand. He broke the seal and began to read.

Bingley was alarmed when Darcy reached a hand behind to guide himself to the ground, still reading his letters.

"Good God, man, what is it?" he asked, putting a hand on Darcy's shoulder. Richard moved quietly over to him to pick up the first discarded note and read it through. When he was finished, he handed it to Bingley and walked toward the stable. He glanced at Darcy, but when his friend made no move to stop him, he began to read. *Oh, no,* he thought, *Poor*

Darcy. It occurred to him that by now, Georgiana might not be the only one ill. *I have to get him home.*

By the time Darcy had finished the packet of letters, his face was white. Elizabeth had asked him not to come, but he had no intention of staying away. He tried to count the days since they had been written, and realized that whatever had happened was likely already over. He had left Elizabeth to help Richard, but he never believed that she would be the one in danger. That Georgiana would. . .

"William," Richard was saying sharply, and Darcy felt his arm being grasped and knew he was being hauled to his feet.

"I have to go, Richard," he said flatly. "I have to go home." It was a tone neither Richard nor Bingley had heard in Darcy's voice since his marriage, the one that masked his deepest emotions when he was in danger of losing control. Bingley had a hand under Darcy's arm and was leading him to the horses Richard had brought, two fine Arabians, fed, watered, and saddled, with the Matlock crest pressed into the leather saddlebags.

"Send word to Matlock as soon as you know anything," Richard said carefully. "I am no more than a half day's ride if you need me." Darcy did not reply, only swung himself into the saddle and began to weave his mount through the crowd of men. Bingley clapped Richard's shoulder.

"I shall look after him, Colonel. Focus on getting the Hawkes to Matlock. Fortunately, it looks as though you have plenty of help. Good luck."

Richard nodded. "Thank you, Bingley," he said gratefully. Any other time, he would have accompanied his cousin to Pemberley, but he felt deeply indebted to Bingley for taking his place. Bingley had made some stupid blunders on this trip, but he had also proven himself intelligent, a good rider, even quite useful during the confrontation with Archibald Hawke. He was beginning to understand his cousin's friendship with the man. Richard sighed, conflicted about where his duty lay, but thanks to Bingley, he would be able to complete his work here. He could deliver the Hawkes to his father and head for Pemberley straightaway.

As he watched, Bingley mounted his horse and deftly maneuvered through the yard. Once in the clear, both men urged their horses into gallops, and they disappeared down the road, tiny bits of mud mixing with dust from the drying road flying out behind them.

That left Richard in charge of the Hawkes, and he turned back to see that Sophia Hawke had not left the doorway. Her face was pensive, and she approached him carefully.

"That looked terrible, Colonel," she said, shaking her head. "I will pray for the Darcys."

"You pray, Miss Hawke?" He was taken aback. After everything, she prayed?

She pursed her lips, anticipating criticism. "I do."

Richard shook his head, thinking of the prayer he had said before Vitoria. That was not a real prayer, and he knew it. "I have not prayed in a very long time," he said absently. Miss Hawke gave him a look of sympathy so unaffected that he hurried to change the subject. "There is fever at Pemberley. His sister, my cousin, is very ill."

Miss Hawke shook her head. "I am sorry to hear it."

The simple words belied the deep compassion in her voice, and Richard could read her sincerity in the way she stood, unmoving, watching his face. When he did not speak, she cleared her throat softly.

"My sister has taken charge of the Briggs boys. She will see to their care while we make plans to leave." She nodded at the saddlebags and said "I see we are for Matlock."

"So it would appear," Richard replied.

"I will arrange new mounts for the Briggs when they are ready," she said quietly. "They should go home."

A large man with short black hair made his way through the yard, stopping to greet a few of Matlock's men before pushing on. Richard stared at him. He had seen this man before, but where? He was moving towards Richard, but his eyes were on Sophia Hawke. He was carrying something slung across his back.

Suddenly, there was a shriek from Miss Hawke. Richard's hand went immediately to his pistol, but she took two large, bouncing steps and launched herself off the small porch into the arms of the newcomer.

"Jack!" she yelled gleefully. Richard was shocked. It was the most emotion she had yet shown in his presence and far from the kind of display he would expect from a lady. After relating her story the day before, he had not thought her capable of this kind of joy. When she smiled broadly like this, she looked years younger.

The man she called Jack spun Sophia Hawke around before dropping her on her feet, none too gently. Richard bristled.

"Jack," she said again, at a normal volume, reaching out to grip his upper arms. "It is good to see you."

He grinned and shrugged a strap off his shoulder. He touched the brim of his hat and handed her something long wrapped thoroughly in rags. She removed the covering to reveal a somewhat battered but very clean Baker rifle. Richard was already shocked, but a sudden recognition of the gun, the man, and Miss Sophia Hawke stunned him into complete silence as he berated his slow mind. *No,* he thought. *It cannot be...*

"Captain," Jack said, looking over her clothes with amusement and giving her a jolly wink, "Good to see you, too."

Chapter Twenty-Eight

*D*EAREST WILLIAM,

Mr. Wright arrived today with your letter. By now you should have seen the Briggs boys and read mine to you. I hope that this is the last I will need to write before you return to us. I long to have you home.

I would wish to end these letters with good news, but alas, I cannot. Mr. and Mrs. Gibbons went home last night. I was sitting with them, and witnessed Mrs. Gibbons softly sighing out her last close to dawn. As sick as he was, Mr. Gibbons knew that she had gone. I whispered my condolences, but I do not believe he heard them. He just kissed her cheek and took her hand. An hour or so later, as the sun was rising, he went to join her. After so many days of pain, the end was almost peaceful. I am resolved to think only on the very end, when they went to eternal life together, holding hands in a room filling with the brilliant sunlight of a warm summer day. I would not have had it happen, and yet I must resign myself. I console myself with the thought that there can be no better leave-taking than this for two people so very much in love. They will be buried tomorrow, and I mean to walk to church with Georgiana this morning to offer our prayers.

It has been nearly a fortnight now, and we are beginning at last to resume our lives as they were before the illness came. Mr. Waters is seeing to the last few patients, issuing instructions and remedies for their convalescence, and then he and John will escort them home. There are very few of the children who are not already playing blind-man's bluff in the garden outside my window as I write. Their laughter, William, is a blessed balm to my weary heart.

This morning we took down the curtains from the windows in the ballroom. I fear they have taken on the odor of the sickroom and are so soiled we shall have to burn them. Mrs. Reynolds has the girls scrubbing the ballroom from top to bottom, and they are working with such enthusiasm that I am quite envious of and grateful for their industry. They have taken very good care of us.

I must speak to Mrs. Reynolds and ready myself for church, William. While we are there, I will offer a prayer of gratitude for our delivery, and will pray, as always, for your safe return to us.

With all my love,
Elizabeth

Elizabeth put down her pen and stepped out to the hall. She walked to the stairs and looked up. They seemed to stretch out forever, but she held the bannister and used it to assist her, putting one foot before the other and dragging herself up by sheer force of will. One last duty to perform before she could rest. Out of the back windows she saw plumes of smoke rising from what remained of the curtains.

"I never cared for that color anyway, Lizzy," said Georgiana from beside her. She was already dressed for church, a simple pendant hanging from her slender neck. "We shall choose something nicer when we are next in town." She held out her hand and Elizabeth reached for it gratefully. Together they walked to her room to wash up and choose a clean dress, one not meant for a sickroom.

Georgiana watched her sister with concern. Elizabeth was so quiet and pale. The dark circles under her eyes were still visible, and clearly she found it difficult to navigate the stairs on her own. She walked with one hand holding Elizabeth's and the other wrapped around her sister's waist. Elizabeth had taken care of her. She had listened to the servants enough to know that her new sister had also taken care of everyone else. She had become, over the past fortnight, not Master Darcy's pretty young bride, but Mrs. Elizabeth Darcy, the Mistress of Pemberley.

It made Georgiana's heart swell with pride to see how Elizabeth had stepped so willingly, so ably, into her role. She hoped that when her own time came to run a home that she would do half so well. As she scrutinized her sister's face and helped her dress, she also knew that this was the last thing she would allow Elizabeth to do before declaring her duty over and insisting that she rest. She was not the only stubborn woman in residence. Georgiana was quite certain that she could see to the tasks required to set the house back to rights. She would not allow visitors until Elizabeth and the staff were better rested, so there would be no visits to endure. She smiled. Visits, even unpleasant ones, would never seem quite so intimidating again.

An hour later, as the two women stood in church, Elizabeth closed her eyes for a brief moment before Georgie touched her arm.

"Are you well?" she murmured.

Elizabeth opened her eyes and smiled. "I am well, Georgie. I am simply tired."

Behind them, she heard the sharp tread of man's boot. Her heart leapt and she turned only to see Mr. Waters sliding into the pew behind them. He caught her eye and bowed slightly.

Elizabeth smiled, hoping her disappointment had not been obvious. She turned back to the front of the church and was soon lost in prayer. She prayed for Amelia, for her boy who had not had a chance to live, for the Gibbonses, who could not live apart. She gave thanks for Georgiana's recovery and for that of all who had been spared. She nearly sobbed with gratitude that she had not been stricken and had been strong enough to care for those in her charge. Whispering, she begged forgiveness for her anger, her impatience, her stubbornness, and her despair. Finally, she asked that her husband be brought home to her soon. Fitzwilliam's absence had settled into a physical ache that could not be relieved until she had him in her arms.

She glanced over at Georgiana, quietly reading and offering up prayers of her own. Elizabeth shivered. It was cold in the church, and she knew her endurance was near its end. She was thankful when the clergyman finally signaled the conclusion of the service, and she could take Georgiana's arm. Mr. Waters nodded as they passed, looking nearly as worn as she felt. As they walked out into the early morning sunshine, she saw him turning to his horse, to head back to town and hopefully his own bed.

"Let us go home, Georgie." She glanced at the girl's face and thought with deep pleasure that it was almost as if she had not been ill at all. Though she knew Georgiana was not quite herself yet, she was reassured that it would come, that a complete recovery was not far off.

As for herself, she was nearly walking in her sleep. Her back ached, her head throbbed, and her stomach was in knots. A little sleep, she thought, would soon put her to rights. She smiled ruefully.

"What was that smile for?" Georgiana asked playfully, ready to be entertained.

"I was telling myself that a little sleep would soon bring me back to myself, Georgie, but I must confess, I do not believe a *little* will do. I feel as though I could sleep for an age."

Georgiana frowned. "You shall, if you wish, Lizzy. Mrs. Reynolds and I will be quite fierce in your protection." Elizabeth laughed at the vision.

Georgiana suddenly giggled, but added, "I am quite serious."

"I know that you are," Elizabeth replied with a smile, "and I thank you for it." She squeezed Georgiana's hand and shivered again.

Georgiana felt Elizabeth tremble and looked up sharply. She gently patted Elizabeth's arm, but there was no heat and her sister's cheeks were not flushed. She scolded herself for her fear. It was sunny but not yet too warm as the morning was still young, and Elizabeth was entirely exhausted. She had not slept completely through the night, Georgiana guessed, in the entire fortnight since she and the children had been taken ill. She had heard the upper servants complaining about that. Everyone had tried to force the mistress to rest, but no sooner would they relieve her of one duty when another would arise. Georgiana did not recall everything from the time she was ill, but she knew that Elizabeth would replace Sarah to sit by her bed all night, and once she had recovered sufficiently, Elizabeth had spent more time downstairs.

In the past few days, she had become accustomed to seeing Elizabeth nodding off in a chair beside a child's cot, or sitting with her head on her arms, dozing on the desk in her study. The night before last, she had gone searching for her after dinner only to find her with her head leaning gently against the back of Fitzwilliam's chair in *his* study. Early this morning, Mrs. Reynolds had entered the sickroom to find Mrs. Darcy standing sentinel over the Gibbonses, gazing out mournfully at the moonlight. Mr. Waters had apparently been quite irritated as he related that Mrs. Darcy had not been to bed at all.

When Elizabeth and Georgiana reached the house, they walked past the open doors of the ballroom where Mrs. Reynolds was still supervising the cleaning. The maids had finished the windows and the walls, Georgiana noted, and had made a start on the floor, dipping their brushes into buckets of hot soapy water and scrubbing so hard she thought they might go right through the polished wood. One of the footmen was about to enter with a bucket of hot water. He stopped to nod his head and smile at them.

"Mistress. Miss Darcy." Elizabeth smiled back and Georgiana did the same.

The gratitude in Georgiana's heart surprised her with its sudden strength, and she did not attempt to quell it. They had been so fortunate. She glanced at Elizabeth's pallid face. So very fortunate.

Georgiana called for Sarah to accompany Elizabeth up to her room and prepare her for bed. She then went into the ballroom to speak to Mrs.

Reynolds and insist that any household matters be referred to her.

"Under no circumstances should Mrs. Darcy be disturbed," she said firmly, and the housekeeper nodded, her relief palpable.

"I must say, Miss Darcy, I am pleased you were able to persuade her to take some rest."

"It was not a matter of persuasion," Georgiana replied, smiling gently. "She could barely stand."

Mrs. Reynolds nodded in silent agreement. She had been afraid that the obstinate mistress would injure herself, fatigued as she was. "And how are you, Miss? Should you like to take a rest before dinner?"

"No, I thank you, Mrs. Reynolds. I am feeling quite well today, and should like to play some music. Do you think it will keep Mrs. Darcy awake?"

Mrs. Reynolds shook her head with a small smile. "No, Miss. I doubt that anything short of cannon fire will be able to wake her before the morning."

Mrs. Reynolds had many things to accomplish, but she stood at the foot of the stairs until the sweet notes of the pianoforte began to fill the hall. She listened to the soft tones of the song, and smiled to herself as she turned back to her work. At last, she thought, with a growing sense of ease and content. At last.

Miss Darcy was playing a lullaby.

Chapter Twenty-Nine

"IT WAS YOU." The Colonel whispered the words, but Sophia Hawke glanced up from her conversation with her friend to meet his gaze.

"I apologize, Colonel. This is Jack Hobson. He is. . ."

Jack laughed as Sophia's face grew puzzled. She glared at him.

"Well, how would *you* describe it, you flea-bitten old clodpole?"

"You're a fine one to talk, *Miss* Hawke. You know," he said in a low voice, green eyes appraising her apparel, hand stroking his jaw. "You looked taller in uniform."

She grinned at both men and made a gesture above her head.

"It was the hat," she laughed. "It gave me two inches at least." She looked at Jack a little wistfully. "I must admit that I miss my boots. These paltry things," she lifted her skirts just a bit to shake her foot in exasperation, "are a poor substitute."

She held out her hand to Richard. "I am truly sorry to have shocked you so, Colonel." She shook her head. "Your father knew. I assumed you did as well. When I realized you did not, I thought perhaps he ought to be the one to tell you. However," she gestured to Jack, "I suppose the cat is out of the bag now."

"Do all the men know?" Richard asked, glancing over his shoulder and feeling like a fool.

"No," said both Sophia and Jack together, rather too quickly. Sophia continued alone. "I doubt very much any of them are listening to us, and they would not understand if they did. Very few people know."

"But you say my father knows."

"He does. He did not know for some time, and when he learned, he was not pleased, but he is aware."

Richard was growing unaccountably angry. "How could you get away with it? Why would you even wish to? What could possibly have possessed you to do such a foolish thing?"

Jack tipped his hat back to look at Sophia sympathetically. She looked at her friend but all he offered was a shrug. She drew in a deep breath, glanced back at the door to the inn.

"Before I begin, Colonel, my sister is never to know any of this."

Richard assented with a nod.

"Very well. Let me be as clear on this subject as possible. Your father could only protect us so far. My uncle had already forced me into espionage and tried to sell me to the highest bidder. As a woman, I am forever a target. Even legal documents do not protect me unless a man is willing to support my claims, and even then, he must be a powerful man. My uncle has had men in constant pursuit of me since I was sixteen, and with your father's help, I was able to hide. On the day I turned one and twenty, I returned to London." She looked up and met the Colonel's gaze without wavering. "I returned to take guardianship of my sister."

"At great personal risk," added Jack through gritted teeth. Miss Hawke waved her hand as if to dismiss that statement.

"She turned me away."

"She what?" Richard was stunned. Jack was angry. Sophia was philosophical.

"We had little contact after I turned sixteen, Colonel. A note here and there when I could get through to her. My uncle had ample time to turn her loyalties." Miss Hawke closed her eyes, and Richard could see the pain the admission cost her.

"I thought I had lost her. I thought he had won. I was sick to death of the whole business." She opened her eyes and looked at Richard, challenging him to judge her. "I was so tired of hiding. I wanted to have the power to direct my own course. I wanted to fight for something larger than myself and my family's property. I wanted to do something with honor. I *needed* it. Can you not understand that?"

Jack shrugged and added, "She went to war to find some peace." Sophia Hawke gawked at her stalwart companion and let out a soft, hooting laugh, her melancholy instantly thrown off. She continued to laugh as she shook her head and eagerly inspected her rifle, choking out, "As usual, Jack, it takes me volumes to say something that requires you only eight words. How I have missed you."

Jack grinned, but Richard was not pacified. "You were nearly killed at Vitoria."

Sophia shrugged. "But I was not. And neither, might I point out, were you."

Richard struggled with his anger. Oliver Hawke was not dead. He was very much alive, except that he was a she, and she was standing here in perfect health with a different name and in a dress.

"Why did you write that letter?" he asked almost inaudibly, his bitterness clear. "Why did you make me believe you dead? It has tormented me, believing myself responsible for your death. I dragged my cousin on this ridiculous chase with me when he ought to have been with his wife. I agreed to allow his friend to assist when he is a newlywed himself. I put them in danger so that I could fulfill the request that letter made of me. How could you do it?"

Sophia Hawke was furious, but she did not answer. Her cheeks flushed bright red, one hand clutching the stock of her rifle so tightly that her knuckles were white, and she struggled to regain her voice. Jack put his hand on her shoulder briefly.

"She did not write the letter, Colonel." Jack continued to rest his large hand on her shoulder until her cheeks began to return to their normal color and she was able to shake it away.

"Then who wrote it, *Jack*?" Richard would not be put off by this woman's anger. She had saved his life, yet followed that by putting them all in danger. No, *he* had put them all in danger, but, he defended himself, he had done it in *her* service. What were Elizabeth and Georgie facing on their own now because of his selfish decision to involve Darcy in this? What might have happened to Bingley's wife, had things gone badly the day before?

Jack Hobson stood to his full height, roughly equal to Richard's, perhaps even a bit taller.

"I wrote that letter, sir," he said formally, "and I would do it again."

The leader of the Matlock men chose that moment to call out from the other side of the yard, "We shall be ready to depart in thirty minutes, Colonel. Will you ride in the carriage?"

Richard did not wish to ride in the carriage. He desired more than anything to ride away from this whole sorry mess, from the Hawkes, from his father, from this insolent man who stood before him. He could not, however, as he had given two horses to Darcy and Bingley, and there was no horse left for him to ride.

"In the carriage," he responded without taking his eyes off of Jack. "Well?" he asked coldly, "Why did you write it? What were you about? Do you work for my father?"

Sophia Hawke rolled her eyes. Actually rolled her eyes. At him. He could barely restrain his temper.

Sophia Hawke was equally irritated. "He works for *me*, Colonel. He is the son of Darlington's steward, a man I hold in high esteem, and he is the only one who realized what I meant to do. He found me in London, intending to help the two of us escape. Instead, with his father's permission," she grimaced at him, "and without mine, he went into the regulars with me. He did spend an inordinate amount of time trying to dissuade me, but I would not give way. You must remember him, he was there with me at Vitoria. It was Jack who discovered you were near and thought we ought to keep an eye on you. We knew you were the Earl's son and thought you were looking rather ill."

Richard knew he had been ill. Exhausted, weak. Still, the letter had certainly not helped.

"Why did you write the letter, Jack? I have been punishing myself since I received it."

Jack shook his head, apologetic. "That was not my intention, Colonel. Miss Evelyn's birthday was fast approaching. Captain Hawke had tendered her resignation, and we planned to travel in a week's time to make one last effort to protect her sister. When the Captain was wounded, I needed to know someone would be able to look after Miss Evelyn, were she unable. I checked on you and knew you would be well enough. You are the Earl's son." He shrugged. "And you were headed home. You were the perfect choice. The Captain," he smiled wryly, "*Miss Hawke,* knew nothing of it."

"Jack hauled me off the field like a sack of flour," Miss Hawke said, attempting to make it a joke. "Hardly dignified. But as you were hollering something about a woman on the battlefield, I thought you knew my secret, and we had no time to waste on my pride."

Jack guffawed half-heartedly, then fell silent. Richard recalled Beaufort's discomfort when he visited, saying that Richard had been out of his head. Perhaps he had not been as out of his head as he thought. He still could not remember being taken from the field, nor what he had said, and he probably never would. Had he truly known, or was he just thinking about Georgiana?

Sophia Hawke's voice cut into his thoughts. "I should fetch my sister. Jack, thank you. Colonel," here she paused and offered him an expression of true contrition. "It was never my intention to hurt you. I offer my deepest apologies." With that, she turned and walked through the inn's rear door.

Jack Hobson removed his hat and ran a meaty hand through a shock of red hair. Richard assessed him carefully. A few years older than Miss Hawke, he thought, and strong. He had likely made a good soldier.

"Colonel, I did not wish to say anything before Miss Hawke," he said quietly, grimly, "but when I wrote the letter, I was almost certain she would not recover. Her wounds were not deep, but they were extensive. She lost a good deal of blood and I was sure there would be infection. That was indeed the case. If not for the care of her sister, I believe she would have died." He took a deep breath, a barely escaped grief bowing him down for a moment. "Would you have preferred that?"

No, Richard thought, *I would not.* He said nothing in response, however, merely moved around the boy to reenter the inn and gather his things. His trunk was on its way to Pemberley, so he had little to carry. He hoped beyond hope that all was well there. If he had pulled Darcy away from his family at such a time and things did not end well, he would carry that guilt the rest of his life. His stomach ached as badly as his head. *Is there nowhere I might be at peace?*

***

As the carriage rolled through the countryside, Colonel Fitzwilliam crossed his arms, leaned his head back, and anxiously watched their progress through the window. There were two armed men riding outside on the back of the coach and six armed outriders surrounded them. Jack Hobson was riding up front with the driver. Sophia Hawke sat on the forward facing bench and was gazing out the window on the opposite side. Her sister sat next to her, trying to sleep, but every time she began to nod off, the carriage hit a rut in the road and she was jolted awake. Richard knew it was a useless exercise to worry when they were so well protected, but he could not shake the feeling that Archibald Hawke might have one final play left in him. Once they arrived at Matlock and passed through the gates, the game would be up, and even a man as dogged as he would have to admit failure. Miss Evelyn turned one and twenty two days from now. There would be no time to marry her off without her consent, no way even to access her once she was safe with the Earl of Matlock as her protector.

Hawke could still try to kill one or both of them and then make a bid for their fortune, he supposed, but by now even he must have admitted to himself that the Earl would never allow him to succeed. Richard was sure that his father had more political favors to call in than Hawke, and a direct affront to the House of Matlock would not go unanswered. Even Hawke would have to see that it would be foolhardy. Yet the Colonel could not shake the feeling that he would try.

They were heading up into the hills now. If Hawke was going to make a run at them, this would be the best place. The topography would allow his men to hide with horses and weapons far closer to the carriage than on the flats. He watched for anything that might give something away when he heard Sophia Hawke say, "There."

Richard turned to see her pointing to the northwest. "Where?" he asked.

"Right there," she said, pointing again, "between the two hills just ahead. Can you see the sun hitting. . ." She did not have to finish. Colonel Fitzwilliam saw it, the brief flicker of sun on metal. He motioned to the outrider moving alongside, but a scout was already returning with news.

"Four men ahead," he said breathlessly. "On horseback, carrying rifles."

Hawke is likely not one of them, Richard thought. *He would not wish to dirty his hands.*

"Get down," he said to Sophia Hawke, and she pulled her sleepy sister from the cushioned bench and shoved her underneath it. She then lay on her side with her back pressed against Miss Evelyn and facing the door, both her rifle and a pistol next to her on the floor.

"Do not use those," the Colonel warned, "unless. . ."

"Unless they attack the carriage directly," Miss Hawke said, finishing his sentence. "I understand, Colonel. I will follow your orders."

Colonel Fitzwilliam nodded and motioned to the closest outrider. "You, there!"

The scout brought his horse alongside the carriage while the Colonel pointed and explained his plan. There was no room on the narrow road to turn around, and no roads branching off where they could circumvent the area entirely. They would have to go through. *What I would not give for a horse,* he thought, swearing under his breath. He held one pistol with another primed and loaded on the bench beside him and crouched, blocking the door.

As they approached the site between the hills, two of the outriders broke off to circle behind the waiting riflemen, and the remaining four rode in tighter formation. Richard heard a banging noise on the opposite door and turned to see Jack Hobson swinging over to ride on the small outcropping on that side of the carriage. He, too, was armed.

There came the sound of two shots. Three. A pause. Four. The driver urged his horses to a gallop, hoping to carry the carriage through the pass while their assailants were busy with the attack from behind. Sophia Hawke pressed her back against her sister to keep her from bouncing out of her protected position. Richard held his gun at the ready, but no riders approached. The rattling of the carriage as it sped along the rutted road made it difficult to remain in place, but Sophia Hawke braced one hand against the underside of the bench seat and the other against the floor over her rifle. The Colonel still held his pistol in one hand while hanging on to the window frame. Neither would be able to hit a target being tossed around as they were, so they simply held on and hoped for the best.

Finally, the carriage slowed and there was silence. The shots had stopped. They were through the pass and those both inside and outside the carriage breathed a sigh of relief. They heard hooves pounding from behind as the two riders who had split off now returned. The Colonel nodded at Sophia Hawke, who rose to her knees to help her sister back to the seat.

Then they heard it. Yelling outside and another shot, close by. The Colonel grabbed Sophia Hawke's arm and pulled her down just as there was a splintering of wood and a scream from Miss Evelyn. Sophia Hawke felt the shot blow past her with a gust of wind and heat. Then the Colonel was on top of her and holding Evelyn Hawke to the floor with a palm on her back. There was one more final shot, another hit to the carriage, and then the sound of clomping hooves as the shooter galloped away, three outriders on his trail.

A trap. It had been a trap. There had been a fifth rider waiting to take his shots on the other side of the pass, where he must have known the horses would need to slow. Richard glanced up from his position on the floor to see two holes in the sidewall just above the bench where the women had been riding, two balls buried in the wall opposite. Had the Hawke sisters been sitting on the seat rather than sprawled upon the floor, the shots would have been true, and all the years of Sophia Hawke's endeavors to retain control of her family's legacy would likely have amounted to nothing.

"Are you hurt?" demanded the Colonel, pushing away from Sophia Hawke. He rolled her to one side and then another, looking frantically for a wound.

"I am not," she said, her voice thin and pinched. She sat and removed her bonnet, which had been knocked askew as the Colonel leapt over her. With slightly shaky fingers, she held it in her lap and traced two holes, one entry, one exit that had appeared in the crown. Richard saw them, too, and sat heavily on the floor as the wild pounding of heart began to slow to a more normal rhythm. *Damn it all,* he cursed silently, *if I ever catch that fat, bacon-faced, beetle-browed bellweather, I shall baste him until he is nothing more than a grin in a case.* He caught his breath and noticed Jack, hanging on the outside of the coach, gazing at Miss Hawke and the bonnet with a dark, murderous glare before he worked his way back to the driver's bench. *Perhaps I shall have to invite Hobson along.*

"I would say, Colonel," the woman tried to jest, though her voice was tremulous at best, "that any debt you may have thought you owed me is now paid in full." Miss Evelyn sat up, grabbed her sister's bonnet, and stared at the holes, her face entirely without color.

"How can you stand this, Sophia?" she whispered, exhausted and shaking but not crying. She leaned against her sister's shoulder.

Her older sister bent to lay her cheek on top of the younger woman's head. "As usual, my dear," she said, a stoic mask overtaking her features, "I do not believe I was given a choice."

***

The gates of Matlock opened wide to allow the party to enter, and were closed quickly behind them. It took only a few minutes to reach the gravel drive, a few more before they were pulling to a stop before the grand entrance to The Earl of Matlock's country seat.

At the top of the marble stairs, the Earl himself awaited the arrivals. His heart was heavy, but he had vowed he would make certain Evelyn Hawke retained the inheritance he knew her sister had fought to give her. He watched as his second son handed a small young woman with dark hair out of the carriage. He started to walk down the steps to welcome her to his home, frowning as he noticed that the carriage had sustained damage. His attention was pulled back to his son when he realized that Richard had not moved to stand beside the young woman or offer his arm. Instead, he reached back into the carriage and took the hand of someone else. Her head was down, so he could not tell for sure, but her height, the blonde curls...

"Sophia," he whispered hoarsely.

The Earl of Matlock was a fierce man, a fiery orator, and an implacable foe once engaged. He did not believe in allowing emotion to show on one's face. He considered it, in fact, as a weakness of the first order. He had often told his sons "The enemy should never be allowed to gain advantage from the expression upon your countenance."

Yet all of that carefully cultivated reserve, the studied lack of emotion, the refusal to reveal to the world that he entertained a feeling so commonplace as love was summarily discarded. He took the rest of the stairs faster than he believed possible to stand directly before Sophia Hawke, place a hand below her chin to tilt her face to his, and sigh out all of his wasted grief in one shuddering breath.

Then, for nearly the first time in Richard's memory, the Earl did something fully, unabashedly emotional. He gathered Sophia Hawke into his embrace and held her as though she was a long-lost child at last returned home.

"Thank God," he said in a strangled voice. "Thank God."

"Thank God if you must, sir," Sophia's voice was clear and strong considering how tightly the Earl was holding her. "But you must not neglect to also thank your son."

Chapter Thirty

ELIZABETH CURLED UP in her bed, laying on her side, knees pulled to her chest, watching the hypnotic movement of the branches outside the window as they swayed and danced in the summer breeze. She was too warm beneath the covers and kicked them off. The air through her open window smelled faintly of roses and lavender. After all the time shut up in the house over the past weeks, she relished the fresh air as she lay there, exhausted but unable to shut her eyes just yet. As she watched the leaves move back and forth in rhythm with the light, calming strains of the lullaby wending its way up to her from the music room, she at last fell into a deep, dreamless sleep.

She slept all day, through the night, and well into the next morning. She did not hear the horses pounding up to the door at a reckless speed or the deep voice booming in the entry, calling her name.

***

"Elizabeth!" roared Fitzwilliam as he burst through the front doors, thrusting off his coat and hat and leaving them in a heap on the floor. "Elizabeth!" He heard footsteps and turned to see Mrs. Reynolds hurrying towards him. James was already folding the discarded coat over his arm.

"Please, Mr. Darcy, Mrs. Darcy is resting upstairs. She is well."

"Georgiana?" he asked hoarsely, reaching out to take Mrs. Reynolds' arm.

"I am well, brother," came a soft voice from the doorway of the drawing room. Georgiana stood there, healthy, blooming, beautiful in a pink dress and shawl, looking only a little thinner and a bit paler than she had when he left. A smothered sob escaped his lips.

"Thank God," he whispered and strode to where she stood to gather her in his embrace. He held her for a long time, leaning down to kiss the top of her head, and then, pulling away, said abruptly, "I should not keep you standing." He led her back into the drawing room. "Come, dearest, and sit. Should you not have a fire? Do you need a blanket? Are you entirely well?"

Georgiana kissed him on the cheek. "The day is quite warm enough without a fire, brother. I am well, thanks to Elizabeth and Mrs. Reynolds. I was ill, but am now recovered, as you can see. In fact," she continued, with a smile, "I should rather ask if *you* require anything. How long have you been riding?"

"Two days," came a voice from the doorway, and Georgiana looked up to see Charles Bingley standing there apologetically, quite as muddy and unshaven as her brother. She felt a stab of grief that she should have been the cause of their pain. She moved to stand, but he shook his head at her and held up a hand.

"There is no need for formalities with me, Miss Darcy." A smile lit his weary, dust-streaked face.

Georgiana nodded. "I am very pleased to say that your haste was for naught. You have missed it all, and I am glad of it." Her voice softened. "We were about to have a late breakfast. I will have Maxwell show you to your room and you may join us at your leisure." Bingley nodded, bowed, and backed out of the room, closing the door as he left.

"Is Elizabeth in her chamber?" Fitzwilliam asked.

Georgiana nodded and touched his arm. "Please, brother, if she is still abed, do not wake her. She was so weary yesterday she went to bed immediately following church and has not yet risen." She paused, unwilling to cause him further uneasiness, but wanting to be truthful. "I do not believe she has slept in her own bed since I was first taken ill." She looked up into his face and saw him struggling to maintain his composure.

"It has been nearly a fortnight, Georgiana," he said softly.

"Yes," she replied quietly.

Fitzwilliam kissed her once more, nodded his promise, and left the room. She heard him pounding his way up the stairs, taking them three at a time, she imagined, and then stood and rang for the maid.

Fitzwilliam quietly opened the door to Elizabeth's room to gaze at his sleeping wife. Her face was drawn and pale, thinner, he thought, than it had been a few weeks before. There were circles under her eyes and her dark curls were scattered across the pillow. His chest tightened with the knowledge of all he had left her to face alone, but his heart swelled with the certainty that she was safe. Georgiana was safe. The rest he would wait to hear until she was ready to tell him. He could feel the fear, the agony of the past two days draining away, leaving him suddenly weak.

Elizabeth murmured something in her sleep and he sat on the side of the bed, careful not to disturb her. Her right hand lay on the pillow, fingers closed in a fist. They uncurled slightly as she shifted, and he nearly wept when he saw his miniature tucked securely in her palm. He unconsciously touched the pocket of his waistcoat, where he kept hers, and could not resist bending to kiss her forehead. She stirred, her eyelids fluttered, and then she was staring at him. So deeply had she been sleeping that it took a moment before she was fully awake and he smiled at her confusion. She sighed and reached out to touch his face, but not until he caught her hand and kissed it did she believe it was not a dream.

"Oh, my love," Elizabeth whispered, her voice low and strained. "You are *home*." He could not pretend that he did not hear both joy and anguish behind the words. She sat up, threw her arms around his neck as his encircled her, and for a time they did not move in the silent elation of being restored to one another.

When he finally pulled back, he reached to touch her cheek. She held his hand there and closed her eyes. He studied her face with concern, and when she opened her eyes to watch him, this simple loving act made her breath catch. She felt all the pain rising to the surface, and for the first time since she had heard Mr. Harrison's fearful news that the children were ill, she began to weep, her sobbing quiet, controlled, but profound.

Fitzwilliam pulled her close again and stroked her hair, rocking back and forth gently as she wept. "Oh, my love," he whispered as though his heart would break. "I am so sorry. I should never have left."

She wept for some time, making him more wretched with every passing minute. All the misery, the fear for Georgiana, the abandonment of Mr. Harrison, the anxiety for so many ill children, their parents depending upon her, the stunning loss of Amelia and her child, the final agony of losing the Gibbonses, forcing herself to lock all heartache away so that she could do what was required, all of it poured out in her tears, leaving her at last feeling empty but also with a sense of peace.

When she had at last finished, she looked up at her husband, smiling though her cheeks were still damp. He wiped them gently away. Elizabeth burrowed into his chest for one more embrace and then pushed herself from the bed.

"Let me wash my face and call Sarah, dearest, and we shall go downstairs for breakfast. It is time for breakfast, is it not?" She smiled. "You must be hungry." She reached to touch his face gently, tracing his cheek as though reassuring herself he was real. Her eyes twinkled then, and he fervently thanked God for it. "You may wish to call your valet while I dress, my dear," she said, appraising him critically. "You look quite wild this morning."

He smiled and replied, teasing, "And this is the thanks I receive for rushing to your side?"

"Indeed, William," she said, quite serious now, putting her hand in his. "I am pleased that you are here."

He kissed her tenderly. "You shall have a difficult time getting rid of me hereafter, Mrs. Darcy."

"I shall hold you to that, Mr. Darcy. Now go and make yourself presentable and I shall do the same." He stood and strode to the door, but looked back one more time.

"Elizabeth," he said brokenly, but she interrupted him.

"None of that, my dear," Elizabeth said with compassion. "I will tell you all, but you must be patient with me and you must also have faith." She paused, longing to ease the grief she saw on his face. "There was no way to foresee what would happen, and I do believe," she said solemnly, "that were you meant to be here, you would have been."

He released a breath he did not realize he had been holding. She was asking for his patience? His faith? Knowing he would need to ask the same of her, these were still not simple requests. He shook his head.

"I will try, Elizabeth," he said quietly, and left the room.

In half an hour he was washed, shaved, changed and at her door to escort her downstairs. She smiled brightly at him and he felt the corners of his own mouth begin to tug upwards as she took his arm. She tilted her face up to his and hugged his arm to her side.

"*Now* you are the man I remember," she said with a little laugh.

As they arrived at the table, Darcy saw that Mrs. Cronk had provided far more food than the four of them could possibly eat, and understood without explanation that she was happy to have the master home. Darcy pulled out a chair for Elizabeth and sat next to her. Georgiana and Bingley were already awaiting them, Bingley rising as Elizabeth entered. She greeted him warmly and inquired after Jane.

"Your sister is very well, and sends her regards. She did not know, when we left, that there was illness here." Elizabeth raised her eyebrows slightly at this, but did not pursue it. They had not come from London?

"You must be famished, Elizabeth," Georgiana said cheerfully. She shot an exasperated look at her brother and he lifted his shoulders slightly in a shrug.

"No," Elizabeth replied carefully. "I am not hungry, though I will have some tea, if I may." She was still tired, but in a more ordinary way. The crushing weight of her fatigue had lifted.

Georgiana smiled, but she was not pacified. Elizabeth seemed pleased to have her pour the tea rather than take over the duty herself, and she could hardly credit Elizabeth's answer about her appetite. How could she not be hungry? She had had nothing to eat since a light breakfast before church the previous day.

The men, she noted, had piled food high on their plates and proceeded to gorge themselves as though they had been absolutely starved. Distracted for a moment, she shook her head. How they managed to stuff themselves without breaking a single rule of etiquette! *This is really quite a performance*, she thought laughingly. Elizabeth sipped her tea and met her sister's amused eyes with her own, her lips quirking up at the corners. Then, suddenly, Elizabeth's face paled.

"I pray you would excuse me for a moment," she said suddenly, and rose. The men stood, but she bade them sit. "I will return shortly," she assured them, a little too quickly, and walked out without saying anything else. Darcy remained standing, his eyes following Elizabeth's retreat.

Georgiana tapped her spoon on the table impatiently to draw his attention. He turned to face her, and saw her irritation.

"I asked you not to wake her, brother. Do you not see she should still be resting?" Her blue eyes flashed with annoyance.

"Georgiana," he said gently, in a voice he might use with a child, "she wished to come downstairs. Was I to lock her away?"

She blew out an aggravated breath. "If you had not awakened her, you would not have had to do *anything*."

Bingley was looking at Georgiana with amusement. She noticed, but was not deterred.

"I would say, Darcy, that your sister is fully recovered." He smiled into his coffee, even in the face of Darcy's scowl and Georgiana's annoyance. Darcy tossed his napkin on the table and went to seek his wife.

Elizabeth escaped into the hall and spied one of the maids taking a basin upstairs.

"Emily," she called out, and the girl stopped and curtsied, her black hair tucked neatly under her cap.

"Yes, ma'am?"

"You may leave that with me." Emily handed it over, curtsied, and returned the way she had come.

Placing the basin on a table in her study, Elizabeth leaned unsteadily against the wall, her head tilted back, taking slow, even breaths. Even the tea had been difficult to take with her stomach in revolt against her, but the smell of the food was too much to bear. Her stomach lurched. She took two steps, put one hand on either side of the basin, and was suddenly, violently, ill.

When she had finished, she felt a familiar hand on the small of her back. When had her husband entered the room? He was handing her a glass of water, and she took it gratefully. When she had sipped a little, she tried to smile, but she was aware even before he frowned that it would not deter him. His eyes were dark with worry as he led her to a chair and helped her sit.

"Georgiana is correct. You should be back in bed," he said brusquely, and stepped out into the hall. She leaned back and closed her eyes, breathing carefully. She heard his low voice giving instructions to someone. She heard "Mr. Waters," and sighed. The poor man was as exhausted as she, and she would not like him to be dragged back up to the house for nothing. She was just tired.

Fitzwilliam kneeled by the chair and took her hand, wrapping his free arm around her waist as he stood with her. "Come, dearest," he said firmly. "Allow me to help you."

Elizabeth knew that this was not a request, and while she normally would have laughed him out of his overprotectiveness, today she was grateful for his assistance. She had learned in the past fortnight that there was a difference between being stubborn and being unreasonable. She felt shaky from lack of food and weak despite her long, deep sleep the night before. After a few unsteady steps, Fitzwilliam would not allow her to take the stairs.

"It will be easier this way, my dear," he said, sweeping her up into his arms, heedless of her protests. She nestled against his chest, feeling safer than she had since his departure.

Darcy carried his wife to her chambers, set her gently down on the bed, and drew the covers over her. Elizabeth did not bother to tell him it was too hot for covers. Instead, she leaned back upon the pillows. Perhaps it had been too soon to rise, but she had felt fine. At least her stomach had now stopped complaining. He sat next to her on the bed and she put her hand over his. He took her hand in both of his own and held it gently.

"Try to sleep," he said, brushing a curl from her forehead, checking, she thought, for fever. She nodded and closed her eyes. It was not difficult to fall back to sleep, and her breathing soon slowed and deepened.

When she opened her eyes, Fitzwilliam was sitting in a chair next to the bed. He had removed his coat and his sleeves were rolled up. She noticed that she had kicked off her blankets and was only under a light sheet. He smiled at her.

"Are you feeling any better?" he asked, reaching out to stroke her cheek.

"I am, thank you."

"Mr. Waters is on his way up."

"It really was not necessary to bother him, William."

"Elizabeth, please, if you will not see him for yourself, do so for me. I will not sleep at all tonight if he does not see you."

She sighed. "Very well," she said, resigned.

There was a tapping at the door. Fitzwilliam stepped out into the hall and returned with Mr. Waters and Georgiana, who shooed her brother out of the room with an insistence that surprised him even more than her sharp words earlier.

Elizabeth studied the young apothecary from her position on the bed. The young man was still tugging absent-mindedly at his rumpled waistcoat. His eyes were bloodshot and his sandy hair was wind swept. He was unshaven. She could see that he had likely been asleep, but had answered her husband's summons immediately. She knew he was still upset that he had been away when the sickness began, and her heart went out to him.

"Mr. Waters," she said mildly, "I apologize that you were disturbed. I know you must be quite tired."

"No matter, Mrs. Darcy," he said quietly. She could see he was silently evaluating her. After a moment, his expression registered both relief and confusion.

"What seems to be the trouble?"

Elizabeth noticed the change immediately. For nearly a fortnight, they had been equal partners in a grim business, but now things would be different. Would have to be different. He took her pulse, checked for fever, all while asking a string of questions. How long had she felt ill? What had happened at breakfast? Had she eaten? Were there any other symptoms? Was her fatigue persistent? She nearly rolled her eyes at the last, but he gave her a silent warning look that told her these were the questions he had to ask. Under Georgiana's watchful eye, he began his examination. When he had finished, he took a step away from the bed.

"Mrs. Darcy," he said suddenly, pursing his lips, "forgive me, but. . ."

"Yes?"

"When did you last have your courses?"

She looked at him, trying to remember. It had been so long since she had even thought about it, thought about anything other than the calamity unfolding before her, that she could not be certain. She thought that she had missed her courses the month before, but that had occurred in the past once or twice, and she had not thought much about it. The epidemic had driven it completely from her mind.

"I am sure I do not recall, Mr. Waters." she replied archly. "I have been rather busy of late."

He looked at his feet and then at Elizabeth, a small smile working itself into a grin. His meaning hit Elizabeth a moment later.

"Truly?" she asked, incredulous. Georgiana moved to grab Elizabeth's hand with a gasp of delight.

After being permitted to examine her more completely, he stepped away from the bed and nodded.

"I would put you at about two months, ma'am. Perhaps a little more." His grin was contagious, all signs of fatigue vanished. "We should know for sure when you quicken." Georgiana placed an enthusiastic kiss on her sister's head.

"May I get up now?" laughed Elizabeth.

"While you are perfectly healthy, Mrs. Darcy, there can be no harm in allowing your husband to care for you for a while," Mr. Waters said with a laugh. "To be sure, I am not the man to gainsay him." She saw the genuine pleasure in his smile, as though he felt indebted to her for such a gift after their trial, and she thanked him warmly. Georgiana threw open the door. Fitzwilliam was leaning against the wall, waiting to be allowed inside. Elizabeth smiled, her face suddenly warm as she watched Georgiana take her brother's hand and lead him to her.

"Well?" he asked gruffly. Elizabeth saw his misery and patted the bed beside her. Georgiana and Mr. Waters left the room, closing the door behind them with a soft click.

"Dearest," she said quietly.

"Yes, my love?" he asked tenderly, taking her hand and gazing into her eyes. He saw the twinkle then, and he felt his heart begin to pound erratically. Her lips stretched into a smile so joyful and loving that he could not help bending to kiss her. She stopped him as he approached, her free hand on his lips.

"Shall we name our son after your father or mine?"

For two long days, Fitzwilliam Darcy had been preparing for the worst. When he arrived and all was well, he could scarce believe it. When Elizabeth fled the breakfast table, his fears had been reignited. Clearly Elizabeth was ill with the same fever Georgiana had suffered, and as he watched her sleep, he was already trying to adapt to what such an illness might portend.

What Fitzwilliam Darcy was not prepared for was joy.

It took a few moments for his wife's words to wash over him and penetrate his understanding. When comprehension at last dawned upon him, he took a very deep breath and let it out slowly, lifting his wife's hand for a soft kiss and then holding her hand to his forehead while he bowed his head and uttered a brief, grateful prayer of thanks. He leaned in to kiss her forehead, her eyelids, the tip of her nose, and then, after regarding Elizabeth with a kind of boyish delight, he placed one gentle hand reverently on her stomach.

"When?"

"It is early yet, my dear. We will know for certain when the babe quickens, but Mr. Waters seems very sure. It would be. . ." she counted the months, "Late February or early March."

"March." Fitzwilliam said quietly. He felt in his heart that Waters was right. His beautiful wife was now carrying his child. After what he had just been through, he was determined not to leave her side until well after she had given birth, if ever. His mind was awhirl with the letters he would write, the staff he could trust to take care of business in London, how to explain to Lady Matlock that they would not attend the Season in town. Elizabeth's soft, laughing voice broke into his thoughts.

"You need not plan your way through this just yet, my dear. There is plenty of time."

"Quite right, love." He took both of her hands in his, looked directly into the chocolate brown eyes he loved so much and said, very simply, "Thank you."

Chapter Thirty-One

*R*ICHARD,

All is well. Bingley and I raced to Pemberley like prize idiots only to learn we had missed everything of importance. Georgiana was quite ill but is well into her recovery, and Elizabeth, thank God, was not taken ill at all. I returned to discover that my indomitable wife has fully assumed her role as mistress of Pemberley with compassion and resolve. I doubt not where the staff's loyalty now lies, and it is not with the master.

I am relieved that the entire party is safe at Matlock. While I look forward to your story, cousin, I will not be traveling in the near future. I am afraid that this time, you must come to us. We would be pleased to see you as soon as you are at liberty. As always, there is no need to wait upon an invitation.

Please relay our regards to your parents, the Viscount, and the Misses Hawke.

Your cousin,

F.D.

Richard set down the letter with a deep sense of relief. All was well at Pemberley. He had slept the entire night without waking for the first time in weeks and was able to finish reading Darcy's letter without his eyes tearing or his vision blurring. The letter was brief and reading still made his head ache, but the pain was only an echo of what it had been. It was a start. He folded the letter and placed it securely in the pocket of his coat. Then he walked out to the gardens in search of his father.

The Earl was walking with Miss Sophia Hawke. She was speaking softly to the older man and he wore a serious expression as she concluded. Her expression, as always, was difficult to read. *No*, Richard thought, *when she is angry, the mask does slip a bit*. He recalled the expression of joy upon her face when she spied Jack Hobson approaching, her shaking fingers as she traced the crown of her damaged bonnet, and amended his analysis. *In times of great emotion. Anger, joy, fear*. She reminded him of Darcy in many ways. His emotional reserve was nearly impervious when faced with crowds or those he did not know. Both expected the worst of people. Even now, after his marriage, Darcy still did not reveal his feelings easily. Both had been hurt deeply. Neither trusted others easily. Yet neither was as stoic as they would like to appear.

He stood motionless for a few moments as he watched Sophia Hawke discussing something distasteful with his father. Her scowl was fierce. His eyes traveled the length of her and noted that she now filled out her gown quite admirably. She seemed to be wearing stays, making a noticeable difference in her figure, a difference he was not sure he cared for overmuch. She was still wearing her sister's dresses, he noted, glancing at the hem. No matter. His mother would soon have that sorted. He chuckled as he finally allowed himself to admit the obvious. *Sophia Hawke may have a lot in common with William, but she is a damn sight prettier.*

When Miss Hawke noticed the Colonel approaching, she made her curtsy and excused herself to return inside. She seemed pained, somehow, beneath that mask of indifference she wore. Richard watched her go, her golden hair finally properly styled into ringlets that bounced cheerfully as she walked, a stark contrast to her controlled features. Without changing his expression in any way, he turned to face the Earl and handed him Darcy's letter. His father read with a relieved nod. "Good, good," he said, and returned it to his son.

They resumed walking away from the house, passing behind several walls of roses. When they had reached a decent distance from the main house, the Earl spoke.

"She is ruined, you know," he said.

Richard nodded. He had not thought on it much, but it was not unexpected. "I would imagine. She ran away from her uncle and has been traveling with a male companion for years. Who else knows?"

The Earl cleared his throat. "Only a few. The Hobsons, me, you. Even her sister is unaware. However, I think we both know that these things have a way of getting out." He looked at his feet. "I have been speaking with Miss Hawke all morning. I suggested that she consider marrying the Hobson boy, despite their differences in station. His father has run the estate essentially on his own for years, and could teach his son well."

Richard was surprised at the resentment he felt in response to his father's admission. What did it matter to him whether or not Sophia Hawke married or to whom? He felt some sympathy for her situation, but she had brought much of it on herself. *That was ungenerous,* he thought immediately.

"Perhaps," he said to the Earl, "she would not wish to have anyone else run the estate after having fought so hard to keep it."

The Earl was gazing at something in the distance, so he missed the flash of consternation on his son's face.

"She assured me," the Earl mused, "that they are not lovers, that she is still a maiden. But she has no illusions, either for her or her sister. She intends to return to Darlington and rebuild."

Richard frowned, thinking about those two round holes in the side of the carriage. "Is not her uncle still a threat?"

The Earl grunted. "It seems he headed straight for Dover when you and Darcy removed the girls from his care." He smiled a little. "Sophia says he turned tail when she told him that she had his secrets and his gun."

Richard snorted. "She did disarm him rather smoothly."

The Earl grimaced. "She threatened to reveal all of his secrets, and that was enough to propel him out of the country posthaste."

Richard remembered Sophia Hawke whispering to her uncle before he released her. "Then who attacked the carriage?"

"His final orders." The Earl said bitterly. "Apparently that little entertainment was carried out purely for spite." He paused. "I will not pretend that he was not hoping you would be a casualty as well. It was his last chance to strike out at me." The Colonel shrugged. It would not be the first time someone had wished him dead. Collecting the right enemies was merely a sign that one was living an honorable life. As honorable as possible, in any case.

"Where is he headed?" Richard asked. If anyone knew, it would be the Earl.

"It is impossible to say for certain, Richard," his father said solemnly. "But I do suspect he has fled the country for a purpose. I believe. . ." he met Richard's gaze and did not break it. "I believe him to be headed for France."

"*France?*" Richard sputtered. He stopped walking. "He is a traitor, then?"

"So it would seem, Richard," the Earl mused. "So it would seem."

"Does Miss Hawke know?"

"I have just informed her. She knew he was spying for someone, but she did not know for whom. He may have thought her better informed."

"No wonder she believes she will never marry. Even should her secret never be revealed, his defection cannot be hidden. It will affect her name. It will damage her sister's chances as well."

The Earl waved a hand impatiently. "They have a tremendous fortune between them, Richard. There will always be a man who will wed for financial considerations."

"Father," Richard began, but Lord Matlock put up his hand.

"I will not pressure either of them to marry where they do not choose, Richard, and I will not abandon Miss Hawke. The fact that she fought her uncle so tenaciously that he made an attempt on her life should help sway opinion in her favor, as will my public support. I would not like to see her lose Darlington to the crown because of a convenient misunderstanding on the part of the Prince Regent."

"How do you plan to avoid it, Father?" Richard asked skeptically.

"I will write to Prinny," he said simply, "and mention to him that the Misses Hawkes are patriots and that I would not like to see them hurt."

"You would threaten the Prince?" Richard asked, incredulous, wondering what secrets the Earl held in his possession. *No, never mind. I do not wish to know.*

"Not threaten, Richard," his father scoffed. "I am not a simpleton. I will explain that Miss Hawke helped me to expose her uncle at the risk of her own life and that she should be publicly thanked for her efforts." Richard knew full well that there would have to be some significant piece of information to compel acquiescence to such a request, but he remained silent. His father would never reveal it anyway. A thought came to him unbidden. *Father is the man Filbee mentioned. Father made sure those documents were released to Darcy's men. There is no other way we would have found the information so quickly.*

They walked on in silence for a time before turning to make their way back to the house.

"Richard," the Earl said, breaking the silence. "I am sorry you were drawn into this. I never thought your world would collide with mine in such a way, but I suppose once Sophia made the decision to. . . well, it became more likely, I suppose."

"I was pleased to find her an excellent shot," Richard said wryly.

The Earl laughed out loud, his face creasing in mirth.

"She is, she is. In more ways than one, son." He slapped Richard on the shoulder and became serious once more.

"Richard, I hope you know that I care for you. It is difficult for me to show you, and so I have always allowed your mother to do that duty to you boys. But I do care what happens to you. I love you."

Colonel Fitzwilliam was stunned to hear the words. He knew, he always had, that his father was a man of honor. The Earl felt himself obligated to do his duty to the estate, to his heir, to his country. That left precious little time for a second son. However, he also knew he would not have wanted to be the first son, to take on the Earl's title or the seat in the House of Lords, nor would he wish to suffer through all of the required social obligations. He was happy enough as the second son, allowed to seek his life's occupation in his own way, and had long accepted his father's benign neglect as the price for that position. He thus felt more than simply pleased by his father's unexpected words. He felt somehow lighter, as though he had carried a burden that was now lifted.

"I know you do, sir." He paused. It was difficult to say out loud, but he felt it was important. He gazed at his feet, and said, quietly, "I love you too."

***

The Darcys were sitting in the drawing room after dinner, Georgiana having retired early, when Elizabeth mumbled something about writing him during the epidemic. Fitzwilliam was not sure he had heard his wife correctly.

"You kept a journal?" he asked. How had Elizabeth found the time to keep a journal?

"No. Well, yes," she colored slightly, feeling his surprise. "A treatment journal of sorts for Mr. Waters and letters for you. It was my poor attempt to make sense of everything that was happening. Every night, I sat down to try to record what we had done. I suppose that it was also my way of reaching out to you."

"To me?" he asked, silently cursing himself. *Imbecile. Can you not do anything more than repeat her words?*

She was smiling at him then, as though she knew what he was thinking.

"Yes. It was a way to reason though problems and consider what advice you might have given were you here."

He squinted at her, trying not to frown. Surely she must realize he would have advised her to do nearly everything differently. Yet her decisions and actions had saved many lives. Of that he was entirely certain. She flushed under his gaze.

"Indeed, I know what you must be thinking. Why try to conjure advice I knew I would not follow?" She shook her head. "I believe that were you here,

William, I could have made you understand. Perhaps I wrote to convince you. . . or myself." She stood. "I will return. Please wait for me." Darcy nodded once and watched her slip into her study. She returned within a few minutes, the journal in hand with several sheets of paper beneath it. She held the stack from the bottom, then placed one hand on the top cover tentatively before she offered it to him. He took them, but set the pile on the table next to him.

"You have offered me an account of all that has happened, and I am grateful," he said quietly. "Before I read your letters, I must offer you an account of my time as well."

She looked at him, serious and expectant, but trusting. "I know from the letter you sent with Mr. Wright," she said quietly, "that you had some business with Richard, but he is not here with you. I expect it was rather personal? Has it been concluded?"

He swallowed. "No, my dear, it has not. The more we learn, the deeper we sink. I hope to hear from Richard soon to tell us they are all safely at Matlock." Her trust in him was a gift, and he did not deserve it. He was silent for some time.

"William," she said, prodding, "perhaps you could simply begin at the beginning. Did you know Richard had business for you before you left home?"

He nodded. "I received a rather mysterious note the day before my departure. I knew he wished to confer with me, but none of the particulars."

She pursed her lips and a small line appeared on her forehead. "I see."

It was some time before he had finished. When his voice at last tapered off, he sat still, staring at the floor. Elizabeth was quiet, thoughtful. He was grateful she had not berated him or left the room, yet he was anxious for her to speak. When she did, it was not what he had expected. Her voice was low, broken.

"Those poor girls. I cannot imagine being left alone so young, so entirely unprotected." He could only agree. After a moment, the response he was expecting was at last issued.

"William," she said carefully, "I must admit that I am rather offended. Do you think so ill of me that you could not share even your cousin's summons before your journey?"

Darcy winced. She had gone to the heart of it and was hurt, disappointed. This was worse than her anger. Still, what would she have him do? What purpose would it serve to know when there was nothing she could do but wait for him to return?

"I did not wish to distress you, dearest. You already seemed so low." She frowned a little, acknowledging this as truth. Fitzwilliam knew he should stop there, but instead he added, "As it turns out, you had enough to do."

"Do not do that, William." Now she was angry.

"Do what, my dear? Protect you?"

"I concede that my spirits were low, William, but what did you intend to protect me from? You did not know what you were going to face."

"It was a note from Richard. I was fairly sure it would not be pleasant," he snapped, and then thought, *I am digging myself deeper still.*

"Do you have so little faith in me, then, to believe I should not know when you are putting yourself at risk?" She met his gaze, would not allow him to look away. "I would have been worried. That much is true. Yet it is still better to know. I can face anything so long as I am not *protected* from the truth."

He tapped the pile of paper she had handed him. "I know you well enough to suspect you have not told me all, even in these letters. I am not the only one who has put himself at risk, my love."

She shook her head, a little amused at his attempt to change the subject of their conversation, but satisfied, believing he had at least heard her complaint. "You are well aware, very well, William, that it is not the same. I did not know before you left that I would be required to face what we did. I had to make decisions very quickly, and we had no way to send you word. Indeed, we did send word at the first opportunity." Darcy ducked his head, ashamed that he had not been in London to receive those letters. "I will acknowledge that I was loath to part with you, but I am not a child and I would not have my husband treat me as one." He looked her in the eye, pleading. She would not look away, her gentle reproach meeting his tortured gaze. He struck back defensively.

"Shall I speak with John, my love? From the little I already know about your actions here, you put yourself at far more risk than necessary. The letters that reached me. . . I cannot tell you. . ." his voice broke and she took his hand.

He closed his eyes, remembering the moment he had read them, how his entire body had suddenly become numb, his legs unable to support him, how he had no power to answer Bingley's increasingly intense questions as they wended their way through the inn's yard. Never had his life been so entirely full, and he had realized, with a stomach wrenching certainty, how much more he now had to lose. He clasped his hands behind his bowed head, trying to dispel the abject terror of that moment. He felt her kneel before him, her hands on his, her lips on his forehead.

"Very well, William," she said softly.

He looked up. "Elizabeth?"

"I do not wish for there to be secrets between us. Not even the unpleasant ones. I do not need to be spared. It would hurt me to discover that you had not been forthcoming. It would hurt more than knowing." She sighed a little. "You have now told me your tale. Have you told me all?"

He nodded.

"Then I will tell you everything as well. Are you sure that *you* want to hear it?"

"I do not want to hear it, but I must. Are you feeling well enough to tell it?"

She smiled and rolled her eyes. "You are impossible. Read the letters, and I will fill in the rest."

He swallowed hard and tried to smile. This was going to be more difficult than telling her his story. He had almost hoped she was too fatigued to speak of it now so that he might have more time to prepare. He picked up the letters and began to read. Every so often, he would point to a line on the page and ask her a question. When he asked who she had sent to find Mr. Waters, she actually grinned.

"I could not find John, my dear, so there was nothing to do but to go myself." She raised her eyebrows and tilted her chin up in a small show of defiance. Dear God, he loved it when she did that.

"The entire story, my wife. That was our agreement."

She pursed her lips and he was surprised to see a blush spreading across her cheeks.

"Elizabeth? Are you well?"

"I am well, William. You must not tell anyone what I am to about to tell you." He looked at her, waiting. She shrugged. "Well, John knows. He caught me when I returned."

"Elizabeth. . ."

"I think I looked quite fetching," she said teasingly.

"I beg your pardon?"

"I believe I looked quite fetching in trousers and a boy's hat." He would have been alarmed but for her soft laugh.

He shook his head impatiently and took her hands in his. "What are you saying, woman?"

Elizabeth grew more serious. "My love, there was no other way. I had to find Mr. Waters. Georgiana was very. . ." she paused, gathering her courage, "very ill. She was delirious. I could not continue without his help. When I could not find John, I dressed as a boy and rode Plato to town."

"Why was there no one around?"

"It was the middle of the night."

Not safe, he thought. *At night on muddy roads. With child*. He bit back the retort, instead asking with a calm he did not feel, "Why did you dress as a boy?"

She raised her eyebrows. "It was safer to ride as a boy than as Mrs. Darcy. Further, there was no time to ride sidesaddle, my dear."

Elizabeth watched her husband's face as several competing emotions fought for precedence. Finally, after a struggle, a thin humor seemed to win, so she added, "You know, you never told me how wonderful it was to ride astride. Perhaps you should teach me how to do it properly."

He shook his head. Infuriating, teasing woman. He would not take her bait. He had to think more on this. He briefly imagined her in trousers, but had to stop almost immediately as a sly grin broke his grim countenance. "Perhaps after the babe arrives, my dear." He laid one warm hand gently on her abdomen and continued reading. When he reached the part about Amelia Blunt and her child, he shot a look at his wife. She was not laughing now.

"Did John find them?" he asked, with more hope than belief.

Her eyes met his with a deep and terrible sorrow he would have protected her from the rest of her life. It struck him, then, how entirely incapable he was of doing so. Terrible things would happen despite his best efforts to keep her safe, to protect her. All he could do was be there with her when they did. He removed his hand from her stomach to take hers and read on, finishing with the letter about the Gibbonses. He set it atop the small pile and put his arm around her shoulder.

"I love you," he whispered into her hair.

She let out a breath she had not been aware she was holding.

"I love you too, William," she said, putting her head on his shoulder.

The two of them sat there, silent and exhausted, until Mrs. Reynolds came to announce dinner.

***

Darcy took the express from Wilkins with a nod and waited until the butler left the room to open it. As the door to his study clicked shut, he broke the seal and began to read.

Cousin,

We have all arrived in safety and are ensconced at Matlock. There is far too much to relate in a letter and I fear you would not believe me in any case. When I next see you, we shall open a bottle of your best brandy and I will explain the rather epic tale in which you and I have played a small role.

Please convey my thanks to Bingley for his help the past week and wish him happy in his hunt for a new estate. Should you need me for anything at Pemberley, you need only send word and I shall set out directly.

Gratias tibi ago, frater.

Richard

Darcy rubbed his forehead tiredly. Had something happened between his departure and Richard's arrival at Matlock? Had Archibald Hawke attempted another approach? He should send another letter to expedite Richard's visit. He would not be separated from Elizabeth and she was not feeling well. She could not travel. His cousin would have to come to Pemberley.

There were two firm knocks on the door, and his wife slipped in without waiting for a response. He rose to greet her, placing his arm around her waist with a smile and guiding her to the settee.

"William," she said with a shake of her head, "I am not an invalid. My mornings may be difficult, but even Mr. Waters agrees that this will be temporary."

He said nothing, just crouched before her and brought her hand to his lips. His heart was too full to speak. His wife seemed to understand his silence and laid her free hand gently on the side of his face.

"I heard that an express had come," she said quietly. "Is it news from Richard?"

He nodded, no longer surprised that she would be told immediately about the post. He retrieved the note from his desk and handed it to her. She rewarded him with a bright smile that he could not help but return, and sat next to her. He watched her read it, a small furrow appearing just above the bridge of her nose.

"I wonder what happened?" she asked thoughtfully. "At least they are all well. I would imagine Matlock to be quite safe. Miss Evelyn should now have achieved her majority without being forced to wed. Still, to be required to remain for one's safety, particularly after Miss Hawke had fought so long for her independence," she said, shaking her head, "it cannot be pleasant."

Darcy nodded, considering how difficult it was even to keep Elizabeth in the house when the weather was poor. "What he has to tell me must be something quite astonishing if it will take a bottle of my best brandy in recompense."

Elizabeth laughed softly, but quickly sobered. "What shall happen to the Hawke sisters now?"

Her husband looked at her quizzically, as though he had not yet considered the question. "I do not know, Elizabeth," he replied solemnly. "Once

Richard and the Earl are assured of their safety, I suppose they will go home."

They sat there for some time, Elizabeth placing a hand over her abdomen and Fitzwilliam covering her hand with one of his own, entwining his fingers with hers. Elizabeth thought of her own recent trials and how grateful she had been that the staff had accepted her authority despite their initial misgivings. What might have happened had they given in to their fears and fled like Mr. Harrison? She was also more than grateful that Mr. Harrison had shown what he was early on. Having to fight him on every decision would have been more than she could bear. While she would forever regret not confirming that he had been to the south meadows, she had largely forgiven herself the error, though she grieved its result. No, it was the man who had lied about his actions that was guilty, and she would place the blame where it belonged, directly upon the head of the cowardly Mr. Harrison.

Elizabeth's tender heart grieved that it had been necessary for Sophia Hawke to flee her uncle's home for her own safety. She was indignant on Miss Hawke's behalf that the documents showing her to be the heir of Darlington and her sister's guardian had been summarily dismissed, that because she was a girl that her wishes to remain with the Tildens had been ignored. She had herself been very fortunate that she had not needed to wage such battles. Elizabeth's imaginative mind was already sketching out endless possibilities for where Miss Hawke had been and what had brought her back to the rooms in Seven Dials. She leaned her head upon her husband's shoulder. It was, she thought, far better to spin stories with such plots than to actually be forced to live them.

Fitzwilliam watched his wife wrestle silently with something. Most likely, he thought, she was considering the Hawkes' plight. Elizabeth had four sisters and had been dependent upon the good health of her father. Had a fire taken him, they would all have been homeless. Unsurprisingly, she had been horrified at the idea of the two girls losing their family in such a way, and her first question after their argument had come to a close had been to ask whether anyone knew how the fire had started. He had not even thought about it, but then, Tilden had never mentioned any doubts about the fire's origins. He would have to speak to Richard about that when he arrived.

In the meantime, he did what came naturally. He made plans. He wondered whether the Hawkes would remain at Matlock while they tried to rebuild, or whether they would require other lodgings. It was best to remain as close to the site as possible so as to keep a sharp eye on the workmen. Her steward would likely help with that as well. Miss Hawke was no longer a child, but it would be difficult to find men who would take their orders from a woman.

It was too late in the year now to begin building in any case. They would have to survey the site and work on the plans, then begin to lay the foundation next spring. He would speak with Richard to see whether they might need recommendations for the architect or builders. If they required assistance with negotiating prices on stone or lumber, he might be of service there as well.

Elizabeth's hand squeezed his, and he returned the pressure. He gazed down at her twinkling eyes. "Are you planning their house?" she asked with a sweet smile. He smiled back, abashed.

"I must admit that I am," he replied. "Am I so transparent, then?"

"Only to me," she said, leaning over to put her head on his chest. He bent to kiss the top of her head.

"I was planning, and you were making a list of impertinent questions to ask, no?"

She giggled like the young woman she was, and the sound made his heart leap. "As impertinent as possible, sir."

Lord, he had missed her. He discarded all thoughts of building houses and creating lists. He stood, took his wife's hands and carefully pulled her up with him.

"We need not solve everything tonight, my love," he said softly.

Elizabeth blinked a few times as her thoughts fled in the intensity of her husband's steady gaze.

"Shall we go upstairs, Mrs. Darcy? I have missed you terribly."

"Of course, Mr. Darcy," she said, standing on tiptoe to kiss his cheek. She put one hand on the back of his head and pulled his handsome face closer to her own. As he bent to meet her, she moved to place a feather-light kiss upon his lips. He groaned, took her firmly by the hand, and led her out into the hall and up to their chambers. There would be time enough for reflection tomorrow.

Tonight, they had one another. It was enough.

Epilogue

THE SUN WAS DIRECTLY OVERHEAD as John Briggs pulled his horse to a stop. This was the fifth coaching inn he had visited in the past two days. This one was the smallest, but the stones were whitewashed and the roof tightly thatched. Across the road, two young men were sliding crates of vegetables onto the back of a wagon, covering them with blankets, while the two mares hitched to the front gently tossed their tails to distract the flies accosting them.

John dismounted, removed his hat, and wiped the sweat from his forehead before tying up his mount and walking inside. His younger son Harry, tall and lanky at fourteen and feeling all the pride of being asked along on the ride, tied up his own steed and stood next to the post, arms crossed over his thin chest. *Nobody will dare approach the horses with such a guard*, John thought fondly, as he replaced his hat and walked inside.

The inn was dark and cool, and John stood just inside the doorway for a moment to allow his eyes to adjust to the dimmer light. When he spied the innkeeper behind the bar, he strode over to take a seat, order a drink, and ask his questions. The innkeeper was a heavyset man of about fifty years with a florid complexion and a full head of gray hair that curled over his ears but otherwise fell straight, ending near his frayed collar. He remained silent until John reached the end of his speech.

"Chestnut stallion, white flash, seventeen hands. Taps his front foot twice if you offer a carrot. Would have been left maybe a month back. My master is anxious to have him returned and will pay for your trouble."

The man's eyes narrowed. He leaned on the knuckles of his fists, bending his corpulent frame closer to John's face. His eyebrows were tufted, gray, too short for his wide-set, muddy brown eyes.

"How much?"

John flashed an austere smile. "Depends upon the condition of the beast. Do you have him?"

"Might." He eased himself back to a standing position and hollered for his wife. Once she arrived, red-faced, flustered, issuing a loud complaint over being summoned in such a way, the innkeeper ambled slowly towards the back of the building, exiting into a courtyard. He crossed through the dusty yard to a small stable beyond. While the front of the building had been well tended, the stable was neglected. The thatched roof was beginning to separate on one side while the walls were haphazardly maintained. The whitewash had faded long ago and long weeds sank their leafy tendrils into the chinks between the stones.

John tried not to show his disdain for the condition of the horses as they made their way past several stalls. He instead focused on what he might do to Isaac Harrison if he ever got his hands on the man, taking a grim satisfaction in devising his penance before admitting to himself that he would likely need to hand him over to the magistrate. It would be the master's wishes, not his own, that would be followed, and Mr. Darcy upheld the law.

They reached the last stall. Tossing his head and snorting was Ares, looking every bit the member of nobility he was in this stable of worn out mares. He moved quickly into the stall to run his hands along Ares' forelocks, checking from knee to hock for swelling or soreness, each hoof for cracks or worn shoes. Then he stood to run the flats of his fingers lightly along the stallion's neck, withers, and muscles, and checked his eyes and his teeth. Finally, he pulled a carrot out of his pocket and held it directly in Ares' line of sight. The stallion neighed, bobbed his head, and gently tapped the ground twice with his front left hoof before John gently moved the treat from side to side, up and down, watching to see that Ares could follow without pain.

"Be ye done yet?" asked the innkeeper impatiently.

John rubbed Ares' nose and offered him the carrot. He had not been well fed and was a little thin. He could certainly use some grooming. Otherwise he appeared unharmed.

"Who left him here?"

"Didna ask his name."

"Short man, bald, squat?"

"Nay. Young, dark, rough-looking."

"How long has he been here?"

"Month or so, like ya say."

John frowned. The man could not be trusted, he thought, but for all that John believed him to be telling the truth about who had brought the horse here. Harrison might have sold the horse or had it taken before he arrived. After he was sure Ares was finished with the carrot, John began to fit him out for return to Pemberley. When he was finished, he tossed a handful of guineas to the man who grunted.

"Had to feed 'em an' all."

"You have not fed him much," was John's retort, though the horse had been watered well. He flipped the man a few additional shillings and threw him a look that said clearly enough there would be no more. The innkeeper had clearly been hoping for better but was wise enough not to complain. He shuffled back off to his wife as John spoke softly to Ares and began to lead him outside.

Harry was still standing next to the horses at the front of the inn, doing his best to appear fierce and unapproachable. His face lit up like a child's when his father walked Ares around the far side of the inn.

"You found him!" he cried, his eyes alight with pleasure before he reigned in his emotions by crossing his arms over his chest and offering a curt nod. "I knew you would. Is he well, father?"

"He is, though he will require some additional care once we get him home," John replied, trying not to laugh. He was pleased, very pleased, to recover Ares, and his son's face had reminded him of times past, when both boys were small and his wife still alive. He well recalled being his son's age, not young enough to be a boy, not old enough to be a man, and he felt some sympathy for Harry's predicament. "Do you think you could take that on?"

Harry drew himself up to his full height. "I could," he said, sounding confident. "Thank you, father." He scratched Ares between his ears and stroked his long neck. The stallion gazed at the boy languidly and swished his tail from side to side.

"We must visit the magistrate before we depart, Harry, but let us make a start, shall we? I should like to eat my dinner at home tomorrow."

Harry grinned. "Aye, father," he agreed. "So would I."

As the two Briggs men led Ares down the road, they ambled past a small, well-tended church with a cemetery behind. John never thought to speak with the pastor to check the burial grounds or the death registry. If he had, he would have seen the relatively fresh mound of dirt heaped on an unmarked grave and a hastily penned line on a cramped page. *Isaac*, it read, and then, *Influenza*.

***

Miss Evelyn Hawke adroitly guided her chestnut mare to the top of Widow's Peak, stopping at a plateau just below the craggy rocks at the top that overlooked Darlington, her sister's estate. It was wooded here, lush with evergreens and painted red and orange by the arrival of autumn. Miss Evelyn relished the opportunity to return to the family lands she barely remembered, and both she and her sister were very comfortable in the country, far from London. Here on the small plateau, she could view the long, flat fields below, the site of the original house just beyond, a small glittering lake to the south, and then, to the west and north, several of the tenant cottages, the farmland stretching out to the horizon. She knew these were only a few of all the farms on the property, but she was not much interested in the business workings of the estate. Though she had accompanied her sister to many meetings with Mr. Hobson and the solicitor who had arrived from town, she far preferred the stillroom, learning about treatments for injuries and illnesses.

She was hoping to be able to assist Sophia by helping to care for the tenants, and she believed she had a talent for it. She had tended Sophia through her injuries and fever, though she had never been enlightened as to their cause. She knew her sister had led a life quite apart from her own, a dangerous life, and could only hope to have Sophia's confidence eventually.

It had been nearly four months since Jack Hobson showed up at the servants' entrance at her uncle's London townhouse, begging for her to accompany him to nurse her sister. Increasingly uncomfortable at home and uncharacteristically desperate to see her sister for the first time in three years, she had immediately agreed. Her residence in Seven Dials had meant nothing compared with the opportunity to be of use to Sophia, particularly after her behavior at their previous meeting. When her sister seemed to be nearly recovered, Evelyn had sent a note to her uncle, hoping to effect a reconciliation. How misguided she had been, how foolish!

Below her, a rider appeared, thundering across the flats on a gleaming black thoroughbred, and Evelyn smiled. Sophia was an accomplished rider and had a wonderful seat sidesaddle, but rarely rode that way when traveling on her own estate. When she had answered her correspondence, gone through the accounts, spoken with the surveyor, discussed the kind of house she wished to build and where best to locate it with the architect, she would declare quite abruptly that she had taken in enough information for one day and would head out to ride in order to sort it all through. She wore a specially tailored set of riding breeches beneath a proper woman's riding habit, but everyone on the estate knew it was a fool's errand to point out that riding a horse astride was hardly ladylike. Sophia would grin, hitch up the skirt around her hips, and throw herself up into the saddle. She only wore the skirt at all, she would say with a laugh, in case a stranger came to visit. After all, she was disinclined to shock strangers. That was something reserved for friends and family.

Only Jack and Mr. Hobson were never surprised by anything Sophia did or said, not even when she challenged Jack to a shooting contest to settle an argument. When she had beaten him soundly, hitting a target some two hundred feet away with a single shot from her rifle, he just laughed and challenged her to a fencing match, and she was finally forced to give way. Fencing was not a strength. Yet she took her losses nearly as well as her wins, and in her unconventional sister Evelyn saw a woman she could model herself after, even if she was herself more comfortable following society's dictates more closely.

She and Sophia had taken up temporary residence in the dowager's cottage. When they first arrived, she and Mrs. Jamison had set it to rights, airing out the entire house, cleaning, dusting, and replacing things that were worn or broken, preparing the guest rooms with fresh linens and curtains should the Earl come to visit. Thus far, however, the Hawkes had been left to their own company. Evelyn was not complaining, of course. She cherished the evenings when she read to her exhausted older sister and they talked, often far later than they should, about her life and future plans. Very rarely did Sophia speak about herself other than the ideas she had for Darlington.

On the fields below, Sophia's thoroughbred leapt cleanly over a hedge, his rider perfectly positioned for the jump. Then the horse pulled up and slowly trotted back the way they had come. Sophia Hawke held a hand up high to greet her sister, and Evelyn, not surprised in the least that her sister had spotted her perch, returned the gesture.

As she lowered her arm, she noticed another rider approaching Sophia, this one on a large, dappled Arabian. It made her a bit anxious to see the speed at which he rode until she caught a flash of a red coat and smiled more broadly than she had since they had settled here in the north. *At last*, she thought, pleased, *I wondered when he would finally make an appearance. Matlock is not so very far away.*

She clucked at her horse and led it down the hill, heading towards the stables. Perhaps tonight they might discuss something about Sophia's life and her plans. *Yes*, Miss Evelyn Hawke thought happily, *there is plenty of room for guests.*

Excerpt from *Courage Requires*, Book 2 of 2, The Courage Series

ELIZABETH DARCY STARED at the ceiling in the master's chambers and tried not to move. She had finally found a position on the bed that did not make her stomach clench and roll, and if she remained perfectly still, there was a chance she might not be ill this morning. Next to her, lying on his stomach with his face turned towards her, was her husband, whose rumpled hair and soft snores made her smile. He had grown more anxious about her every day, more so now because she was long past the time Mr. Waters had suggested would mark the end of this constant nausea. The local midwife simply harrumphed at such pronouncements. Mr. Waters was a man, after all, nothing more than an apothecary, and should not have presumed to make such a statement. She would not hear that he had only offered Mrs. Darcy some general assurances but had indeed been wise enough not to make promises.

"The worse you feel," the heavyset woman had said with an unsympathetic cluck and a toss of her head, "the healthier the child." Elizabeth could have wept at that breezy dismissal of her misery, but she had decided to be angry instead. She wanted to eat, truly she did, but even when she could manage to force something down, it did not stay down for long. She was nearly desperate to eat something other than broth, but nobody seemed to be able to help. The ginger tea and biscuits Mrs. Cronk sent up had no effect, the peppermint tea was useless. Fitzwilliam, in his deepening anxiety, had dismissed the midwife altogether in favor of seeking out an accoucheur, who had also had little of help to offer other than going through the menus for foods that might trigger her illness. As she was not eating much, it seemed a useless exercise. She closed her eyes and tried to think of something other than how sick she felt, how sore her stomach and back muscles were, how the room swirled relentlessly after every attack. One morning feeling well. One walk in the garden without dizziness or concern about casting up her accounts. Was it so much to ask? *This had best be the healthiest child in the kingdom*, she thought with irritation, holding her limbs rigidly in place.

As she lay unmoving on the bed, Elizabeth could hear the vague sounds of the house coming to life. The soft footfalls in the hallway, the gentle murmuring of voices, the slow opening of the chamber door as a servant entered to tend the fire. After a wet summer, the harvest months had been mercifully dry and mild, but the days had begun to grow cooler at last. The day before, resting in the garden trying to find a comfortable way to be outside, she had noted the men coming in from the orchards and walking the roads across the meadow. They carried large sacks of what she knew must be the last of the apples, and she had thought how wonderful one crisp apple might taste. While she realized she would almost certainly not be able to abide it, she was still thinking about the harvest at Longbourn and what a wonderful time of year this was. She only wished she could enjoy it more if for no other reason that she would like William to worry a little less about her.

Cautiously, she breathed in and then out. She still felt all right. Slowly, she established a calm rhythm and felt able to open her eyes. There was gentle pressure on her hand, and she turned her head very carefully to see her husband watching her.

"Are you well, Elizabeth?" he asked, his fingers lacing with hers as he leaned just a little closer.

"As long as I do not move, William," she replied stiffly. The anticipation faded, and while very few people would have said that he looked any different, Elizabeth could see his face fall. Every morning he woke hoping she would feel herself, and each morning he was disappointed. He attempted to hide it, but she could read him too well. It was an added burden, his anxiety, but it was impossible to disguise her suffering.

"It is temporary, love," she said, forcing the words to sound encouraging. "It will pass."

"You need not reassure me, my dear. Just tell me if there is anything I can do to help." Fitzwilliam shifted, leaning over her to brush a soft kiss on her cheek. As he pulled away, Elizabeth felt the bile begin to rise again. She rolled away from her husband with a moan, grabbed the pail sitting on the floor next to the bed, and was ill.

Darcy placed a hand lightly on his wife's back as she bent over the side of the bed retching. When she was finished, he helped her settle back onto her pillows. Once she was comfortable, he rose to walk around the bed and remove the bucket. He placed it out in the hall and picked up the one that had been placed near the door, clean and empty, to set in its place. Then he moved away to wash his hands. Finally, he poured his wife a glass of water and sat next to her. He brought the drink to her lips carefully, tipping it a little to help her sip.

He had been away when his sister was ill in the summer, arriving home just in time for his wife to begin showing indications that she was with child. Four months along now, nearly five, and she was still ill, more so now than the earlier months. Mr. Waters had little of help to offer, and the midwife had made Elizabeth even more wretched than she had been before the visit. The babe seemed to be progressing well, Elizabeth's abdomen clearly rounded and growing, but she had not gained any weight. Instead, all the weight that had settled on her abdomen appeared to have come from somewhere else on her body. Her face was thin and drawn, and she was unsteady when she walked. The intense relief he had felt upon arriving home to learn that she and Georgiana were both well had given way to a paralyzing panic that he might still lose Elizabeth. He could barely stand to be away from her, but she insisted he tend to the estate, and because hovering was all he had to offer her, he reluctantly did as she asked. When she rose from her bed late each morning, she allowed a footman to assist her on the stairs and sat in the drawing room just for a change of scene. She had not walked in ages and her easy agreement to being attended by a footman wherever she went alarmed him as much as any of her symptoms.

"You will feel improved soon, my love. I am sure of it," he said softly, stroking her hair.

"William," she said in a breathy voice, exhausted.

"Yes, Elizabeth?" Fitzwilliam asked, kissing her hand.

"If we ever want another child," she said faintly, though her eyes sparkled just a bit, "we shall have to find one to adopt."

Afterword

The positive reception of *Courage Rises*, my first *Pride and Prejudice* novel, was a wonderful confirmation for me, and I am very grateful to the readers who have been very supportive and enthusiastic. I cannot tell you how pleased I am that *Courage Rises* struck a chord for so many of you.

There are, of course, those who felt that the story was entirely implausible. Oddly enough, however, it is the facts that I plucked from historical accounts that seem to have caused the most consternation on this score. So let's look at them.

First, of course, was the idea that Sophia Hawke could disguise herself as a male soldier. Such an action is not out of the realm of possibility, as there have been women like Sophia in every war perhaps until WWII, when standards for accountability were higher and there were places for women to serve without having to pretend to be men. While it would be difficult to pull off such a deception today (and certainly less necessary), women dressing as men and fighting in wars, sometimes to follow their husbands, sometimes to escape their home lives, and sometimes for the adventure of it, was not unheard of in Jane Austen's time.

A few women who we know dressed as men and fought in the Napoleonic Wars include Nadezhda Durova (cavalry, awarded the Cross of St. George), Eleonore Prochaska (drummer, infantry, killed in action), Freiderike Krügar (Infantry, Iron Cross, discovered to be a woman but allowed to remain in service), and Anna Lühring (who, inspired by the death of Prochaska, joined the Lutzow Free Corps).

Though she did not fight as a soldier, Margaret Ann Bulkley/James Barry dressed as a man in order to attend medical school as a teenager and never returned to life as a woman. Barry joined the British army after graduating from the University of Edinburgh Medical School in 1813 and served in Africa, India, and Jamaica. She is credited with one of the first successful Caesarean sections (both the mother and child survived). Barry eventually became the Inspector General of Her Majesty's Hospitals in

Canada, and her sex was discovered only after her death.

Another issue seems to be the accuracy of Sophia's shot. The Baker rifle, the one Sophia Hawke carries, was a bit more than a decade old at the beginning of our story, and it signaled a significant change in wartime weaponry. It could fire two shots before requiring reloading, and its accuracy was unparalleled at the time. It took a bit longer to reload than the standard Brown Bessie musket carried by other troops, but its longer range and increased accuracy made up for that. The Baker rifle was selected for use by the rifle corps specifically because it was accurate up to three hundred yards which, as you might guess, had the potential to greatly influence the outcome of a battle. It had been in use since 1800 and was adopted by the rifle corps (later the 95th Regiment of the Foot) in 1802.

Other readers opined that Elizabeth would never have dealt with an epidemic in the way that she does in the book, setting up her own hospital so as to gather the afflicted in one place. What I can tell you is that while we are very fortunate to have access to modern medical care, the early 1800s were not, as some might claim, quite the same as the Middle Ages in terms of scientific knowledge.

The institution we recognize as the modern hospital was born a good deal earlier than our story (Westminster Hospital was opened as far back as 1719). It was during the Regency period that French doctors began to toy with the idea of antiseptics, and British chemist Humphry Davy, in 1800, published his findings on nitrous oxide, suggesting its use as an anesthetic for surgical patients.

Old practices such as bloodletting were still in use, but not universally accepted. While older doctors were often staunch advocates, younger doctors like Dr. Hughes Bennett, born in 1812 (a little late for *Courage Rises*), fought just as strongly against it. The point is, the tide was turning, particularly after the famous and sought-after London physician Sir Richard Croft routinely bled Princess Charlotte during the pregnancy that ultimately killed her. Christian Stockmore, her regular physician, had declined to be a part of Croft's team because he did not agree with the treatment and, as a foreigner, did not want to be blamed if something went wrong. So these types of treatments were certainly being actively questioned.

Most physicians at the time also had some knowledge of germ transmission. Most knew to wash their hands before working with patients and the importance of keeping the sickroom clean. They did not yet know *why* this was important, but most would likely have performed the function anyway, as it had been reported to reduce cases of secondary infection. By 1854, John Snow, a London physician, had published the first modern theory of disease transmission.

Sometimes we believe that the marvels of modern medicine began to arrive only relatively recently, but it has actually taken a very long process of building upon the discoveries of previous generations to achieve these accomplishments. Those who came before us were not entirely without medical knowledge.

I enjoyed all the historical research I conducted in the writing of both *Courage Rises* and *Courage Requires*. In the end, writers should take the literary license to do what they must for their stories, but I caution readers that just because it sounds impossible doesn't mean that it is!

If you enjoyed *Courage Rises*, I encourage you to finish the story of the Darcys, Fitzwilliams, and Hawkes in the second and final book of the series, *Courage Requires*!

Acknowledgements

Many people were instrumental in the writing of this novel. I thank all my reviewers, readers, and supporters, those who pointed out errors or inconsistencies and who mused about potential storylines. Thanks to you, the story is better and stronger than it would have been without your assistance.

Thanks must also go out to my family, who put up with my many hours spent typing away on my computer when I might have been cooking, cleaning, or doing the million other things it takes to run a house. Thank you for your love, support, and the invaluable gift of time.

About the Author

MELANIE RACHEL is a university professor and long-time Jane Austen fan. She was born in Southern California, but has lived in Pennsylvania, New Jersey, Washington, and Arizona, where she now resides with her family and their freakishly athletic Jack Russell terrier.

Website: melanierachel.weebly.com

Facebook: facebook.com/melanie.rachel.583

Made in the USA
Monee, IL
29 November 2019